MW00531766

DEADLY SINS

STACY M. JONES

Deadly Sins Copyright © 2018 Stacy M. Jones

All rights reserved. No part of this publication may be reproduced, distributed, or transmitted in any form or by any means, including photocopying, recording, or other electronic or mechanical methods, without the prior written permission of the publisher, except in the case of brief quotations embodied in critical reviews and certain other noncommercial uses permitted by copyright law.

ISBN: 978-0-692-12630-1
Imprint: Stacy M. Jones
First printing edition 2018

Any references to historical events, real people, or real places are used fictiously. Names, characters, and places are products of the author's imagination.

Book design by Sharon Aponte, Chick & a Mouse Graphic Design.

For more information and to contact the author:
www.stacymjones.com

DEDICATION

For Mom for her constant support and encouragement

ACKNOWLEDGMENTS

Special thanks to my family and friends who were all a source of support and encouragement throughout this process. Thank you to my early readers whose feedback was invaluable. Sharon Aponte, a wonderfully skilled and patient graphic designer, a huge thank you.

To the countless detectives, prosecutors, child protective case workers, forensic nurses, and medical examiners I've worked cases with over the years, your insight, expertise and experience was my early classroom and on-the-job training that laid the groundwork for this novel even to be written. Any law enforcement procedural mistakes are my own.

DEADLY SINS

CHAPTER 1

I SHOULDN'T HAVE COME BACK to Little Rock, Arkansas. It was nothing but a city of unfinished business for me, and this was a fool's errand. The call that brought me here came three nights ago at two in the morning. On the nightstand next to my bed, my ringing cellphone woke me from a sound sleep to awake in seconds flat. I am not a heavy sleeper as it is, and the ringing phone cut through the silence of my slumber. Four words were all it took for me to drop my entire life in New York, pack a bag, leave my yellow lab Dusty at my mother's, and board a flight to Little Rock.

I let myself believe I was putting up a good resistance about coming back here, but all he had to say was that he needed my help. A stronger woman wouldn't have even taken his calls. *A simple quick trip* were the delusional words I told myself as I drove to the airport and boarded my Southwest flight. Truthfully, there was nothing simple about the man on the other end of the phone that night or his request.

It was a long turbulent flight from New York, and I was happy to have had an easy check-in at the downtown Marriott, formerly the Peabody Hotel. I'd had more than one night of misplaced passion at this place.

After a refreshing shower, I now stood barefoot with a simple emerald green tee-shirt on and jeans riding low on my ample hips. I blinked several times at my reflection in the hotel's bathroom mirror while I struggled to tame my long auburn hair and throw on just enough make-up to look presentable. Once finished, I took another good long look at my reflection. Not bad. But I knew I was unprepared, and there wasn't much I could do about that. As a licensed private investigator, it's the worst feeling I could have.

I swiped some tinted lip gloss across my lips just as three loud raps reverberated against the hotel room door. I put the lip gloss back in my makeup bag, gave my reflection one last half-hearted smile and took a deep breath. I walked to the door to let in my visitor. I didn't even have to look through the peephole. I knew who was standing there. I also knew there was no turning back.

"They found a woman's body, Riley. She's in the river, right down the road behind the River Market Pavilions," George Brewer barked as he brushed past me into my room. He had an edge in his voice I had never heard before. He looked awful.

This was the first I had laid eyes, or anything else, on him in two years. He definitely looked older than his forty years and heavier than when we dated. His face round and belly swollen. At five-ten, he was only three inches taller than I was. The rumpled blue Oxford and pleated khakis he was wearing didn't do him any favors. His face sported a few days old dark stubble, and the dark hair on his head had thinned.

Is it wrong that I'm glad he looks terrible? Isn't that every woman's best hope? You get dumped. You see him again, and he looks dreadful. But most ex-girlfriends aren't private investigators called into a missing person's case to find the very woman who was the cause of the aforementioned breakup. As I said, I shouldn't be here.

His wife Maime has been missing for five days. Vanished. Gone. No one has seen or heard from her. The police and her family suspect George, of course. They always do when a wife goes missing. Husbands generally have means, motive and opportunity. I was sure George had all three. When it came to Maime, there were times I had all three. Luckily, I was in New York when she disappeared. George broke our very comfortable two-year silent stalemate to ask me for help. That, in itself, was the act of a desperate man. The last time we had spoken, it hadn't ended well.

"I know, George. I got Cooper's text when I landed," I said in response to George's abrupt entrance. Cooper Deagnan, a local private investigator and a great friend, was going to be my saving grace in this situation, running interference between George and me. He just didn't know it yet.

"Is it Maime?" George asked as he paced small circles around my room. He always did that when he was nervous.

I moved from the door, walked past George without touching him, and planted myself in the desk chair at the far end of the room.

"No, Cooper didn't seem to think so. Maime's blonde and this woman had dark brown hair. I believe she's taller than Maime."

George stopped pacing. He let out a long sigh and sat on the edge of the bed. His arms lay limp at his sides. He looked defeated. George looked over at me and made eye contact for the first time since he barged into my room. His dark eyes bore into mine. It was a long intense stare. He searched my face for what I don't know. Pity? Anger? Love? I broke eye contact and looked away.

When George finally spoke, he said with an edge of annoyance, "Tell me again why Cooper has to be involved."

"I have no authority to investigate here," I explained matter of fact. "My private investigation license is only good in New York. Cooper's licensed here. He'll be the primary investigator."

I didn't like having to run my investigations with anyone, but if I had to pick, Cooper would do.

George stood up and ran a hand down his face. He pointed at me and said with anger in his voice, "I trust you. I don't trust him." Then he paused and looked a bit uncertain but said softer, "You know this could get delicate."

"Delicate?" I asked with my eyebrows raised.

"You know, given our history." George deadpanned, as if I'd forgotten.

"We went over this. You want me. You got him. I trust him. That's all that matters." In our relationship, George was accustomed to getting his own way. I wasn't in that place anymore.

"Have you heard anything more? Any signs of her?" I asked.

Let's face it, all I really knew of Maime was that she was all drama. Who fights so hard to keep a cheating man? I never understood it.

"Nothing. The last I saw her or talked to her was Friday morning. We were both headed to work."

"George, we both know Maime has taken off before. Did something happen?"

He stared at me with a blank expression on his face, but I knew he knew exactly what I meant. When Maime found out about me, there was a storm that raged on for weeks. When I found out about her, I walked away.

But she carried on. She cried, screamed, begged. I even heard things were broken. George called me once, his booming voice taking up space on my voicemail for a full five minutes. He yelled forcefully that I had to leave him alone. That I was nothing but a stalker, and he wasn't leaving his girlfriend for me. I could hear Maime crying and screaming in the background.

George called me thirty minutes later and told my voicemail how sorry he was and asked if I was okay. Pretending to tell me off was just something he said he had to do and to call him. I never did. As I said, drama to a whole other level.

Finally, not meeting my gaze, he said, "Nothing, nothing has happened. Everything was normal."

I knew he was lying, but I also knew sometimes it's just not the right time to push for the truth. "The cops question you again?"

"Yesterday. They wanted me to run through the timeline again. Nothing has changed in what I've said. I know they don't believe me. Maime's father thinks I killed her. He's been asking me to take a leave of absence from the firm."

George was a lawyer at LaRue & Associates, a successful high-priced corporate law firm owned by Maime's father. The firm handled corporate litigation as well as being known for its ferocious lobbying work. They were rarely on the moral side of an issue.

"Have you taken the leave?"

"No, I refuse to give the old man the satisfaction."

"The break might not be bad for you," I suggested. When George didn't respond I added, "You know perception is everything in these cases. You do things to look guilty, you'll be guilty. I don't know how you could focus on work anyway."

George watched me. The same blank expression on his face. I couldn't really read him, but I knew he wasn't going to take the leave of absence no matter what I said.

George asked, "You think this woman they found today is connected?"

"Connected how?"

George shrugged.

I thought for a few seconds and then said, "I have no reason to believe that. But I haven't talked to anyone yet. Cooper's already down there. I was going to let him handle it and then meet him in about an hour for dinner. We were going to get a game plan together and meet with you in the morning."

George turned towards the door, exiting just as abruptly as he entered. Clearly, our initial client meeting was over. As he turned the door handle, I said to his back, "I don't want to ask this, but I have to. Did you have anything to do with Maime's disappearance?"

He opened the door and then turned to face me. This expression I could read. He looked angry. For a few seconds, he didn't say a word, just watched me, but then he asked, "Have you ever thought about what life would be like for us if I never married Maime but married you instead?"

He didn't wait for my answer. George walked out as I watched the door shut behind him. He left me sitting there stunned by the question. It was moments later that I realized he never answered mine.

CHAPTER 2

IT WAS A WARM CLOUDLESS NIGHT in November. By-standers along President Clinton Avenue in downtown Little Rock stood in eerie silence at the edge of the yellow crime scene tape that blocked the way down to the river. Cooper Deagnan, former Little Rock detective turned private investigator, took in the familiar scene. He watched the police diligently doing their work.

The crime scene techs made their way through the debris that littered the ground while looking for evidence. A few uniformed officers with notepads and pens in hand jotted down information they gathered from a few of the stunned onlookers who might have heard or seen something suspicious. The area, which was usually filled with tourists and locals visiting the River Market area to shop, dine and take in live music at the amphitheater, was now an active crime scene.

Cooper got a tip from a Little Rock homicide detective so he ditched out on an insurance fraud surveillance that wasn't yielding much anyway and drove straight to the scene. He navigated through the throngs of people, took in the scene before him, and then nodded to the officer standing guard as he slid effortlessly under the crime scene tape unbothered. He made a beeline directly to where his long-time friend Detective Lucas "Luke" Morgan stood. Being a former Little Rock detective still had its privileges.

Cooper watched as three detectives including Luke surrounded the half-naked body, clad only in her bra and underwear. She lay motionless on the cement, already showing signs of bloat. Cooper's stomach lurched at the sight of her. He had heard she was initially spotted by two women taking a stroll after their dinner. Her body was caught up in old tree limbs and slapped against the retaining wall, driven over and over again by the Arkansas River's current.

When Cooper was standing among the crowd, he had heard people saying they could hear the screams pierce through the normally festive downtown streets. Cooper wasn't surprised. It was a grotesque sight even for a seasoned detective. Not so much the condition of her body but the look on her face, eyes wide open and mouth contorted as if she died mid-scream.

"How long has she been dead?" Cooper asked his friend.

Luke got up from his crouched position over the body and made his way to Cooper. The two men stood eye to eye both about six foot. Cooper's messy blond hair and green eyes contrasted against Luke's darker African-American features. Both thirty-seven years old and single, neither had been short-changed in looks.

"Medical examiner's not sure. More than a day less than two is his rough estimation," Luke responded.

"You know for sure it's not Maime LaRue Brewer?" Cooper asked, looking over at the body and back before nausea set in again.

"She doesn't fit the description at all. I haven't bothered to call her husband or family. No point dragging them down here," Luke said, looking across the parking lot back the way Cooper had entered. He added, "But with all this attention, I wouldn't be surprised if they came down anyway."

Cooper nodded along in understanding but didn't offer up anything else. He hadn't come to the scene just to make small talk. He had a purpose. There was something he had to tell Luke. He knew as soon as he did, his friend's mood would go from bad to worse. Luke had to hear this from him though.

Finally, Cooper just asked, "Speaking of that case, you got anything yet?"

Luke eyed him. "You on the case? I figured the old man would just get one of his in-house investigators."

"No, I haven't been hired by the LaRue family," Cooper said, shaking his head and pausing a beat too long.

Luke gestured impatiently with his hand for him to go on.

Cooper spat the words out in one breath as quickly as he could, "George Brewer hired Riley. She's here in Little Rock."

Cooper barely got the words out when he heard Luke curse under his breath. Cooper couldn't quite make out what he said. He could only imagine. Luke and Riley had some history. What happened between them was anyone's guess. Cooper wasn't privy to the details, but he knew from past conversations Riley was an off-limit topic with Luke. She certainly wasn't going to be welcomed with open arms and certainly not in the middle of Luke's investigation.

Luke folded his arms over his chest and looked down at the ground. After a moment he asked softly, "She tell you her connection to George?"

"No," Cooper responded truthfully. "What do you know?"

"Bring her in tomorrow morning. We all need to talk."

"Okay, I'll try. You know Riley though," Cooper responded with a shrug.

"Too well," Luke said and then got quiet.

Cooper let the subject drop. He knew better than to push. "What have you got here?" Cooper asked, hitching his jaw towards the woman on the ground.

"I'm not too sure yet, to be honest. Woman probably in her late thirties, maybe early forties. The medical examiner said it looked like possible strangulation from the marks on her neck, but he won't know until he opens her up to see if she was alive when she went into the river," Luke detailed and then added, "No matter what happened, there are no defensive wounds. She didn't put up a fight."

They stood in silence for a few seconds looking over at the woman. A longtime native of Little Rock, Cooper said, "We get crime here, but this is different. Isn't it?"

"Sure feels that way." Luke shook his head in disgust.

"Any other missing women reported?"

"Not that I'm aware of. Once we get prints, we'll run her in the database and see what pops," Luke said and then more seriously, "I don't like this to be honest with you. We've got our fair share of homicides in this city but not in this part of town. First a missing woman from the Heights and now a floater in the river. Something's not right."

"You think it's connected?" Cooper was struggling to think it was all just a coincidence.

"No idea," Luke said with a sigh. He looked back over to the woman's body.

"You okay? I'm sure it reminds you a little of Lily?" Cooper knew a case like this had to hit home. Luke's sister had been murdered during their senior year of college when she was just a freshman. To this day, it went unsolved.

Luke didn't respond but started to walk back toward where the dead woman remained. He turned back to Cooper, paused for a beat, and then asked, "How's Riley?"

"Spitfire as always."

"So nothing's changed." Luke gave Cooper a half-hearted smile. "Be there at eight-thirty tomorrow morning."

CHAPTER 3

"RILEY SULLIVAN NEW YORK," Luke spoke each word aloud as he typed them again into Google, mentally thanking Cooper for the tip. After Luke got all he could at the crime scene, he left and headed back to the police station. The medical examiner and CSI unit would keep him up-to-date with anything relevant and important.

Luke viewed his computer screen carefully and scanned link after link. He found old articles Riley had written, her business website, and some reviews from some of her clients. Nobody had a bad word to say. He scrolled down further finding an animal shelter website that listed her as a donor. He wasn't surprised. Luke knew she had a soft spot for dogs.

Luke kept going until he was sure there wasn't anything but article after article with her name listed in the byline. He knew he couldn't get into her social media account. Her Facebook page was locked down tighter than Luke's house. He hated to admit it, but he pulled up that page with her profile photo at least once a day, hoping some hint of information would be available. He was left disappointed each time. Luke clicked back to her business website again, *Sully Investigations*, and printed off a couple of pertinent pages. Luke grabbed those pages off the printer and the Maime LaRue Brewer file and headed back to the detective's conference room for a meeting.

Entering the room, the first thing he saw was the familiar chalkboards with case notes and strategy. The photos of suspects and witnesses lined the walls. Both Captain Kurt Meadows and his partner Detective Bill Tyler, who sat on opposite sides of the conference room, were waiting for him.

Luke was the head of the violent crimes division, a post he took up four years earlier. Each case seemed to get a little tougher. Luke could have farmed out the Brewer case to one of the detectives in his unit, but he chose to keep it for himself. It was a high-profile case. Really, he just wanted the satisfaction of taking down George Brewer himself.

Luke was as sure as he was standing there that George killed his wife. They just didn't have any evidence yet. Luke pulled out a chair at the conference table and sat down next to his partner and pushed the folder of information across to his captain.

Captain Kurt Meadows just turned sixty and was close to retirement. He had a head of sparse white hair that most times couldn't be seen under his captain's hat. His hands were as sun spotted as his face, and his blue eyes were dulling with age. Luke knew he just wasn't quite ready to hang up his hat, literally.

"Anything on the floater in the river?" Captain Meadows asked as he kicked off the meeting.

"Not yet. Medical examiner and CSI are down there now. Once we get prints, we'll see what we get back. Won't know anything until then. We got statements from the women who found her and a few others who came running to the scene but not much else," Luke detailed.

"What have we found here?" Captain Meadows asked, tapping his index finger on the open Brewer file. It was filled with useless statements and photos of the Brewer home. No sign of struggle, nothing of significance.

"We don't know much. Maime left work midafternoon last Friday and hasn't been seen since. Still no word to her family or friends and certainly none to her husband," Luke explained regretfully. Every lead they initially had turned out to be a dead end. Five days in and they had already run out of leads.

Luke went over the details again for his captain. "Her husband called us on Sunday morning. He said she usually goes out on Fridays after work with her girlfriends so when she didn't come home Friday night and hadn't called, that wasn't unusual. When she wasn't in by her usual time on Saturday, he checked with her friends and family and realized they hadn't seen her on Friday night. He got worried, spent most of the day Saturday driving around, checking out spots she frequents and then called in a missing person's report when he ran out of options."

Luke's partner Tyler asked, "You mean it's normal for her to leave work Friday afternoons and sometimes not come home until Saturday morning? What kind of marriage is that?"

Tyler had been married for close to seventeen years. He had been a detective for twelve of those years and Luke's partner for seven. Tyler was in his forties, a decent detective and even better husband. He always had Luke's back. He also adored his wife. Luke was sure Tyler couldn't imagine his wife not coming home on a Friday night and instead staying out with the girls. Tyler stared at Luke. He felt like he needed to explain further.

"I know it's weird, but it's what he says and a few of her girlfriends have confirmed. They like to have a few drinks, shop, maybe see a movie and have girl's night. Except this Friday, she never showed. The girls assumed she went home instead. They didn't think anything of it. It had happened before, and then Maime would call them on Saturday with an apology and explanation for her absence."

Captain Meadows thumbed through the file and noted, "Last positive eye on her is at her office in the middle of the afternoon Friday. One of the coworkers saw her leaving the building, correct?"

"Yes, that's correct. She said she was going to a meeting but nobody seemed to know where. We don't know where she went. I think the husband is involved. Nothing points to any other direction and the many volunteer searchers haven't recovered anything. I think he'll lead us to her eventually," Luke said, and then added thoughtfully, "I think he called in the report to cover his own butt. He beat her friends and family to the punch."

"You think she's dead?" Cap asked directly.

"No signs of life. So yeah, not sure what else we are supposed to think. It's been several days and no sign of her. People don't just disappear. Something's obviously happened to her."

"Her SUV hasn't been found. Couldn't she have just driven off somewhere?" Captain Meadows offered in response.

"She could. It's possible I guess, but we've notified every surrounding state, put her photo and SUV info on the national news and only a handful of calls have come into the hotline. Not one has turned out to be a decent lead," Luke countered.

Then he added, "Plus, she was never known to carry much cash. There has been no bank activity on her personal account or credit cards. From what George says no money seems to be missing from their joint accounts either. Her family and friends said that Maime didn't like being alone at all. Taking off would be completely out of character."

Captain Meadows flipped through more notes, and then reminded them, "Ask for the bank records and to search the house again. I want everything documented. We've got to cover our butts on this one. Her father is already calling everyone he knows. We've already handled calls from the mayor and the governor's offices."

"Cap," Tyler interrupted, "you hear George hired some female private investigator from New York to search for Maime?"

Luke shot his partner a look. He didn't want to go into this now.

"Really?" Captain cocked his head to the side and laid the file folder down, looking at Luke across the table. He didn't look happy. "What do you have on that?"

"Riley Sullivan. She's licensed and runs her own firm in New York. She was an investigative reporter previously. She lived here a few years ago and worked for the Little Rock Record."

"She lived here? What's her connection to the Brewers?" Tyler asked.

"Cooper just told me about an hour ago," Luke responded sarcastically, hoping he could convince them this was a waste of time. When he saw their faces, he quickly realized his attitude wouldn't help anything. He toned it down. "She should have arrived this afternoon. I asked them to meet tomorrow morning."

"Keep her out of the way. You asked Cooper to run interference for us?" Captain asked, and Luke nodded yes. "Good, keep them both out of our way."

It was at that moment the conference room door banged open and a uniformed officer stuck his head in and shouted, "Let's go! Fisherman just spotted another woman's body floating down near the boat launch at Murray Park."

CHAPTER 4

THE CRISP FALL AIR ENVELOPED ME as I walked out of the hotel and onto the sidewalk. The historic Capital Hotel was directly across the street. I was flooded with the memory of George and me seeing the beautiful Christmas tree they put up in the lobby each year and having a romantic dinner there one holiday season. I shook it off and headed down the street farther into the River Market District.

The President Clinton Library was directly at the end of the road. I couldn't see it from where I stood, but someone once described its long rectangular design as a trailer home on stilts. They joked it was fitting architectural design for Arkansas. I didn't really see that in the design but to each their own, I guess.

As I walked, I was happily surprised at just how many new bars and restaurants lined the streets, their lights brightening up the sidewalk and road. There hadn't been this many places when I lived here before. I had spent a bit of time at the few places here back in the day so I was half expecting to see people I knew, but so far, no one looked familiar.

I crossed the road, stepping over the trolley tracks. Downtown now had a trolley, which made me smile. The area wasn't really big enough to warrant one but a fun addition nonetheless. I walked by couples holding hands, walking snug against each other. I felt a pang of jealousy. It's been a long time since I've felt anything even remotely close to being a part of a twosome. I hadn't realized how much I've missed it. A little tumble between the sheets and kicking them out right after certainly didn't qualify as a relationship.

The truth is I missed living here. Deciding to leave and go back to New York had been a hard decision, but it had to be done. I tried to shake off the crappy mood setting in as I watched the few onlookers standing at the yellow crime scene tape. This was usually an area of downtown known for fun with family and friends. Now it was marred by police searching for clues. Death just didn't seem fitting. It sent a shiver down my spine.

I turned my back to the scene and kept walking. Arriving at my destination, I pulled open the door to the Flying Saucer. It seemed crowded for a Wednesday night with the servers in their plaid mini-skirts, tight tees and knee socks. They ran from table to table taking orders and depositing food and drinks. Looking around, I spotted Cooper at an empty table in the far-right back corner.

"I thought we could use some privacy," Cooper said, smiling as I sat down across the table from him. Our server Mandy came over to take our order. I noticed that while she was writing down what we said, Cooper was checking her out - all five-feet-ten-inches of her, long legs clad in black thigh-highs and her red and black plaid skirt coming just inches below her bottom. I waited until she left to call him a pig.

"What?" he asked, feigning innocence.

I spent a few minutes trying to get out of him who he was dating and what he was doing for fun when he wasn't chasing down cheating spouses or insurance fraudsters. No go, he wouldn't tell me a thing. He remained tight-lipped about the women in his life, but it was clear there wasn't a Mrs. Cooper Deagnan on the horizon.

Mandy came back and laid down drinks. Cooper spent some time watching her behind sway as she walked away. Then he turned to me and said, "You're going to have to fill me in sooner or later, you know, so why don't you just tell me the history between you and George. I'm having trouble believing you would be involved with a guy like him." Cooper raised his glass to his lips, took a few sips of his drink, and waited.

I filled Cooper in on how I met George at a coffee shop in Boston. Hit it off right away. Then about the calls, emails and letters over the months that followed. I told him about the plane tickets

George kept sending me and the hotel reservations in Little Rock. I also mentioned George's frequent trips to New York to visit me.

"I admit I was attracted to him. He was funny and sweet, and even though it's hard for you to believe, we had things in common." I purposefully left out that George was seeing Maime at the time. That although I was separated, I was still technically married, which to this day George still doesn't know. I guess we both had our secrets.

Cooper held up his hand interrupting me, "This was before you moved to Little Rock? Is George the reason you moved?"

I hated that question. The truth was pathetic. The answer was yes, but I couldn't admit that to Cooper, so instead I said, "I had been visiting a lot and had met some reporters down here. I ended up getting a pretty sweet deal at the Little Rock Record that made a move worthwhile. I was building my reporting career and the offer made sense at the time."

"When were you seeing George in relation to when you lived here?" Cooper asked, ever the investigator. "Where does Maime fit into this?"

I waved my hand dismissively and lied through my teeth, "Things ended with George well before I moved. He and Maime got together and the rest is history." I shrugged for good measure. This was definitely territory I didn't want to go into tonight.

Cooper leaned across the table, stared me in the eyes and said, "You're being dismissive. I think you're lying to me about something. I'm just not sure what yet."

"You know much about the woman they pulled from the river?" I asked, desperate for a subject change.

"No. I saw Luke earlier, but they are still processing the scene."

I took a sip of my drink and asked as nonchalantly as I could, "You saw Luke?"

Cooper eyed me. "You know that's the other thing you might want to explain to me. I know there's history there. You dated for a while. Then it ended. What happened?"

"Things end." I shrugged again.

"Riley, what are you doing?" Cooper asked, cocking his head to one side and shooting me a look like I was one toe over the ledge of insanity.

"What?"

Cooper watched me closely, maybe waiting to see if I was going to open up on my own. I wasn't one of his witnesses though. I knew the wait and see game in interrogation.

He caved first and said, "I don't understand what you're doing here. You dated George and you dated Luke. The alleged perp and the lead detective. Isn't this one heck of a conflict of interest for you?"

"That, my friend," I said as I picked up my glass, took a sip and peered at him over the rim, "is precisely why I need to be here."

CHAPTER 5

LUKE GRIPPED THE SUV'S STEERING WHEEL so tightly his hands were cramping. He drove with measured determination, getting to Murray Park as quickly and safely as he could. Tyler and Captain Meadows rode in silence watching Luke navigate the winding Little Rock roads on the way to the river's edge.

Although Luke hadn't admitted it to Cooper earlier, his friend was right. Whenever Luke was called out on a case where there was a dead young woman, it always brought him back to the day his little sister Lily's body was found in the woods near the University of Arkansas in Fayetteville. She had been a freshman, and like many young co-eds, walked home alone from a party one night. She never made it back to her dorm.

Luke had been living in an off-campus apartment with friends and didn't know Lily was even missing until his parents called. He felt helpless at the time. Guilt had set in over the years as he replayed those hours he was drinking and laughing with friends while his sister was murdered. Cases like these brought back the same feelings of guilt, anger and dread. To do his job, Luke had to keep that in check.

His sister's death was the reason he went into police work. Lily had been missing for eight months before her skeletal remains were found tossed among the leaves. His once beautiful little sister reduced to bones. They never did find her killer or even any evidence for a real cause of death. Lily's murder had devastated Luke's parents.

He didn't think they had ever fully recovered from the loss of their only daughter.

Lily was Luke's only sibling. He still felt like a part of him was missing. His relationship with his parents only got stronger through the years. But because he still hadn't been able to solve his sister's murder, Luke felt like he was disappointing them, and himself, if he was being honest. That's why he worked so hard on murder cases, pushing himself beyond a breaking point at times. He had more to prove than the others. At least, he felt like he did.

Luke was almost to the crime scene. His stomach knotted and rolled. He released the tight grip on the steering wheel and tried to take a few deep breaths. Showing up to a crime scene tense and already agitated wouldn't make his job easier. Murray Park was generally safe. It was a family place with eight pavilions, three soccer fields, two playgrounds and the boat dock. Runners, walkers and families with their dogs were a common sight at the park. Not dead bodies.

Passing the Rebsamen Park Golf Course on the right, Luke noticed the line of cars on the side of the road. He passed slowly, taking in the news vans and onlookers, some standing in groups and others moving slowly down the walking path towards the park entrance. The street was ablaze in light. He didn't like that such a crowd had already started to gather.

All Luke knew from the initial call to 911 was that a woman's body had washed up near the boat ramp at the park. An older man in his sixties coming in from a day on the Arkansas River spotted the body and made the frantic 911 call. There was a woman's body. She had long blonde hair and was face down in the water. Her body was caught between two rocks just out from the boat ramp.

The fisherman had left late in the afternoon. The report didn't specify a time. He told the 911 operator he hadn't noticed anything when he took his boat out, but when he was coming back in at dusk, he spotted a body in the water. Uniformed officers were holding him at the park for Luke to question.

Luke approached the entrance to the park and was thankful a police barricade was already in place. He slowed down and navigated his unmarked police car through the crowd. A uniformed officer waved him through. He pulled in, drove past the playgrounds and open field directly to the back parking lot that overlooked the river.

Marked and unmarked police cars littered the parking lot. Luke was surprised to see the Pulaski County Medical Examiner had already arrived. Luke had just seen him down the road at the other crime scene. Two dead women pulled from the Arkansas River in one night. Unprecedented in Little Rock.

Luke steered his SUV in line with the other police vehicles. He stepped out, barely closing the door behind him. He moved quickly, walking ahead of Tyler and Captain Meadows. He wanted to see the body and get the initial shock he always felt first on the scene over and done with so he could get to work. No matter how many times he had rolled up to a scene like this, nothing could prepare him for the sight of the deceased. Luke never understood when he heard other detectives tell him they were numb to it. That wasn't him. He wished for numbness to wash over him. It never came.

Luke walked to the top of the boat ramp and looked out at the river. Ed Purvis, the Pulaski County Medical Examiner, was with two of his employees knee deep in the water. They were flanked on each side by members of the Little Rock Dive Team who carefully moved the woman's body, clad only in her bra and underwear, out of the water onto a dive board. They carefully moved her into a heavy black body bag.

Luke moved down the ramp towards the water and called out to Purvis, "What do we know so far?"

Purvis, fifty-five and balding, wore black waterproof rubber overalls and a county issued medical examiner white shirt. He looked up. "Hold on, let me get out of here, and I'll fill you in."

Purvis and his team carried her body past Luke and up the boat ramp.

Luke felt his impatience rise. He wanted to know right now if it was Maime LaRue Brewer or not. She was the daughter of the most high-profile, richest lobbyist in the south. He knew the whole community would be watching the police department on this case. The pressure he felt was already intense.

Luke stood halfway down the boat ramp. He turned to see Captain Meadows and Tyler at the top, watching as Purvis moved past them to the medical examiner's van and placed her on a stretcher. Tyler was clenching and unclenching his fists. Captain Meadows wiped his brow as he asked, "Any chance we can get a photo comparison before you take her, Purvis?"

Purvis responded as he positioned the body on the stretcher. "Might. She's bloated but not much else. Don't want to guess, but if I had to say, she hasn't been dead more than a few days. Looks like ligature marks are around her wrists, ankles and neck. Petechiae is present and lips, fingers and toes are bluish. Can't call it now, but my guess would be a homicide. Like the one earlier, no defensive wounds that I can see here. I really can't imagine she was taking a swim half naked in the river this time of year."

"Fits with the timeline," Tyler reminded them without saying anything else.

Luke couldn't wait any longer. He had to know. He walked back up the ramp to the van while pulling on heavy purple medical gloves from his back pocket. He side-stepped around his partner and his captain and unzipped the body bag, partially exposing the deceased woman's face. He peered down, looked closely, and muttered curses under his breath.

Luke looked up at Captain Meadows and Tyler and shook his head side to side. He would have to wait for the official identification, but he was pretty sure this was not Maime. Not that he was hoping it was Maime. It's just that this meant he now had three cases – two deceased, one missing. He certainly wasn't one to be dramatic, but he felt like Little Rock was under siege.

CHAPTER 6

I TOSSED MY NAPKIN DOWN and pushed my empty plate to the side. The dinner's arrival had delayed the discussion about Luke, thankfully. More than anything, I wanted to learn what Cooper knew about Maime and George. "I've read the news reports and only spoke to George briefly. What can you tell me about this case so far?"

"Before we really get into this, you have to promise me that tomorrow you'll come with me to meet Luke and his partner Det. Bill Tyler who are in charge of the investigation."

I sipped my drink. I hadn't planned on seeing Luke so soon. Meeting with him and getting things out in the open might prove useful. I couldn't keep my eye on him if I didn't get close enough. "All right," I conceded. "I'll meet them tomorrow."

"You'll make nice?"

I held my hands up in surrender. "I promise. Now tell me what you know so far."

"I don't really know a lot either," Cooper admitted, leaning forward, his elbows on the table, hands folded in front of him. "I guess Maime said she was going to be with friends on Friday night, but she never met up with them. George claims she didn't go home either. On Saturday morning, after George said he hadn't heard from her, he called her several times. Then he called friends and family.

When no one said they had seen her, he made a police report. She hasn't been seen or heard from since Friday."

"Her friends didn't bother to call her when she didn't show up on Friday night?" From what I remember, she had a tight-knit group of girlfriends.

"No, but I guess they never did. A big group of them met up, and if you showed, you showed. If not, they assumed you had other plans," Cooper explained.

I let that sink in for a minute because it meant there was a lot of time for Maime to be missing without anyone realizing it. George thought she was with friends and her friends thought she was at home. I didn't know if she spoke to her mother or other family every day, but I doubted it. She was a grown woman after all. Then again, if her mother was anything like mine, we might get lucky and find she had a tracking chip in her.

"There haven't been any other sightings of her since Friday afternoon at work," Cooper said.

"Where does she work?"

"She was doing some pharmaceutical sales from an office out on Chenal in West Little Rock. After she left the office, there were no other sightings of her. No bank transactions either from what Luke tells me. It's like she just vanished," Cooper explained, gesturing with his hands as if into thin air.

If it was George, his motivation was anyone's guess. Husband or boyfriend was the usual prime suspect. And that was the first time it occurred to me that Maime might have a boyfriend on the side, which could also be motive for George. That wouldn't help.

We would have to start with George and get him to tell us everything he knows that will help this case. He has to help himself before we start anywhere else. I didn't even know where else to start other than the girls she was supposed to see on Friday night. Her parents and coworkers might know something as well. They would be my next step.

"You know if Maime was seeing anyone?" I asked, hoping Cooper might know. While I didn't think he really knew George well, they did run in some of the same circles. Little Rock was surprisingly small in some regards.

"Not that I'm aware of. If anyone was the cheater in that relationship, my best guess would be on George."

I nodded in agreement. Unfortunately, I had learned the hard way. I started to ask another question when I overheard the two women behind Cooper talking about a text one of them just received. It was from the one woman's husband who had come back from a fishing trip and was down at the dock at Murray Park. We heard her screech to her friend that another woman's body had washed up close to the dock.

CHAPTER 7

LUKE LOOKED DOWN AGAIN, closer this time, at the woman's face and then unzipped the body bag down her torso. She was probably in her thirties, blonde hair and what he assumed was probably a pretty face, now ravaged by death. Her eyes were closed and she was slender. Like the woman earlier in the day, she was found only in her bra and underwear.

Tell me who did this to you, he mentally asked the deceased, scanning her body for clues or some sign of what might have occurred. Luke was sure it wasn't Maime, but he'd still need a positive identification from her husband or parents. He didn't want to make that call.

Luke slowly looked her over again from the top of her head to her shiny red fingernail polish. He was just about to cover her back up when he noticed the bracelet on her right wrist. It was a silver bracelet, intricate in design with a squared jeweled clasp. He wasn't sure of the design. Celtic possibly, trinity knots maybe, but either way it looked of quality. Strangely enough, it looked familiar. Luke searched the recesses of his brain for where he might have seen this before. He couldn't place it. Feeling defeated, he reminded Purvis to bag and tag it. Maybe prints would be present. He hoped.

"This is crazy, Luke. Two in one day. Any ideas?" Purvis asked, staring at Luke over the dead woman.

"Unfortunately, not a clue," Luke let out a long sigh. "Get me what you can on prints and time and manner of death, and it will be a start."

Luke stepped back as Purvis and his team zipped up the body bag and began to load the stretcher into the back of the van. Purvis was good. He would get Luke the information he needed and as quickly as he could, given the circumstances.

Luke looked to the dock area and the witness sitting on a bench with two officers on either side. The witness was an older guy probably mid-sixties with little hair, and what he did have left was gray. He had on glasses, khakis and a white Razorbacks tee-shirt.

As Luke approached, the older man stood, extended his hand and told Luke his name was Walter Thomas. He spent the next thirty minutes filling Luke in on how he fished the Arkansas River for forty years and nothing like this had ever happened to him. Walter said he didn't notice anything else unusual and wasn't certain whether the body was there when he went out earlier in the day. But as he said, "How could I miss a dead body?"

A uniformed officer standing with them informed Luke that other witnesses in the area confirmed that Walter had started yelling for help as his boat approached the ramp. That's when a group of them in the park noticed the body. Luke asked the officers to double check witness statements, make sure they had all their names and contact information, and put them on notice that, if needed, the police would be in touch.

Luke didn't think there was a suspect among them. They seemed like ordinary folks enjoying what otherwise would have been a pleasant fall day at the park. Same as the first two women who spotted the woman found earlier in the day. Average people on an average day that now would horrifically be remembered forever.

Luke took in the crowd once more. He knew it wasn't uncommon for the killer to revisit the scene or be among the spectators when a body was found. Luke looked around at the families and scared confused faces. If the perp was here, it sure didn't seem like it.

Luke stood for a moment deciding what to do next. He was overwhelmed. His cellphone buzzed against his hip. He answered, "Not a good time, Coop."

"We know. Riley and I are standing on the other side of the barricade with the news media out front. Let us back. We heard you found a woman's body."

"Not now. And definitely not with her." Luke looked in the direction of the park entrance but couldn't see them from where he was standing. He wasn't ready to deal with Riley yet.

"Is it really a woman?" Cooper asked, and Luke confirmed. Cooper went on, "If it is Maime, Riley has met her. She can help with the identification."

Luke was torn. For as much as he didn't want to see Riley, he really wanted a positive identification out of the way. It would save him a call to George and to Maime's parents. He kicked the dirt in front of his foot. "All right," he said hesitantly, "I'll be right there."

CHAPTER 8

I COULDN'T BELIEVE that Luke was actually going to let us back. After leaving the pub, we drove straight to the park. It was only a few miles but seemed to take forever with each second painfully ticking by. When we arrived, we were both surprised the media was already stationed around the scene. Cooper had to park far down Rebsamen Road. We walked to the park entrance, and on the way, Cooper called Luke.

Cooper ended the call, looked down at me and asked, "You okay with taking a look and helping with a positive identification? Sorry I spoke for you, but I didn't know how else to get us back there."

"I'm okay with it. It's been a couple of years since I've seen Maime in person. I'm pretty sure I'll know if it's her or not." Of all the times I'd wished she'd disappear from my life, I never wished her dead. If it was her, I wasn't sure how I'd feel.

We waited at the barricade for Luke. The uniformed cop nodded to Cooper but didn't make a move to let us back. The crowd seemed to grow with each passing minute. I always found it strange how many people seem to flock around tragedy.

"Excuse me," a male voice called from the right of me. "Did I overhear you say you know Maime? I assume you're talking about the missing woman Maime LaRue Brewer?"

Cooper and I both turned to look at who was speaking to us. Neither of us said anything at first. It was obvious the guy was media.

They used to be my kind of people. The guy was a little shorter than Cooper. He was about five eleven with sandy brown hair that hung over his forehead almost covering his right eye. I guessed he was right around forty years old, with light-colored baggy jeans, sneakers and a long-sleeve black tee-shirt. He carried a camera, a digital Nikon D4. I knew Cooper would be jealous. He just said at dinner he'd been saving for that very camera for surveillance.

"I'm sorry. We can't really answer any of your questions." I turned back around. Hoped he went away. The last thing I needed was Luke thinking I was passing information on to reporters. Unfortunately, the guy didn't take the hint. Instead, he moved even closer next to me, stuck out his hand and introduced himself.

"I'm Ben Prosser with the Little Rock Times. What about you?"

I shook his extended hand. "Waiting."

Cooper smirked, but he didn't say a word either. The Little Rock Times was the only other paper in Little Rock covering local news. It was a direct competitor to the Little Rock Record where I had worked.

Ben went on undeterred, "I've been covering the missing person's case since it was reported. I work the crime beat a lot. I was there for an interview of the husband and her parents over the weekend. Real nice people. Maime's family thinks the husband did something to her. I think we all suspect that."

I took a deep breath so loud that I'm sure Cooper heard it above the noise of the crowd. I turned and said slightly exasperated, "Good for you, Ben. I'm sorry, but I really don't want to talk. We have work to do. Now just isn't a good time."

Before Ben could respond, Luke walked up to the barricade. He stopped in front of us, but he didn't even look at me. He turned to Cooper and spoke directly to him like I wasn't even there.

"Cooper, you ready to come back?" Then he turned and said to Ben, "You're out here fast, Ben. You got any ideas who called the media?"

I was a little surprised Luke was so familiar with Ben, but then again, that is how I met both Cooper and Luke. Different cases, different scenes but still the same way. I raised my eyebrows and shot Cooper a look. He shrugged.

Ben said he didn't know who made the call. His editor Cathy called and sent him out. Luke must have caught my look. At least he finally looked at me. Ben, Luke explained, had been known to look through Little Rock's cold cases for new leads. He was a bit of an amateur sleuth. Luke told us Ben had actually found new leads on two homicides from the seventies, and the cases were later solved. Most of the cops knew Ben pretty well.

"Ben, I'll give you a call with our statement as soon as we have one. Right now, I can't confirm anything," Luke explained as he moved the barricade aside and let Cooper and me through. Ben smiled and then shot me a nasty look. It seemed I was making friends already.

CHAPTER 9

WE WALKED BACK to the crime scene in silence. I was already regretting being snarky to Ben. I was used to asking the questions, not answering. I probably shouldn't have been rude, but I just wasn't in the mood to talk. We could chalk it up to the fact that I'm a "Yankee" in the south, but I needed to remind myself to stay friendly with the media and everyone else. It's a great way to get information or at least the gossip about a case.

We walked past the uniformed cops and through a second barricade. Luke and Cooper walked side by side. I trailed behind a few steps. I watched Luke as he walked, long strides and sure of himself. I admit I was still attracted to him. He always looked good, but there were moments, like now, where his attractiveness caught me by surprise. I couldn't really explain it. It made my stomach flip a little.

I met Luke when I was a reporter in Little Rock. We met on a homicide case in the southeast part of the city. Luke was the detective that eventually gave me a statement. I thought he was attractive from the moment I saw him. It was an odd emotion to have while covering a homicide. He was tall, broad-shouldered with dark smooth skin and close-shaved head and face. There was no denying our chemistry.

Later, after that case, I noticed his beautiful smile and dimple in his left cheek. Whenever I saw him, he was well-dressed, preppy almost. He looked the same to me now. I felt that old physical attraction coming back. If I wasn't reading too much into it, he still seemed to hate me. Not that I could blame him.

As I was lost in thought, Luke abruptly turned to face me, folded his arms over his chest and said, "Ms. Sullivan."

"Nice to see you again, Detective," I said, putting my hand out to shake his. He didn't return the gesture. He just glared down at me, then turned and started walking again. I stood there awkwardly for a moment before I retracted my hand and put it in my pocket. Cooper shot me a look with his eyebrows raised.

We started to walk towards the river. Luke turned on me again. I almost bumped into him this time. We stood almost toe to toe. He bore down on me and asked angrily, "Why are you here, Ms. Sullivan? Do you assume we are incompetent and can't solve a case?"

His anger made me take a physical step back. I wasn't prepared for it to be so blatant and obvious to those around us. Cooper hung back, not saying anything, definitely not coming to my defense. I scrambled for an appropriate response.

"No, of course not," I stammered. "George Brewer called me. He told me his wife was missing and that he needed an investigator. I know Maime, too. I know what she's like, and what she's capable of, Detective."

"That means what?" Luke asked me with a sarcastic tone of voice.

"Could I please just see her and get this over with?"

Luke started to say something and stopped. He uncrossed his arms and pointed his finger at me and said, "Fine, but I want you both in my office early tomorrow morning by eight. Follow me."

Luke, Cooper and I walked over to the medical examiner's van. We stood together at the back of the van, and Luke introduced us to the medical examiner and his team. Ed Purvis was short and stocky. He wore wire-framed glasses and reminded me of every medical examiner I've ever met. Someone you'd never really remember. He'd blend into the crowd. I've always been a little amazed by anyone that would choose that as their line of work, but then again, most people say the same thing about me.

Purvis reached into the van and rolled the body out on the stretcher. The stretcher's legs folded out on their own. I braced myself. No matter how many times I've done this, I've never really found a good way to prepare myself to come face-to-face with death.

Cooper was by my side. I felt his hand on my back as Purvis unzipped the bag, uncovering her face and upper body. I looked down, held my breath, and stared at the dead woman's face. It definitely wasn't Maime. It wasn't her nose, her chin or her hair. I'd never seen this woman before.

I looked farther down over her body and sucked in an almost audible breath, shocked by what I saw. On her wrist she wore a bracelet I'd know anywhere. I also knew who gave it to her.

"Well," Luke said, looking at me waiting for a response.

I nodded toward Purvis indicating he could zip up the body bag. He pushed the stretcher back inside the van. I waited until Purvis rejoined the group. I stood there with all of them looking at me, waiting for a response. I wasn't sure if I was going to let them know about the bracelet or not. I wasn't sure how much I should say.

"Riley, you okay? You look a bit shaken," Cooper said, watching me. He reached his hand out and squeezed my shoulder.

"I'm fine," I said evenly, and then paused to take a breath. "It's not Maime. I'm positive about that. I've never seen this woman before."

"I didn't think it was her," Luke explained. "I've seen photos, and while the age is about the same, hair color close enough, I didn't think it could be her."

We stood in silence, taking in what this meant. Maime was still missing and now two women had been found dead in the Arkansas River on the same day. This quiet upscale part of Little Rock was being turned upside down.

"Have there been reports of other missing women?" I asked.

"No, not recently," Luke said. He turned to Purvis. "When you pull her prints, let me know. We'll run her in the database and see what pops. I want to be cautious with the media so we have a chance to notify her family before this is made too public."

He turned to me and added, "You think you can keep your mouth shut? What you saw tonight is not a matter for public consumption."

Before I could defend myself, Luke stalked off towards a group of other cops who turned to look at us as he approached them. Purvis nodded goodbye to us.

Cooper and I walked back out of the barricade and through the throngs of bystanders and news crews. Luckily, they were more focused on Luke who walked behind us toward the barricade. I could only assume that meant he was going to make some kind of statement to the press. Thankfully, they let us pass without question.

CHAPTER 10

COOPER TOOK THE STAIRS to his loft two at a time. He was surprised he still had that much energy left after the day he had. All he wanted was to flop down on the couch, open a cold beer and check some scores on ESPN. It was moments like this that he was glad he lived alone and didn't have a wife who was going to nag him to take out the trash or pick up his clothes as soon as he opened the door. He had yet to find a woman he could tolerate for more than a night or two.

After leaving Murray Park, he dropped Riley off at the hotel. She seemed distracted and quiet. Too quiet to be typically Riley. Cooper tried several times to talk to her about what was bothering her, but she remained pretty closed off. Maybe it was seeing a dead body that was throwing off her evening. It sure threw off his. Cooper was still having trouble wrapping his head around it all. He saw crime all the time but not like this.

After making sure Riley made it into the hotel lobby, Cooper drove down the road to the other crime scene and noticed the techs still hard at work. Then he went a few blocks over to his condo on Third Street. He loved living in downtown Little Rock – always something to do, but then again, temptation lurked around every corner. He could almost hear his father Leo asking him when he was going to settle down like him. Cooper laughed at the idea. Leo had been married four times. Cooper's mom passed away when he was young, and there were a series of stepmothers that followed.

After parking his truck in the lot and taking the stairs to the sixth floor, Cooper slid his key in the bolt lock and was just about to turn the key when the door across the hall from him opened. Cooper turned in time to see his neighbor Jenny Pike step into the hall.

"Cooper, can I talk to you for a minute?" Jenny asked quietly. Cooper could just about taste that cold beer that waited for him. He didn't want to talk, but she looked a little bit worried.

Cooper hadn't really spoken to her much in the three months since she moved across the hall from him, other than exchanging some pleasantries in the hallway when they saw each other, which was rare.

Cooper knew she was around his age and was a nurse at UAMS, but that was about the extent of it. He didn't like to get involved with women so close to home. She was still dressed in her scrubs, and her dark hair pulled back in a ponytail. He guessed she hadn't been home from work very long.

Cooper opened his door and turned, leaning into the door jamb. "Sure, what's up? Is everything okay?"

"I'm not sure. You're an investigator, right? I'm hoping you can help me." Jenny was wringing her hands together. Cooper glanced at his watch. He wished she'd get to the point. It was almost eleven, and he wanted to catch the news before he switched to ESPN.

"Yeah, I'm a PI. I'll do my best," Cooper said honestly.

Jenny took a deep visible breath and said, "You know the case of the missing woman Maime LaRue Brewer?"

Cooper stood a little straighter and crossed his arms, ready to listen. "I'm familiar with the case," he said casually.

"I might know something. I don't know if it's important or not so I thought you could tell me what you think," Jenny explained.

Cooper nodded and let her continue.

"For the last six months, a friend of mine had been dating George. She shouldn't have been, but she was," Jenny said, sounding nervous to Cooper's trained ear.

"Are they still seeing each other?" Cooper had suspected George was a cheater, but this was the clincher.

"I think it stopped a few weeks ago. I saw them together at the hospital pretty often. He would visit her, and she confided in me about the affair. Then a few weeks back, she came to work pretty upset. She was obviously crying and her work suffered. When I asked, all she would say was that it was over with George."

"Any idea what happened? Do you know if Maime found out?"

"I don't know about Maime. My friend didn't say, and I didn't press her for details. I figured when she was ready to talk about it, she would. I can tell you George wasn't trying to hide the affair, at least at the hospital. He was affectionate and more than once her supervisor had to speak with her about her behavior in front of staff and patients, if you know what I mean. Shouldn't she tell the police?"

"I think she probably should. You can have her ask for Det. Luke Morgan. He's in charge of the investigation," Cooper said. He wished he could have a crack at interviewing her before the cops, but that wouldn't happen. That's the problem with getting involved in an open law enforcement investigation. There was always a fine line you had to walk.

"Thanks, Cooper, I'll talk to her. I don't know if she will, but I'll try. I'm worried about her. If he did kill his wife, who knows what he's capable of," Jenny said. She looked at Cooper like she wanted confirmation that her friend would be safe. Cooper couldn't give it.

Instead, he reached over and laid his hand on hers, hoping to calm her. "It will be okay. Det. Morgan is a good guy. Any information your friend or you have will help the investigation. What's your friend's name?"

Jenny hesitated. Cooper figured she was trying to decide if she wanted to share that much information with him.

Finally, she said, "Let me talk to her first. I don't want her angry with me. I'll try to call her tonight or in the morning and talk with her. I'll let you know."

Cooper gave Jenny his and Luke's cell numbers, and again, reassured her that she was doing the right thing. Jenny said she was concerned her friend would be angry with her for meddling in her life, but she just didn't feel right about the situation. Cooper assured her that he understood.

They said goodnight, and Cooper let himself into his loft. He sat down on the couch and was asleep before he could even think about calling Riley or catching any ESPN updates.

CHAPTER 11

MY RINGING CELLPHONE broke the late-night silence. I didn't even want to bother looking to see who it was, but I picked it up anyway and saw that it was George. I sent the call to voicemail. I assumed he was calling because he had seen the report about the woman's body found in the river. I should have answered. He was technically a client. I just couldn't be bothered. I had enough for one day.

I wanted nothing more than to be home in my own bed, in my own house. And that's exactly where I was. After leaving the park, I went back to the hotel, quickly pulled my things together, and checked out. George had made the reservation, and it served as the perfect spot for the initial meeting. Now I wanted the feel of home.

I drove my rental car out of downtown Little Rock, up the winding Cantrell hill, and into the historic Heights neighborhood that George first introduced me to. It's the very same neighborhood in which George and Maime currently lived. I navigated the streets like the back of my hand and finally pulled the Jeep into the driveway of my house on N. Tyler Street. There were only a handful of people who even knew I still owned a house in Little Rock.

I loved this house. It suited me. I pulled my luggage out of the SUV, took out my keys, and opened the front door. The cold air and silence of a house standing empty rushed me. My best friend Emma and her husband Joe lived next door. They watched my place for me.

I hoped Joe had some firewood ready for me so I could light a fire in the living room fireplace and bring this place back to life. I had called them before I left New York to let them know I was coming back.

The house, for the most part, had been empty since I left Little Rock. Emma came over from time to time when she needed a break from Joe and their three-year-old daughter Sophie. The furniture I bought when I purchased the home was still here, but other than that, the house was unoccupied.

The house meant too much to me to sell it when I left. I was in a holding pattern trying to decide what I was going to do with it. It was costing me money. I didn't care.

A few months after moving to Little Rock, I saw this house for sale and knew immediately I wanted it. It was a 1925 two-story, four-bedroom bungalow with a large wrap-around front porch, eat-in kitchen and high ceilings decorated with the details found during that era including built-in bookshelves, crown molding and hardwoods throughout.

The house, much like me at the time, just needed some love and attention. Mending a broken heart, I threw myself into renovating. With each room, I restored the house including hardwoods refinished, walls freshly painted and the original crown moldings restored. I restored myself as well. I brought myself as much back to life as I did this house. It wasn't just a project for me. It was the very reflection of who I was and what I was going through at the time. It was not just a house to me but my home. I was never so happy to be back.

Standing inside the front door, it was a straight shot through the foyer to the kitchen. I could see the back door from where I stood. The living room was off to the right of the foyer and the dining room flowed from the living room with a door that led back into the kitchen. The back door led to a small enclosed porch and out onto the deck. The laundry room was off the kitchen as well. I wandered through the house turning on lights, running my hands over the furniture and walls, noting that at least the housekeeper I paid to clean the place twice a month seemed to be doing a decent job.

I opened the fridge and realized it was stocked with food as were the cabinets. My housekeeper must have taken care of it when I called to tell her I'd be back. I knew she couldn't have spoken to my mother because even my mother didn't know about this house, but the food was all healthy and some even listed as organic. I'd definitely have to shop for myself. I rummaged around in the cabinets until I finally found a package of chocolate chip cookies and poured myself a glass of milk. Some investigators had their vices — sex, smoking, or alcohol. Mine was milk and cookies.

I took the stairs to the left of the front door and headed up to the second floor. I flipped on the hall light as I went. A small hallway connected all four bedrooms. Two larger rooms in the middle, either of which could be used as the master bedroom, and two smaller on the front and back end of the house. One I used as a small library and the other my office. The only drawback to the house was the somewhat small second story bathroom, which was the only one in the whole house. The house was perfect in so many other ways, it was easy to overlook.

I stepped into the smallest of the rooms in the very front of the house and set my milk and cookies on an end table. I moved to my bookshelf and pulled down the old tin jewelry box I bought at an antique shop in town. I sat in an oversized chair that was positioned in front of several bookshelves filled with both fiction and nonfiction alike. I stared at the jewelry box in my lap, knowing what was inside, delaying the inevitable.

Finally, after a couple minutes went by, I did what I had to and opened it. Inside, lying neatly against some tissue paper, glaring back at me, was the very same bracelet I had seen earlier on the dead woman's wrist. The bracelet with its same silver Celtic design taunted me, telling me all I needed to know. George had given me this bracelet. If I had to bet money on it, I was pretty sure whoever the dead woman was, George had given her the same bracelet. It was supposed to be rare. George said he had designed it specifically for me.

Clearly, I wasn't the only one to receive such a beautiful gift. Once when the clasp had broken on mine, I had taken it to a local jeweler to be fixed. He was the one that had made it, a special design both he and George told me. I knew it was not something commonly bought.

That meant that not only was George's wife missing, now he was connected to a dead woman from the river. I laid my head back on the chair and stared at the ceiling. I couldn't wrap my head around it. This definitely wasn't the George I knew. I wasn't dumb enough to think I had been his only affair, but I really didn't think he was capable of murder.

The plan was to meet at the Little Rock Police Department in the morning. I was going to have to tell Cooper about this, and more importantly Luke, which meant I was going to have to explain more than I ever wanted to.

CHAPTER 12

LUKE CLICKED AWAY at the keyboard in front of him. His vision blurred the lines on the screen. He hadn't slept well the night before after coming back from the river. He was frustrated. After speaking to the media and wrapping up at Murray Park, he went back to the station and dug through old missing person's reports to see if there was anything that might give some clues to the identities of the deceased women. He didn't find anything significant.

At two in the morning, Luke finally went home, crawled into his king-size bed alone, laid his head on his pillow, and willed himself to sleep. It didn't happen. His mind raced with thoughts of the missing and the dead, and in between, old memories of Riley crept in. He tried to push those out of his head as soon as they entered, but after seeing her earlier in the evening, he failed at that too.

Luke expected that since so much time had passed he wouldn't feel that old tug of emotion, but he had. The more he thought about it, the angrier he became. He hadn't intended to lash out at her the way he did, but he really couldn't help himself. So much had remained unresolved. Luke had to admit though, Riley still looked good. Her face still heart-shaped, lips full, eyes still dark as night. She still wore her hair long, and although he knew she was always trying, she hadn't lost any weight. Not that he minded. She was the perfect hourglass shape, but he knew for some men, she probably had more on her curves than they would have liked.

For him, Riley was perfect – a little thick in all the right places. Earlier, when he was standing inches from her, breathing her in, he had resisted the urge to reach out and brush those auburn strands of hair away from her face the way he always had when they were lying in bed together.

Really Luke had been hoping that in some small unrealistic way that Riley would have gotten ugly or lost all her hair or something else ridiculous like that. The truth was, that even if she had, he imagined he'd still feel the same about her.

Sleep never came. Luke tossed and turned until he just couldn't take it anymore. He gave up and climbed out of bed, dressed in sweats and went for his typical morning run at six before he headed into the station to start another day's work.

Now that Luke was sitting at his desk, he was paying for his restless night. A full day ahead of him and his head felt like it was going to hit the desk at any moment. It was only through sheer will and practice that he would be able to get through a day with little to no sleep.

Luke was getting older though, felt it in the way his body betrayed him. Although still muscled and toned, his bones creaked at times and his energy depleted quicker than in his youth. He even noticed a gray hair had found its way among the hair on his chest. Time, it seemed, was having its way with him.

Luke rubbed his tired eyes as he continued to scan George and Maime's financial documents. He had already reviewed them. He hoped he had missed something on the first look. They both made a decent income but were living close to their means. Luke wondered if they ever ate at home with the number of credit purchases for local restaurants and pubs.

Maime liked to shop, too. She spent hundreds of dollars each month at local specialty retailers, online and at Dillard's. Even with all those purchases, there was nothing to indicate where she might be or that gave any hint to a financial reason George might have harmed his wife.

Luke was about to pull out more financial documents when he heard the squeak of shoes in the hallway and raised voices. He got up, smoothed his blue tie over his white dress shirt, and navigated his way through the other detective's cubicles to the main hallway to see what was happening.

Luke pulled up short. He hadn't expected to see George Brewer standing in the hall with Maime's father Edwin and another man. They looked to be arguing with Captain Meadows. From Luke's vantage point, he couldn't hear the nature of what they were arguing about. Edwin's face was red, and he was jabbing his finger into Captain Meadows' chest. George hung back not saying anything. The other man with them looked enough like George that he could have been his brother. To Luke's knowledge, George only had a sister.

Luke stepped through the door in enough time to hear Edwin demand to know why they hadn't found his daughter yet and what they were doing to find her. He also wanted to know the identity of the woman pulled from the river. Luke wanted to know the very same things. Edwin could yell and demand all day. They couldn't give him what he wanted.

"Sir," Luke interrupted and pointed to a room down the hall, "I'm sure you'd be more comfortable over in the conference room."

Edwin stopped long enough to take a deep breath and then followed Luke and Captain Meadows into the conference room next to the captain's office.

As they each took a seat around the large table, Luke reached across to the man about to be seated next to George and said tersely, "I'm Detective Lucas Morgan. You are?"

"I'm Dean Beaumont. My firm represents LaRue & Associates. I'm also a good friend of the family. We spoke on the phone earlier this week. As I told you, George was with me on Friday," Dean stated as he shook Luke's hand and then sat down.

George's alibi. Luke didn't like having to speak with Dean on the phone, but the man said he'd been out of town, and the information needed to be confirmed. Luke didn't like him on sight. His handshake was womanly, and his designer suit was too high-end for a meeting at a police station. The man had slick written all over him, from his perfectly coiffed black hair down to his Italian shoes. Luke thought this was probably the kind of guy that gets manicures and pedicures on a regular basis. Too perfect all the way around.

Luke sat and got right to the point. He assured them they were doing all they could to identify the deceased woman but no leads had confirmed her identity yet so there was nothing new to share.

"You're sure it's not Maime?" George asked. Luke noted how pulled together he looked in his polo shirt, pressed khaki pants and jacket. Luke thought he looked too well-rested for a man whose wife was missing. He was also curious why he had not received a call last night from George inquiring about the woman they found.

Luke wanted to know if the reason he didn't get the call was because Riley had told him or if George knew it wasn't Maime because that wasn't where he disposed of her. He'd have to remember to ask Riley if she spoke to George last night. Edwin had called the station around midnight and spoke to another detective. But they should have received a call from George.

"Yes, we had someone who knows Maime make the identification last night." Luke explained. "In fact, Mr. Brewer, it was Riley Sullivan, the private investigator from New York that you hired."

Luke watched Edwin grip the sides of his chair and turn to look at George, shocked. George lowered his eyes and didn't meet Edwin's gaze. Luke wondered why hiring a PI would be such a secret or maybe it was something about Riley that George was hiding. Luke didn't like that he wondered about George and Riley or that his curiosity was more personal than professional.

"Who is this investigator, George? How does this person know Maime enough to make the identification? Why hire someone from outside the state when we have our own investigators at the firm?" Edwin fired away questions not even giving George time to answer.

Luke thought Edwin made some excellent points. Before George had a chance to explain, Tyler opened the door and was followed by Cooper and Riley. Luke had forgotten he demanded their presence here first thing this morning. Tyler must have assumed they were a part of the meeting.

CHAPTER 13

THE LAST THING I EXPECTED to see this morning was Luke and George sitting at the same table. It was hard enough to agree to come to a meeting with Luke. I had contemplated backing out of the meeting altogether, and seeing both of them at the table, I wanted to turn and sprint out of the police station. Cooper and I planned to meet with George at his house after this meeting. He never told me he'd be here.

George was seated in between two men; George's father-in-law Edwin and another man I didn't know. I had never met Edwin in person. He definitely had a commanding presence. Physically, he was an average guy but power seemed to ooze from him from the way he sat to the look on his face. It definitely looked as if he was controlling the meeting.

I knew George didn't like him. He never went into too much detail why, just said that Edwin was always too involved in their lives. That made sense. Edwin was George's boss. He met Maime at work when her father hired her as a secretary after she graduated college.

Prior to getting involved with Maime, George said he and Edwin always got along. After he found out George was sleeping with his daughter, there was an immediate decline in their cordial relationship. As soon as they married, George said Edwin was downright overbearing at work and at home. I was surprised they were here together.

I trailed behind Cooper who followed Det. Tyler into the room, which didn't serve me well because I was stuck taking the only seat available between Cooper and Luke directly across from George.

I had been running late that morning and had grabbed clothes blindly from my closet. I wore a black knee-length skirt, knee-high black boots and purple v-neck shirt. The skirt seemed to be riding up inch by inch and the shirt was riding low. I bet if I leaned my head down I could rest my chin on a pillow of cleavage. Maybe my mother was right, and I had gained a few pounds. It had been awhile since I wore these clothes. Even Cooper did a double take this morning when we met outside the police station.

Luke turned slightly to look at me when I entered the room. I caught his eyes glance down towards my cleavage but then quickly shoot back up. He glared at me. Just as easily as he bored his eyes into mine, he turned his head away as I sat down next to him. Luke made quick introductions around the table.

The man on George's right was Dean Beaumont. I knew the name. He and George had been best friends since middle school. They attended the same high school and college and were fraternity brothers. From George, I knew Dean ran his own high-end public relations firm. Or at least that's what he called it. He cleaned up a lot of politicians' messes. I wondered why he was here.

I was hoping to get Edwin on my good side so I spoke up first and extended my hand to him across the table. "It's nice to meet you, Mr. LaRue. I'm the investigator that George hired to help find Maime," I said and then added nodding towards Cooper, "Cooper is a licensed investigator here in Arkansas. Since I'm not, and only licensed in New York, I'll be working with him."

Edwin didn't respond to me and didn't shake my hand. He barely even glanced my way but addressed Cooper instead, "You'll be helping to find my daughter?"

Cooper shifted in his seat. I'm sure he was wondering if he should respond or not. He didn't so I jumped in. "Actually, sir, Cooper is assisting me, but yes, we are here to help find your daughter."

"I've never heard of a female investigator before and certainly not one that looks like you," he said, taking a long hard look at my cleavage making no pretense at hiding his actions.

I wanted to reach down and pull my shirt up but that would be too obvious. I ignored the remark. "I've been an investigator for several years including a few years as an investigative reporter here in Little Rock. I know your daughter and her friends as well as having other resources available to me. I'm hoping that we can work with the police to assist in finding her as quickly as possible."

I was hoping that if I threw it out there that we were willing to cooperate that Edwin would put a little pressure on the cops to make sure we had access.

No one spoke up so I continued. "I just arrived yesterday. I haven't even had a chance to meet with George to fully go over the situation. Maybe we can all get an update now," I said, turning to Luke, hoping to toss the conversation back his way.

It didn't happen. Edwin glared at me and accusingly asked, "How do you know George? Are you one of his whores?"

CHAPTER 14

SO MUCH FOR SOUTHERN hospitality. Cooper looked like he was about to leap across the table. I held my hand out to stop him from saying anything. Captain Meadows, who had remained silent up until that point, leaned forward resting his arms on the table, looked directly at me and then added, "Ms. Sullivan, we'd also be interested to know the nature of your relationship to George."

I waited for George to come to my defense since he was the one who dragged me into this. When he didn't respond, I finally did and tried to sound as professional and emotionally detached as I could.

"We are acquaintances from several years ago. Other than his reaching out for investigative services a few days ago, I've not spoken to him in close to two years." That was all technically true.

"Yes, but did you bed him?" Edwin added directly to the point.

I felt the anger rise up inside me. I slammed my chair backwards, crashing it into the wall behind me. It was only once I was standing that I realized I was stuck between Cooper and Luke. I needed one of them to move so I could get out. I just stood there fuming. I couldn't get out words.

Luke spoke up while George remained noticeably silent. "Edwin, that's enough. We are here to discuss your daughter not Ms. Sullivan's sex life." His eyes betrayed his words though. He shot me a look I knew meant this discussion wasn't over and to sit back down. I did so begrudgingly.

"Fine, fine," Edwin said, folding his arms over his chest clearly angry he wasn't going to get a response. "What, if anything, have you been doing to find my daughter?"

Captain Meadows gave us all a brief rundown about their efforts so far. It seemed the police had taken this report very seriously. They had already spoken to Maime's family and friends. They pulled her phone and credit card records as well as did a thorough sweep of her house. They were going through financial documents. I'm sure to see if there was a financial reason Maime either took off or for motive to see if George killed her.

They had set up a hotline for tips and were working with local search and rescue groups to search for Maime on foot. What I didn't realize until this meeting, what hadn't even occurred to me, was her vehicle. When Captain Meadows mentioned that her 2015 Land Rover hadn't been found either, it caught me by surprise.

"Wait," I said, interjecting but not directly speaking to anyone in particular. "I didn't realize that her car was missing, too. Anyone check video surveillance from her office or the routes she might have traveled that night?"

Luke barked, "This isn't our first case, Ms. Sullivan. Of course those things have been checked but nothing of any significance has been found. None of our leads have yielded anything of significance at this point, unfortunately, but we are going to keep working at this until she is found."

"The women found yesterday, how are they connected? Who are they?" Edwin demanded, interrupting us.

"We are working on identification. We have no reason right now to believe the cases are connected to Maime," Luke explained. Then he directed his attention to George. "We would, however, like to speak with you again. We have some more questions."

Dean leaned over and whispered to George. I couldn't hear what he said but it was an awkward moment. When he was done, George turned to Luke and said calmly, "I guess I could do that, but I don't think I really have anything else to say."

Luke was visibly annoyed at their exchange. He turned to Dean and asked what I was thinking. "What is your role in this?"

Dean straightened his tie, made direct eye contact with Luke and said smoothly, "As I'm sure you are aware, George is employed at LaRue & Associates. They are a very important corporate law firm that has a lot of VIP clients. I'm here simply to make sure their reputation stays intact."

Why on earth would Maime's father think the law firm's reputation was at stake unless he thought George had something to do with her disappearance?

When no one responded, probably all thinking the same thing that crossed my mind, Edwin slammed his fist on the table and snarled, "He's here because I told him to be here. I trust him more than I trust the lot of you."

Luke didn't comment. No one else did either. Edwin looked like he was going to have a stroke.

The awkward moment just hung in the air. Finally, Luke turned back to George and said in a calm and measured tone, "I think there are some things you can help us understand from some of the financial documents we were looking through."

"Sure," George said with a slight catch in his voice. "I can come back tomorrow morning at nine if that works for you. I have an appointment to get to now, if that's okay?"

"The sooner the better, but I think that will work," Luke said. Then he addressed Edwin. "Please let us know if you or your wife hears anything from your daughter or if you think of anything that might help us. Please know we are doing everything we can to find Maime."

Edwin stood. "I expect to hear as soon as you know anything." It wasn't a question. It was a command.

Dean, George and Edwin got up to leave. When they moved by us on the way out the door, George stopped, grabbed my arm and pulled me into him. With his hot breath directly in my ear, he whispered, "I love that shirt, sexy as ever. I expect to see you at my place when this meeting is over."

I don't know if anyone heard him, but they definitely saw me jerk my arm out of his grip and move backwards.

CHAPTER 15

THE ROOM EMPTIED. Luke, Cooper and I stood alone. Before I could make my way to the door, Luke shut it and held up his hand to block my exit. "Sit down," he demanded, pointing to a spot across the table. "You are not going anywhere until we get a few things out in the open. I may have come to your rescue in front of Edwin, but we've got some things to discuss."

Luke didn't even wait for me to sit back down before he attacked, "What are you doing here, Riley?"

I didn't answer right away. I moved around the conference table and sat down opposite where Cooper and Luke sat. I realized after I sat down that it was the worse seat to take, farthest from the door. If we had been in an interrogation room, this was where the alleged criminal would have sat. All I needed now was a bright florescent light shining in my eyes. I knew what was coming. I still hadn't decided how much I wanted to share. I just watched them across the table. Cooper had his arms folded across his chest. Luke was sitting with his forearms on the table and his hands folded, fingers laced.

"You can go ahead now and answer the question Edwin asked before. When did you last have sex with George?" Luke watched my face, glaring across at me, making intense eye contact.

I felt my temper rising again. Luke was baiting me. I knew it. He knew it.

"Look," I said finally with an air of annoyance. "I'm not going to dignify this with an answer. The relationship I had with George was years ago and isn't relevant now. It certainly isn't anyone's business."

"You understand, Ms. Sullivan..." Luke started to say.

"Riley," I yelled back, losing my poise. "Please stop with the Ms. Sullivan crap and just call me by my first name."

"Fine, Riley," he said with that sarcastic tone of his I always hated. "You understand that the only reason I'm even entertaining conversation with you is because of my relationship with Cooper? That if Cooper was not involved, you'd be out on the sidewalk on your behind. We wouldn't share a thing with you and would keep you as far out of this investigation as possible. Do you get that?"

"I guess I do now." I looked Luke directly in the eyes and said, "You already know about my relationship with George. Why do I need to rehash it? It has nothing to do with this case."

Cooper looked between us and said to Luke, clearly confused, "You know all about her relationship with George?"

Luke didn't bother to answer Cooper. He kept his eyes fixed on me. "It has everything to do with it. Don't play with me or I'll consider you a suspect next," Luke said evenly and calmly, which knowing him the way I did, meant he was livid. His statement was ridiculous, but nobody was laughing.

"Okay that's enough," Cooper said obviously annoyed with both of us. "Look, Riley, we need to know everything about you and George. You have to know that it may change how you see things, good or bad. It makes a difference. We might be able to use it to our advantage if George still has feelings for you."

I hated to admit it, but I knew Cooper was right. My relationship with George was a factor. It was the only reason I was here. I had taken the case thinking Maime was up to her old tricks again. But with the bracelet last night, the other women found in the river, and the number of days Maime had been gone, I knew this was more serious than I was prepared to admit.

I threw my hands up in defeat and caved, "Fine, I'll give you an answer only in the interest of this case and as my own way of playing nice, Detective. Yes, as both you and Cooper now know, I had a relationship with George. It lasted about a year. It ended a long time ago."

"When was the last time you were with him?" Luke demanded again.

Cooper looked at me, pleading for me to play nicely.

"Three years ago."

I could see Luke doing the mental math, and when he looked up, he seemed less angry. He leaned back and relaxed his body. I was hoping that he would stop treating me like the enemy now that he knew.

"Riley, does that mean George cheated on Maime with you?" Cooper asked.

"Yes, it does," I said ashamed for a sin that wasn't even mine. "He lied. I fell for it. I didn't know until I moved here that he was seeing her. When I found out that he was involved with Maime too, she went crazy, and we stopped seeing each other. We tried being friends, but Maime found out and made it impossible."

"Impossible?" Cooper asked, urging me on.

"She harassed me. She would send me nasty emails and call me, leaving threatening messages. She seemed to always know if George and I had spoken. It got too much to take so I eventually cut off all contact with George. Since leaving Little Rock, I've had no contact with him or her." Then I added more softly, "This isn't my proudest moment. It's still embarrassing to talk about so if we can move on from this subject, that would be great."

"Riley, I know this is hard but anything else that you can think of might help. You obviously know George better than any of us," Luke said, his voice much nicer in tone than before.

"I can't really think of anything important, but you have to know that each time George would see me, we'd have lunch or he would stop by my office to say hello, Maime would know and throw a fit. Or she would take off for a few days and have George in a panic. It was all for attention, and it worked. If George was cheating again, then you could all be wasting your time. She will show up in a few days once she has everyone totally in a panic."

I paused and then added, "Although, I admit, this is above and beyond what she's normally done. Before, she would just leave for a day or two."

"I'm only going to ask this once. I want it out of the way. Understand?" Luke asked me. I nodded and he continued, "It seems like you really dislike Maime and for good reason. Why do you want to help find her?"

The truth is I didn't care if we found her or not. I just knew George couldn't have had anything to do with hurting her. I felt a need to protect him. Also, I knew how much Luke hated George.

Before, when Luke and I were together, he often made silly comments about getting revenge. I knew he just said it to make me laugh. But still, I was worried Luke would be blinded by that now. I was here as much to protect George as I was to protect Luke from himself.

I couldn't say all that though so instead I said, "George asked and he seemed desperate. If there's something I can do to help him, I will."

CHAPTER 16

LUKE LOOKED DISGUSTED that I would even think of helping George after the lies he told me and everything he put me through. I started to get up from the table. Cooper waved me to sit back down.

He rested his arms on the table, looked between both of us and said, "I've got something to add that might be interesting. I don't know too much yet."

Luke urged him on, "Anything might help no matter how insignificant it might seem."

"When I came home last night from dropping off Riley, my neighbor stopped me and asked if she should talk to her friend who she said was having an affair with George. She wanted her to talk with the police about the affair. She wouldn't give me the friend's name or any details. I encouraged her to talk to her friend. They both work at UAMS. Luke, I gave her your number."

"Okay," I said, letting that sink in. "So it looks like George continued his old ways." This didn't really surprise me. I was disappointed in him all the same.

"No calls so far, but do you think your neighbor will talk to me?" Luke asked.

"Let me give her a call today and see if she talked to her friend. I'll get back to you. One way or the other, we should interview them both."

"Thanks, Coop," Luke said, but then more seriously he said to both of us, "I know you are here to help, but we have to talk about how you are going to be involved in this case. I can't have you damaging evidence, interviewing witnesses, and getting in our way." Then turning to me he said, "You know I'm going to have to fill in the rest of the detectives about what you just told me."

"I know," I said resigned and then added helpfully, "Luke, you're going to be stretched thin now with these two other homicide cases. How about if we follow-up with the people you've already interviewed? Maybe they will tell us something different or at least add to what they told you. We can see if we can come up with any new leads." Hoping to find some middle ground I added, "Then we can find a way to share information as needed."

"Would you be willing to wear a wire when talking to George? You might be able to get him to confide something to you. I know how good you are at getting people to spill their secrets."

I could see he wasn't going to play nice for very long. I didn't take the bait.

"No," I said, shaking my head. "But I promise you that if he's guilty of something, you'll be the first person I call."

"What do you think, Luke, these cases connected?" Cooper asked.

Luke got up and paced slowly around the conference table. We both stared at him while he thought. Luke did this when he was stressed. Like George, Luke was a pacer. It was how I always knew he had something on his mind.

"They feel connected," he said, stopping and turning to us. "But I don't have anything tangible so far to connect them. It just seems too coincidental to have all this happen at once. I need the medical examiner's report back and to identify the victims before we can really go anywhere. The witnesses didn't have much for us."

Luke turned to me and asked, "What do you think?"

"I think you've got your hands full and no information. Worst kind of case. I don't think you should assume anything at this point including that George killed Maime. You have no idea if she's connected to these two dead women or not. The age of all the women though is similar. That's why you should let us run with some leads on Maime and see what we can turn up. If she's connected to the other two, in time, the evidence will show us that. If she's not, maybe we can dig up some leads to see where she might be."

"You know it's dangerous for you to assume that George is so innocent," Luke said, looking me directly in the eyes.

"Not any more dangerous than for you to assume he isn't."

CHAPTER 17

IT WAS ALREADY TEN-THIRTY by the time Riley and Cooper made their way from the police station to George's house. Cooper hadn't been to the house before but clearly Riley had. She navigated Cooper through the narrow streets of the Heights neighborhood with ease.

When they pulled to the curb in front of George's house on Hawthorne Road, Cooper was shocked to see the condition of the home. He was expecting one of the grander houses in the neighborhood. He was met instead with a one-story bungalow, painted light blue with white shutters. The front yard needed some obvious tending to, and the bricks in the walkway were in need of repair, many chipped away from age and decay. It was still a nice house but not as grand as some of the others in the neighborhood. Not exactly what Cooper pictured when he thought about what George's residence might look like.

George answered on the second knock. He guided them to the dining room table where they all took a seat. Cooper spread out his paperwork. He looked around the house, taking in the worn hardwoods, dusty table tops and tattered throw rugs. The inside didn't look any more together than the outside.

Cooper wondered if anything in the financial documents Luke had pulled had given any indication to financial struggles of the couple. The furniture was older, the walls needed some updated paint, and in general, the place needed a good cleaning. Not that it was really dirty. It just looked neglected, as if the owners were rarely around and used the place as a stopover rather than lived here. Cooper's place wasn't spotless, but his place looked well-lived in. That wasn't the feeling he had here.

"George, if you are going to retain us to investigate this case, then there is a retainer agreement I need you to review and sign," Cooper explained, pushing documents towards George. "Then there is the matter of payment. You need to pay me directly, and I will pay Riley as a subcontractor. I know this isn't how you wanted this to work, but we have to work within the law here. There are rules to follow. I know Riley has explained this."

Before Cooper could really get into the paperwork, Riley blurted out, "George, would it be okay if I just looked around for a few minutes while Cooper goes over all of this? Then we can get started."

George hesitated but agreed. "Sure, the cops already dug through everything so I'm sure if there was anything of interest, they already have it. Feel free to look anywhere you need."

Riley left the dining room and walked into the kitchen, starting her exploration. Cooper wondered what she was looking for while he distracted George at the table.

George started to read over the contract as Cooper assumed he would. He was an attorney, after all, and even though Cooper was sure half his clients didn't read the contract, he knew George would, word-for-word. When George finished and had no questions, he signed. He pulled his checkbook from the sideboard drawer and wrote Cooper a check for $25,000 without blinking an eye.

Just as George handed the check over to Cooper, Riley entered back into the dining room and joined them at the table, sitting next to Cooper. Her backside was barely in the seat when she asked directly, "How long has it been since you and Maime shared a bed?"

George started to protest, but then seemed to resign himself and answered, "Almost five months."

Riley continued to control the interview. Cooper let her as she obviously knew what she was doing. He had to admit, he enjoyed watching her in action.

"Let's start from the beginning," she said. "Go back five months ago, six or seven if we need to and work forward. We need the whole story, George. Don't play me. Don't lie to me and don't sugarcoat anything because you don't think I'm going to like what I hear. Got it? I can't help you if you don't let me in on what's going on. Every dirty detail I need to know. If you don't think you can manage, get yourself a new investigator, and I'll head back to my life in New York. There's more to this story than you've told me and told the police. It's now or never, George."

Cooper realized he was smiling ear to ear as she attacked an obviously startled George. Cooper knew it was effective when George let out an audible sigh and slouched in the chair.

"We don't have much of a marriage," George explained. "Riley, you know how Maime and I got together. Cooper, I don't know what Riley has filled you in on."

"Not much. Enlighten me."

"We met at her father's office where we were both working. We snuck around for a while because she was technically my subordinate and the boss's daughter. When we hit about the eight month mark she told me she was pregnant. We couldn't hide our relationship any longer, and I did the right thing. I married her out of obligation. It turns out she wasn't pregnant and never had been. It was the first of many lies."

Cooper wasn't surprised, but certainly heard motive in George's words. He let George continue uninterrupted.

"About a year after we got married, her friend Cassie told me that Maime had made up the whole pregnancy story to get me to marry her. Cassie was pretty drunk. It just kind of slipped out. I don't think she intended to tell me. When Maime and I got home that night, I was angry and confronted her. Maime tried to lie, but I pushed until she finally told me the truth. She cried and begged me to stay. I did so stupidly. I thought I could get over it. The truth is, if she hadn't been pregnant or rather had I not thought she was pregnant, I wouldn't have married her. That one lie changed the course of my life."

Cooper finally had to say it. "That's pretty big motivation to kill her, George."

George shook his head. "I've been a stable provider, a supportive husband and remained married to her. It's been a marriage of convenience though. We lead two separate lives. Yes, I've had several affairs. I think a man can only take so much and needs to find happiness somewhere."

"Why not just divorce her?" Riley asked what Cooper was thinking.

"I've talked about it, and each time, Maime reminds me of all I have to lose. I work for her father. She owns this house. They have me so tied into them for everything. I'm not just walking away from a marriage. I'm walking away from my entire life."

It was a pathetic excuse, Cooper thought. A job is a job. A house a house but then again who was he to judge. He'd never made that kind of commitment before. Hearing George talk like this reminded Cooper why he hadn't.

"I don't understand," Riley chimed in. "You would rather live a lie than lose everything but find some happiness and have your freedom? She would rather live in a fake marriage than have the freedom to find someone new? That must be a really sad existence."

"You have no idea," George said, shaking his head.

Cooper pushed George further. "Okay, so you've had several affairs and your marriage is a joke. You're tied to the old man for work and finances, and this house isn't yours. But a dead wife certainly would grant you freedom. Sounds again a little like motive."

George didn't respond for a few seconds. His face slowly turned red. Cooper noted that he was clenching his fists on the table. Cooper thought he looked like a five year old about to throw a temper tantrum.

George though seemed to regain his composure. Emotionless, he gave what sounded like a recorded news soundbite. "You are absolutely right, but I didn't kill my wife. We were leading separate enough lives. I could do what I wanted, and she could as well."

"Back up." Riley jumped in waving her hands across the table theatrically. "You mean to tell me that Maime was fine with you seeing other women? I have trouble believing that, George. Remember who you are talking to here."

"No, she wasn't okay with it. She was far from okay with it. That wasn't what I meant. I just meant we had reached a point about six months ago that we were just doing our own thing. I was working and she was working. We had separate groups of friends. As you already pointed out, we weren't even sleeping in the same bed. We were barely speaking, and when we were, it was short. We kept up appearances in public though. I don't know if Maime told anyone how bad our marriage was. I can't imagine she did. She liked to keep up appearances that everything was fine. This is why I didn't worry when she didn't come home right away."

Cooper wondered if this was part of the reason why the house looked the way it did. The house was as neglected as their marriage. Cooper thought George was throwing motive down on the table just daring to be caught. He wondered if Riley felt the same.

He and Riley continued to pepper George with questions, going over in detail Maime's relationships with her friends, family and coworkers. They were checking to see if there were any potential reasons she would have left or if someone would have harmed her. They continued coming up blank, which for Cooper meant George was still suspect number one.

"We know Maime went missing on Friday. She was last seen at her office Friday afternoon. Do you have an alibi for that afternoon into Friday evening?" Cooper finally had to ask.

"Yes, I told the detectives I was with Dean," George said as the phone on Cooper's hip began to buzz.

George continued talking as Cooper slid his phone out of its holder and looked down at the text message. The message from Luke read, "Another woman's body pulled from the river. Not Maime. Come alone."

CHAPTER 18

COOPER HEADED BACK to the Arkansas River just down from where they had been the night before. After receiving Luke's text, he had stopped the interview, excused himself and Riley, and walked her outside. She had been annoyed that he had interrupted the interview until he held up his phone and showed her Luke's text. Riley looked as shocked as he felt.

They talked quickly and decided the best game plan was for him to leave and Riley to stay. They both felt that maybe if Riley was alone with George she might get the truth out of him or at least some leads for them to follow.

Cooper cruised down Cantrell out of the Heights toward downtown. At a light he made a left on Lilac Terrace and then across Riverdale Road where he made another left on Riverfront Drive. He drove the short distance to Morgan Keegan Plaza, and as he approached, he saw the mass of people, cops and news vans. A barricade was up, blocking the entrance into 100 Morgan Keegan. After a quick flip of his identification to the cop manning the barricade, he pulled into the parking lot. It seemed they were expecting him.

It was the middle of a workday and Morgan Keegan Plaza held several different businesses. He didn't envy the police who were going to have to canvass all these people to see what they might know or might have seen. He pulled his pickup truck into an open space, grabbed his cell and hit the ground, walking towards the back of the building. Cooper only made it about a hundred yards when Ben, the reporter from the night before, stopped him in his tracks in the sea of other news media.

"You're back?" Ben asked, drawing Cooper's attention. "Where's that girl you had with you last night?"

"What's your interest?"

"No interest really. Just someone last night said she used to work for the newspaper, and I looked her up. She's a private investigator from New York, which begs the question of why she's here and interested in this case. Are you a PI, too?"

Cooper nodded in response but didn't give much in the way of an explanation. It was then he saw Luke. Cooper yelled to him to get his attention. He walked away from Ben without saying anything more.

Luke got Cooper through the second police barricade and over the grassy hill down to the river where the body had washed up. As they walked, Luke explained that two women who walked down to eat their lunch at the picnic table in the back of the building had made the discovery. One of the women fainted while the other made a frantic call to 911.

Unfortunately, they had gone back inside and told some of their coworkers. By the time the cops arrived, Luke said, the whole area was crawling with employees from the building. People walked over any evidence that might have washed up with her.

Didn't people watch *CSI* enough to know not to walk on a crime scene? Cooper was about to complain about stupid people when Luke pointed to the building. "Maime's father is here. Apparently, this is where his office is located."

"George works in this building, too," Cooper said matter-of-factly.

"Yeah," Luke confirmed, and then looked out towards the road. "Did you just leave in the middle? Where's Riley?"

"She's still there. I thought maybe she'd get more information from him if they were alone. You told me to come by myself." Cooper looked around at the cops talking to people and the medical examiner's team hard at work again. The crime scene folks, wearing blue jackets with CSI on the back and black pants, were doing what they do best especially given the circumstance.

"You think that's safe?" Luke asked with an edge in his voice.

"I guess we'll see. Riley can handle herself," Cooper said as they walked towards the river. "You know it's not Maime, but do you know who it is?"

"No. It's a woman probably late thirties to early forties found only in her bra and panties like the women last night. This woman is much curvier than the other two. She's heavier. Long blonde hair. She's in worse condition though. Looks like someone beat her badly before she died," Luke said, going down the facts they knew so far. Then Luke got closer to Cooper and said almost in a whisper, "I called you because there's something else you've got to see."

Cooper walked with Luke towards the body still lying on the grass not yet covered. Cooper looked down and took in the woman. Luke was right. She was much heavier than the women from last night. She was taller, too. Cooper guessed almost five-ten and probably close to two hundred pounds. He guessed her face would have been pretty but it was badly swollen and bruised. Blood had caked on her face in several places and remained even after being in the water.

Then Cooper saw what Luke was talking about. She had the word *whore* written across her stomach in bright pink lettering. Cooper thought it was maybe marker, but he couldn't be sure. Cooper noticed something else about her. She had on a pair of big expensive looking silver hoop earrings.

He turned to Luke and asked, "You notice the earrings? The woman last night had on a bracelet. The other woman had on a small pinkie ring. You make anything of that?"

Luke ran a hand down his face and said, "Honestly, Coop, I noticed the bracelet, but that's about it. They each wore jewelry. Most women do. What do you think of the writing?"

"Obviously, she pissed someone off. You think it's connected to the women last night?"

"It can't be a coincidence that three women were found in the river less than a mile apart within twenty-four hours. They all have ligature marks on their wrists and ankles."

"What can I do to help?" Cooper asked, feeling overwhelmed. He couldn't imagine what Luke was feeling.

Luke pulled Cooper aside, far from all the other cops and medical examiner staff and said, "Listen, I don't know what I've got here. But something isn't right. Brewer's wife is missing and now three women wash up not far from where he works. This is a lot more than we bargained for. Off the record, I need you to be my eyes and ears. Through Riley, you've got the inside track. I need enough evidence to make an arrest."

"You really think it's George?" Cooper asked cautiously. He thought it was a quick jump to make.

"Don't tell me Riley's convinced you already?" Luke asked, shooting Cooper a dirty look.

"No, but it's a jump. You don't even know for sure Maime's connected."

Cooper felt conflicted by Luke's request. George Brewer was technically his client. He worked for him, not the police department anymore. But since he wasn't working for a defense attorney directly, there was no legal obligation to withhold information from the cops, particularly if that information could help them solve a crime, or in this case, prevent a murderer from seeing justice. Actually, Cooper had a legal obligation to report that information. Ethically, it walked a fine line Cooper wasn't sure how comfortable he felt walking.

Plus, it would betray Riley.

"I'll see what I can do as we were really only hired to help find Maime. If I pick up other information, I'll pass it along," Cooper promised Luke. "You got any idea how the media keeps showing up so quickly? Twice now, they have been out here almost as quickly as you guys."

"Least of my worries right now," Luke called over his shoulder as he walked to where the body was, but then he turned back and added, "Don't tell Riley what we talked about."

CHAPTER 19

"IS YOUR ALIBI TRUE, GEORGE?" We sat down on the couch in the family room across from the kitchen. After Cooper left, I thought if we moved from the dining room table to the couch and sat more comfortably that I might get George to open up more. I decided not to tell him about the woman's body just found.

George didn't say a word as he settled into the couch and slung his arm over the back of the brown leather sofa. He turned his body toward mine. I sat sideways on the couch careful my knee didn't hit against his thigh.

I continued, "George, it's really important you tell me the truth. I can't help you if you're not honest. I need to know about all your affairs. These women will come forward. Think of the cases you have seen on the news. It's important or I wouldn't be asking."

"I don't want to hurt you, Riley," he said, reaching out and giving my shoulder a patronizing squeeze. I wish I could say I pulled away from his touch. I didn't.

"It's a little too late to worry about hurting me. Forget all that and just give it to me straight," I said but didn't quite believe I was ready to hear it all.

"There's been more than a few. Most were one-night stands when I would travel. I'd meet someone in a hotel lobby or local bar and it would be for one night. No strings. No involvement."

He walked me through a few of them and how it would go. George said sometimes he wouldn't even use his real name. It was companionship, conversation and sex for the night. He said he didn't expect me to understand. I understood better than he would've ever thought. Then he stopped talking. I knew there was more, probably a lot more, so I encouraged him to continue. He got up, went to the kitchen and brought back a glass of tea for each of us. He sipped and finally continued.

"About six months ago, I started seeing a woman who works at the local hospital. She knew I was married and knew how sensitive the situation with Maime has been. I broke it off with her recently. She wanted more than I could give. She had called the house a few times and sent some emails. I was worried Maime would find out. Stupidly, I gave in the Friday night Maime went missing and saw her again."

"Did Maime ever find out about her?" I asked, knowing the storm that would rage if she had.

"I don't think so," George said. "I think we both know if Maime found out, I'd know."

"Is she your real alibi? You weren't really with Dean, were you?"

George looked down at his hands for a moment and then back up to meet my eyes. "Yes. I was with Laura. I don't want to get her involved. I was stupid to even see her again. I knew that as soon as I picked her up. I don't want to complicate the situation more."

"She's important to clear your name. Don't you think she's watched the news and knows your wife went missing on the same night she was with you?"

"I know, I know. Detective Morgan asked what I was doing and I panicked and told them I was out with Dean." George looked away from me and said, "Dean covered for me."

"You can't lie and get Dean to lie for you. This is making you look guilty." I was afraid George just wasn't getting it. It was little lies like these that end up making him look guiltier.

George turned back to me. He had tears in his eyes. I'd never seen him cry. He looked older and more tired than I had ever seen him. Then he said with his voice cracking, "I just don't know what to do. I swear to you I didn't hurt Maime. I don't know where she is."

I wanted to believe him. I really did. I was almost there when he leaned across the space between us and kissed me. His hands cupped my face and his lips were against mine, tongue slowly teasing mine. He knew just how I liked to be kissed, and the worst part, I was letting him. I was kissing George in the house he shared with Maime, and she was missing. The thought of Maime snapped me right back to reality. I pulled out of his arms.

"George, we can't," I said, putting my hand up to stop him from leaning in farther. "Your wife is missing. You're lying to the cops, still holding back on me and now kissing me. What is wrong with you?" I pleaded to him still thinking about that kiss.

What was wrong with me? How could I fall back into this so quickly? I was kissing a married man whose wife was missing. Even I wasn't this desperate.

"I'm a mess," George whined. "You deserve the truth if you're going to help me. Her name is Laura Bisceglia. She lives in Hillcrest. I'll give you the address."

"Friday was the last time you saw her or spoke to her?" I asked him.

"Yes, I haven't tried to call or text her since then. I was too consumed with Maime. And honestly, I don't think she'd speak with me. I ended it for good with her on Friday."

"How did it go? Did she cry, argue with you? Did you fight?" I inquired.

George shrugged. "How do you think it went?"

By the look on his face, I knew he realized what was going through my mind. I knew all too well how bad he was at ending things. It brought me right back to that day I moved to Little Rock. George knew I was moving. We had planned it. On the day I moved in, after the movers came and I got settled, I called him so excited to be there. He was so cold on the phone. Told me that he wished I hadn't moved. That he was engaged to someone else and to never contact him again. Then he hung up on me mid-sentence. Didn't answer when I tried to call him back. I left a message, several messages, and he just continued to ignore me. It still hurt.

George reached for my hand, but before he could touch it, I pulled away and stood. "I'm going. Do you have a list of Maime's friends, people that I should interview?"

He stood and went to move past me but stopped and enveloped me in a hug. He wrapped his arms tightly around me. I didn't move or hug him back. I stood rigid in his arms. He squeezed me harder, then released me, and walked to one of the bedrooms down the hall.

When George returned, he handed me some typewritten pages with handwritten notes included. "It should be everything you need. All of her friends' addresses and phone numbers. I noted who they are next to them."

I scanned the list and some of the names were familiar. Some of them were the very same women who took part in harassing me when Maime found out about me. It would be awkward going back to talk to them now.

For the first time, I was really glad Cooper was helping me on this case. I thanked George, gathered my things and was just about out the front door when George said to my back, "Riley, I'm sorry. I think I'm still in love with you."

I stepped through the door and out into the sunlight. I left his home without looking back.

CHAPTER 20

I REALIZED AFTER I LEFT GEORGE'S HOUSE that I didn't have any way home other than to walk. I tried Cooper on his cell, but he didn't answer. I left him a message that I was going back to my place and told him the address. I walked the few blocks to my house. The Heights neighborhood is perfect for a walk so I didn't mind. I even stopped at my favorite Starbucks on Kavanagh and grabbed a bag of coffee.

When I got back, I put on a pot of coffee and sat down at my kitchen table with a notepad and pen to write some notes about what I knew so far. I was still a little shaken from the kiss and George's ill-timed, inappropriate declaration of love. It definitely wasn't what I was expecting. Neither were the dead women yesterday and the woman found today.

I hadn't even been on the case twenty-four hours yet and already I felt scattered. I reminded myself that Maime was why I was here. I had to stay focused on her and not get sidetracked, but it was hard to believe that it was all coincidental, especially after seeing that bracelet last night.

I was lost in thought going over the list of those that I needed to interview. I had started making a list of questions to ask when I heard a loud rap at the front door. Before I could get up to answer it, Emma came through the house and rushed towards me, her arms outstretched.

"Look at you, pretty girl," Emma said, hugging me. "I've missed you. Please tell me you're back for good."

Emma helped herself to the coffee and sat down across from me. Emma was my best friend and the person I trusted the most. She knew all my secrets. She looked good, too. Her black hair was cut in a chin length bob. She looked like she'd lost some of the baby weight. I was a little jealous.

"Girl," Emma drawled getting straight to the point like she was known to do. "Don't just sit there silent, update me about what is going on."

I realized in that moment I felt like I had been holding my breath since I arrived in Little Rock. Now with Emma, I could finally exhale. And with the release, all the pent-up emotions came pouring out.

"George called me. Maime is missing, and the police suspect he had something to do with it. He asked me to investigate her disappearance, find her. See what I can find out. I have such a hard time believing he had anything to do with it. Then I get here and find out Luke is the lead detective. He still hates me. He'll barely even look at me. And if all that wasn't bad enough, earlier today when I was interviewing George, Cooper got a call about another body that was found, so he left. When I was alone with George, he kissed me and then told me he's still in love with me. Everyone thinks he killed Maime."

When I finally ran out of words, Emma laid her hand over mine and said, "Well that certainly is a whole lot to digest. I just heard on the news about the other body they found. The cops aren't releasing any information though. You've got a lot on your plate. What's the easiest to start with?" She knew just what I needed. To problem solve in small bites.

"I guess Luke."

"Have you talked to him about what happened?"

"No, we haven't had a chance. I wouldn't even know what to say." I put my head down on my folded arms. I felt like a ten year old who just failed her first test.

"The truth. Start there. You owe him that. Clear the air and then maybe you two can start putting your heads together. Or you can spend the whole time fighting and not accomplishing anything. Up to you," Emma said, shrugging.

Emma was right. I just needed the guts to have the conversation.

I turned my head and looked up at Emma. She had a look of pity at the mess I'd gotten myself into. "What am I going to do about George? What have you heard about Maime? There's got to be neighborhood gossip. I know you still see some of her friends."

"Most people think George killed her. I hate to say it. I know him, know everything you've told me, and even I have a hard time believing he didn't kill her or have someone kill her. Maime has never been my favorite person, but she didn't deserve to die."

"We don't even know if she is dead," I reminded Emma.

"Do you really think she's alive? I've known Maime since high school. She's not you, Riley. She's not one to fend for herself. I really believe if she was alive she'd contact someone."

Part of me believed Emma was right. "I really haven't had a chance to interview anyone yet. What are her friends saying? Has she been in contact with any of them?"

Emma shook her head no and said, "Not a peep. Claire and Gina, who are her two best friends at this point still left in Little Rock, are heading up the search. They called in a search and rescue dog team from Dallas, who also brought up a cadaver dog. They were up here yesterday and nothing. I guess we can assume he didn't kill her at home. I heard George let them in, gave them some of her clothes. He's being cooperative, which is about the only thing he has going for him."

"I didn't realize they had brought dogs in already. Where's the rest of Maime's family?" I knew she had a sister and two brothers, all of whom were married with kids.

"Not local," Emma said, updating me as she sipped her coffee between tidbits of information. "Her sisters are in North Carolina and her brother is down in Dallas, I think. From what I heard from Claire, none of them have heard from her either. Riley, you have to face it. It just doesn't look good for George. Are you going to be willing to turn him in if you find evidence?"

"What's his motive though?" I persisted harder. "It wasn't financial. The cops ruled that out. They were fine financially. I don't get it. He's had affairs before, and they made it work. I know Cooper and Luke think that's reason enough for murder but come on, really?"

"I don't know. You never really know what happens inside someone's marriage. What about the other women found? Do we know if they're connected?"

Emma caught the look on my face. She put her coffee mug down and her hand on my arm. "Riley, is there something else?"

I didn't respond. I shrugged off her hand, got up and went upstairs. I grabbed the bracelet from my dresser and brought it back down, setting it on the table in front of Emma.

"What's this?" Emma asked, picking up the bracelet and turning it over inspecting it.

"This is a bracelet George gave me for our six month anniversary. He had it specially made. This is also an exact replica of the bracelet found on the wrist of the woman pulled from the river last night."

Emma continued to examine the bracelet, running her fingers over the delicate design. When she looked up at me, I saw fear in her eyes. She held the bracelet out to me and said, "Riley, this is serious. It was serious before when it was just Maime, but now there's Maime and this connection to a dead woman. What did Luke and Cooper say about this?"

"I didn't tell them yet. I was hoping to look into it first. Obviously, it will just make him look guiltier."

"Did you ever stop to consider that it will make George look guiltier because he is in fact guilty?" Emma countered. "You need to stay away from him. Something is off, Riley, you have to see it."

Looking up to the ceiling, I took a few deep breaths, measuring my response. Trying to get a read on my gut. "I know something is off, which is why I'm here. Come on, Emma, do you really think I could have fallen in love with a killer? You know me. I have better instincts than that. Yes, I missed all the warning signs that he had another girlfriend, but could I have really missed all the warning signs that he was a budding psychopath who would kill his wife and other women? I just can't truly believe that, Emma. Can you?"

I was on the verge of crying and Emma could see it.

"Honey," Emma said, putting her arm around me, "I don't think you missed anything. Some people are just really good at hiding what they don't want you to see. George never struck me as the kind of guy to get his hands dirty though. I will give you that much. Now his friend Dean I could see killing people. He's always seemed shady."

Dean's whole line of work was cleaning up; spinning the press and hiding facts about his clients. I never really liked what George had told me about Dean. Meeting him this morning didn't improve my impression of him. Emma was right about that.

Emma pushed her chair back and held up her hands in surrender and said, "You're the investigator. I'll concede for now about George, but it would seem to me if you want to keep him out of prison, where it looks like he's soon to be heading, you have to find someone else with motive. And don't, Riley, don't you dare go off with him alone or hide evidence from the police. Do not fall for his charm again. I will not see you get taken down with him. Sophie needs her godmother around."

"How is my little Sophie?" Thinking about Sophie and her fat little baby cheeks always made me smile. She was just about a year old when I left. Emma sent me pictures through email. We'd video chat by Skype pretty often. Emma was one of the few holdouts not on Facebook.

"She's a holy terror. I'll gladly drop her off to her Auntie Riley and she can stay right here with you when this is all over. Until then, come to dinner whenever you can. Joe has some firewood for you out back, too." Emma washed her coffee cup and placed it on the drying rack. She came over, kissed me on the cheek, and made her way back out the door, reminding me not to work too hard as she left.

CHAPTER 21

"WELL IT SEEMS you've got more secrets than I realized. I didn't know you kept the house when you left," Cooper said. His eyes wide open scanning the room as he walked through my front door. He called as Emma was leaving. I figured now was as good a time as any to bring him over.

Cooper looked around my living room. "You've sure got a sense of style. Love the black and white photos. If you fail at being a private investigator, you should try being a decorator. I could use you at my place."

I laughed. "Yeah not many people know I kept it. I couldn't bear to sell it." I lead him through the living room and gave him the five-cent tour of the house. I offered him something to drink and sat comfortably in the living room. Cooper sat on my black and white square-patterned armless chair. I sat on my favorite robin's egg blue couch ready to get down to business.

"You go first. Tell me about the rest of the interview with George," Cooper suggested.

I filled Cooper in on some of the basic details and left the most interesting to last. "I got George to admit that his alibi was false. He wasn't with Dean, after all, which is what he told Luke. Dean covered for him. George was really with his mistress on Friday night."

"That's not really surprising," Cooper said. "I think we can assume that most of what George will tell us and the cops will be a lie."

"Are you really convinced he killed Maime? I just want to know. Everyone seems to think so. I feel like I'm the only one who isn't so sure." And that was the truth. I was really starting to feel like the whole world was against George, and that I was the only one who still believed him. I didn't blame everyone else. I could understand it. He was someone I once loved. Even my confidence in him had been rocked.

"I don't know. I try not to go into any case with the idea that I know all the answers. What I do know is he is a liar and a serial cheater. Does that make him a killer? No. But, he hasn't been helping himself. His life is one slippery slope after another. Why all the lies if he has nothing to hide?" Cooper asked. He leaned forward in his seat, waiting for my response.

"I think he's hiding the cheating. He went over the last few years with me. He and Maime have no marriage at all at least in the traditional sense. It's all for show. George has had a lot of women, Cooper. More than I ever realized."

Cooper nodded.

I continued. "That is one of my biggest problems with him; the lying. Our whole relationship started with a lie, and his lies continued. If it's not just the affairs he's trying to hide, you're right, I don't know what else there is he's not telling us."

"He's got to stop lying or we aren't going to be able to help him. Did you tell him that?"

"I did. Or at least I tried to anyway. I don't know how much he really heard me. I think I know who your neighbor is talking about, the nurse George was having the affair with. Her name is Laura Bisceglia. She lives in Hillcrest. I have both her address and phone number," I said evenly, handing Cooper the piece of paper that contained her information.

"My neighbor hasn't called me back yet, but we should pay Ms. Bisceglia a visit instead of calling her first. Can you go with me now?"

"That works for me, the sooner the better. I just want to nail down at least one fact George has told us. Tell me about this other body they found."

"I will on our way to Laura's place," Cooper said, stalling me. "Tell me about George's friend Dean first. He left me a message earlier today. I haven't returned the call yet. What do we know about him? I've seen him around the country club, but I don't know much about him."

"You know it's funny you should say that. Do you remember my friend Emma and her husband Joe?" Cooper nodded. "They live next door. Emma was just here. She said something funny to me. She told me that she has a hard time believing George could murder someone. But she said she wouldn't be surprised if Dean could. I hadn't thought too much about him until she said that."

"Since he lied and covered for George, we don't have his real alibi either. What do you know about him?" Cooper asked again and then jotted down Dean's name in the small black notepad.

I shrugged and told Cooper the little I knew. "Not much. Today was the first day I met him. I know he and George are best friends. They grew up together, went to the same schools all the way through college, and played football together. I know they were both members of the same fraternity. Dean runs a pretty successful public relations firm. George's law firm is one of their main clients."

That really was all I knew. Dean wasn't around much when I was dating George so I didn't really know a lot about him. Of course, looking back, I realized that I was just another affair. George had every reason not to bring me around his friends. It's funny what you see in hindsight.

"Maybe instead of calling him back, we should just pay him a visit. I like to watch people's reactions face-to-face," Cooper said and then added, "I found it really strange he was at the meeting this morning and that Maime's father would feel the need to worry about his law firm at a time like this. It seemed cold to me."

"I agree. I think we definitely need to sort out how Dean's involved. George gave me a list of people to interview including Maime's friends, family and coworkers."

I got up and walked to the kitchen table where I had all my case information. I handed the list to Cooper for him to review while I gathered up the rest of my stuff to leave.

CHAPTER 22

WE TOOK MY RENTAL AND LEFT Cooper's truck at my house. After a few moments navigating my suburban streets, I looked over at Cooper in the passenger seat. "Okay, you've kept me in suspense long enough. What's with the other body they found?"

Our eyes met in a knowing glance. Cooper looked shaken. "It's not good, Riley. Same as the others yesterday. Woman probably in her early forties with ligature marks on her wrists and ankles. There were ligature marks across her neck, too. Medical examiner wasn't sure how long she'd been dead. She was really bloated from the water. Looked like she'd been beat up bad."

"This doesn't make any sense. Is there a serial killer in Little Rock?" I was truly perplexed. I knew a lot about serial crime. So far, the similarities in victims, manner of death and dumping place for the bodies were all leading to one alarming conclusion. Worse yet, I still didn't know where George fit in the mix.

"This woman was different though. She was heavier than the women last night, long blonde hair and one other new detail," Cooper said. Then he touched my arm, and I gave him my full attention. "She had the word *whore* scrawled across her stomach in pink."

"Is she? I mean do we know if she was a prostitute or something that would elicit that kind of description from the killer?" I don't recall seeing prostitutes just trolling the streets of Little Rock, at least on the side of town we were on, but it didn't mean there wasn't an underground sex business. Every city has one.

"Luke wasn't sure. There was no identification. Here's the other thing. Did you notice the bracelet on the woman that was found last night?"

I nodded but avoided making eye contact.

Cooper continued, "The woman pulled from the river this morning had on what looked like an expensive pair of silver hoop earrings. Luke didn't seem to think any of it was a big deal, but something felt weird to me about it."

It would have been the perfect time to tell Cooper about the bracelet. I didn't. I wasn't ready to tie George to a murder until I could wrap my head around what it really meant.

"Are you thinking it's some kind of signature? Or did the killer just forget to remove her jewelry?" I asked hesitantly.

"I don't know. As I said, Luke hadn't noticed. I brought it to his attention. He said he'd look into it. I think they are focused on getting the identification of the women and cause and manner of death. But, Riley, there's one more thing."

"Go on, don't keep me in suspense," I urged him, easing my foot off the gas pedal trying not to speed.

"The woman this morning was found washed up behind George's office. The woman last night was found less than a mile down the road and the other a little farther down the river. Luke thinks it's significant. I have to agree it's too much of a coincidence not to be connected."

I rolled my eyes. Yes, the circumstantial evidence was mounting. Once a cop gets tunnel vision, there's usually not much to get him off his one-track mind. They just start digging for more connections, no matter how insignificant.

I sighed at Cooper's predictability and said, "I knew last night that we were right down the road from George's office, but the river runs right behind his building and many others. She could have been dumped anywhere. The same with the others. It doesn't mean anything."

Cooper groaned, slapping his hand against the dashboard. "Riley, come on. His wife is missing and three women wash up dead near his office. You've got to put your emotions aside and look at this logically."

"I am!" I shot back angrily. "We have to keep an open mind. The cops aren't going to. George hired us. We work for him. The least we could do is give him the benefit of the doubt right now until we have something irrefutable."

Cooper didn't argue with me. He didn't say anything for several minutes, just stared out the passenger side window. Finally, he turned to me and said, "We'll have to tell Luke about George's alibi. It's not information we can hold back."

I didn't protest. We drove the rest of the way in silence.

CHAPTER 23

LAURA BISCEGLIA'S HOUSE was a two-story Craftsman bungalow typical of her Hillcrest neighborhood. It had greenish gray siding and white trim with two stone pillars lining either side of the porch. Cooper and I walked up the slate-tiled walkway that cut a path through the neatly manicured lawn. I noticed off to my right there was a Toyota SUV in the driveway. Cooper knocked on the heavy wooden front door. We waited. He knocked again.

Cooper stood on his tiptoes. He peered through the square window at the top of the door. I stepped around him and looked through the living room window to the left of the front door. The blinds were open. I could see into the living room. The house's open concept allowed me to see into the dining room and open kitchen too. The house was quiet and dark.

"I don't think she's home," I said to Cooper while still looking into the house. Something on the kitchen table caught my eye.

"Coop, it looks like there's a purse and cellphone sitting on the kitchen table. Maybe she's out for a walk or at the neighbor's house."

"Maybe. I'm going to walk around back and see what I can find. Maybe knock on the back door. Why don't you check with the neighbors next door?" Cooper suggested as he walked off the porch and around the right of the house, heading towards the back.

As Cooper disappeared from sight, I stood for a moment looking at the neighbors' houses next to and across the street deliberating who I wanted to check with first. It seemed there weren't many people around in the middle of the day.

"Miss, can I help you?" a woman asked, suddenly appearing on Laura's front lawn. Her voice was like honey, sweet and southern. She was older. I would guess in her sixties with short gray hair, and she was dressed like she was headed out for afternoon tea — black slacks and a cream-colored sweater with a bright multi-colored silk scarf tied expertly around her neck.

"Yes, ma'am," I replied remembering my southern manners. "We are looking for Laura Bisceglia. Do you know where I can find her?"

"Are you a friend of hers?" the woman asked. She reached her hand out to shake mine. Her grip was firm but her hand ice cold. "I'm Elaine."

"Riley. No, we aren't friends exactly, but I need to speak with her. Have you seen her around?"

Elaine looked at Laura's front door and then back at me. She turned back to look at her own house for a moment and then back to Laura's. Elaine put her hand on my arm and pulled me to the far side of the lawn closer to Laura's SUV and away from her own house.

She spoke in a voice only slightly higher than a whisper.

"My husband doesn't like me to get involved in other people's business, you understand. Laura is a sweet girl. I'm worried about her. I haven't seen her since Friday afternoon. That man on the news with the missing wife came to pick her up. I know it was him. I've seen him here before. I haven't seen Laura after that. Her car has been in the driveway and no lights on in the house all week. I was going to wait another day and then call her parents."

"Has anyone been by that you've seen? What about friends? Could she be with them?" I asked hopefully.

"Her parents and other family are in Chicago and a brother up in New York. She has a good deal of friends, but they haven't been over in a long while. When she goes away, she asks me to take in her mail. She never mentioned a trip to me."

That feeling down deep in the pit of my stomach was starting to grow. I didn't want to alarm Elaine just yet so I said, "Wait right here, Elaine, let me run around back and grab my partner. We can all talk together."

CHAPTER 24

I WALKED QUICKLY to the back of the house and found Cooper standing on the middle rung of an old wooden ladder looking into the back windows of the house.

"See anything?" I asked, coming up behind him.

"No, just the purse. That's definitely a cellphone on the table. I knocked several more times. No answer. Any luck with the neighbors?" Cooper asked, climbing back down the ladder and moving it to the side of garage.

"Unfortunately, yes. I stopped her mid-story though. I wanted you to be there to hear what she had to say. It's Laura's next door neighbor. Her name is Elaine. The last time she saw Laura she was leaving with George on Friday afternoon. She hasn't seen her since."

Cooper cocked his head to the side and raised his eyebrows. "Out of town?"

I shrugged. "Elaine said she usually takes in her mail if she goes away. It seems they were at least fairly friendly. It's that kind of neighborhood. But Coop, I know from George that it didn't go well between them on Friday night. He ended it with her for good. He said he brought her home and dropped her off. Maybe she did just take off with friends and forgot to tell Elaine. I bet she was pretty upset after the break up."

"Okay, let's go talk to Elaine. We might need to call Luke before we get too far in, but let's see what we can find out before we need to do that," Cooper said. I agreed.

We walked back around to the front of the house where I made introductions. Then we convinced Elaine that we should meet in her house at a table so we could take some notes if needed. Elaine really didn't want to get her husband involved but then admitted it was probably too late for that.

The three of us came through Elaine's front door and were greeted by Elaine's husband Don sitting in his recliner, iced tea in hand watching television. He barely even nodded in our direction as we walked through the house towards the kitchen. Her home reminded me of someone's grandma's house. It was warm and cozy and the kitchen smelled like wonderful things were constantly cooking in the oven. Cooper and I sat around her small kitchen table as she pulled out three glasses and poured us all some sweet tea without bothering to ask if we wanted any.

"Tell me who you two are again before we go any further," Elaine requested as she joined us at the table.

"We're private investigators. We are working on a case where Laura might be a witness. We just need to speak with her," Cooper explained.

"I see," Elaine said. Then she asked, "Is it the Maime LaRue Brewer case? I've been following it on TV. I don't want to get involved in all that."

She said it loud enough for her husband to hear her protest.

"We understand," I said, trying to reassure her. "Yes, we are looking for Maime. We know George was with Laura the night Maime went missing. All we need to do is confirm that with Laura."

Elaine shook her head in understanding. "Laura's a good girl, you have to understand that. She got mixed up with George Brewer, and she hasn't been the same since. We used to sit out on the porch and have nice long talks. She was good at her job at the hospital and has a lot of friends. But since she started seeing him, everything changed for her."

"Tell me what you mean, everything changed? Did she confide in you about the affair?" I asked, taking a sip of my tea.

"Well, she doesn't come out of the house much anymore. She doesn't have friends over like she used to. The last time I saw her, she looked tired and like she had been crying."

I waited, nodding my head to urge Elaine to continue.

"She did tell me a little about the affair. George played mind games. He would pull her in and then push her away if she got too close. He'd never let her go enough for her to move on. As soon as she'd get herself together and take a step forward, he'd come back around again. It was too much for her. She couldn't seem to get out of his hold. I knew she was having some trouble at work, too. Her boss said her performance on the job was suffering."

After a few beats of silence, Elaine pounded her frail fist down on the table and said forcefully, "That man ruined her."

I reached out and put my hand on top of Elaine's arm, but there was nothing I could really say. George had a way of doing that to nice women. It seemed he knew what weakness to play. I always gave him the benefit of the doubt, but hearing Elaine, I was beginning to wonder if George was a little more destructive than I realized.

Cooper interrupted the moment. "When was the last time you saw her?"

Elaine straightened in her seat and wiped her eyes. Turning to Cooper, she said, "Friday. I happen to look out the window at the same time she was getting into that man's truck. I never saw her come home that night, but then again, I don't stay up very late."

"What about before then? When was the last time you really spoke with her?"

"Let's see, it had to have been maybe Wednesday of last week. I saw her bringing in groceries. I went out to say hello. She was in a rush so we didn't get too much of a chance to talk. She did seem happier than usual."

"Do you happen to have a picture of Laura?" Cooper asked. I knew where he was going. I silently said a little prayer she wasn't one of the women found in the river.

"I don't, but I can do you one better," Elaine said, getting up and walking to a kitchen drawer. She pulled out a key attached to a purple grappling hook and waved it at us. "I've got her house key."

CHAPTER 25

"DON'T TELL ME you haven't got anything, Luke. Don't even say it," Captain Meadows demanded as he entered the empty conference room where Luke waited at the far end. Luke had scheduled an impromptu staff meeting with all the detectives that were available to start going over the evidence of the three Jane Does that were found in the river. Finding a connection to Maime LaRue Brewer was also on the agenda.

Besides Luke and his partner, there only five other homicide detectives at the Little Rock Police Department available for the meeting. The three old timers – Jenkins, Richards and Romero – were there. They mostly handled the gang homicides in the southeast part of the city. They were all past retirement age but still hanging on. Then there was the newest promotion Phillips, a young rookie detective who followed the old timers around like a puppy. Phillips mostly fetched coffee and stood around and waited for orders.

Then there was the transfer from Tampa, Florida, David Norwalk – who was frankly a know-it-all that Luke wished was another police force's nightmare instead of their own. Since the first day Norwalk arrived almost a year ago, he rubbed Luke the wrong way. He handled arson, thefts and then homicide cases, when needed. Nobody liked working with Norwalk. He gave fast, often inaccurate opinions but spoke them like they were cold hard fact. He was the kind of guy who spoke first and thought later, if at all. There was a real sense of camaraderie among the detectives. They all helped each other out when they could, pitched in for one another, but not Norwalk. It was like he was in competition with all of them.

Luke stood against the back far end of the table and waited. The other detectives, in their pressed khakis, dress shirts and ties, took their seats one by one and talked amongst themselves as they waited for the meeting to start. Luke noticed Cap looked downright haggard and didn't talk to anyone. Instead, he stared hard at Luke. He wished he had some good news to share. He was at a loss.

After everyone got settled, Luke flipped the switch on the wall and the ceiling fans overhead started to hum. He stood in front of a large dry erase board and an equally large cork board next to it and laid the three manila case files he held in his hands on the table. He picked up a dry erase marker and nervously snapped the marker top off and back on. Once all eyes were on him, he started.

"Thanks for meeting today. As you know, we now have had three homicides and one missing woman. What we don't know is if they are connected. The first woman was found in the River Market District, the second tangled by a boat dock in Murray Park, and the last not even a half mile from her along the side of the river caught in some shallow water. We know very little so far, but a quick look at the cases show they're similar. All were found in their underwear and bras less than a couple of miles from each other, all within roughly twenty-four hours. Something Cooper pointed out, each was wearing a single item of jewelry."

The detectives started talking at once. Luke quieted them back down and continued.

"The first woman had on a ring, the second had on a bracelet and the third a pair of earrings. All of what appears to be expensive quality. The medical examiner is working up toxicology and cause and manner of death. On first glance, it looks like strangulation. One last thing to note, the last woman we just found today had the word *whore* written across her stomach in pink. We don't know if it was marker, or as the medical examiner suggested, maybe nail polish. No idea yet on approximate times of death."

"Any chance we get identification on any of the women?" Cap asked, pulling the file folders off the table and passing them around to the detectives. The files had crime scene photos and photos of the deceased women.

"We're working on it," Luke responded. Then he outlined the details of the files along with the basics he knew about the women; height, hair color and approximate age.

Cap nodded and wrote down some notes. He directed, "When we get enough information on them, let's get it out across the state to all the local police departments, and let's make sure to get it into NCIC and NamUs."

Luke routinely used NCIC – the National Crime Information Center, which helped the department on many cases. They used it to apprehend fugitives, locate missing persons and recover stolen property. Others had even identified terrorists using the system. He was less familiar with NamUs – an initiative by the Department of Justice called the National Missing and Unidentified Persons System. Luke jotted down some notes on his growing list.

A question from the back caught Luke's attention. "Any other similarities?" David Norwalk asked.

"No. Nothing definitive yet. Of course, it's been less than twenty-four hours since the first woman was found and less than six hours since the last. Ligature marks on their wrists and ankles and one around their necks. Clear sign of petechiae present, which the guess of strangulation probably wouldn't be that far off," Luke detailed.

The meeting continued as Luke fielded questions from most of the detectives. He made notes on the board, tacked up relevant documents and engaged them all in discussion.

Unfortunately, Luke couldn't answer most of the questions yet. He had asked for a rush from the medical examiner's office and hoped Purvis would have some answers at the latest by tomorrow morning. They didn't really know any more than the basics. Without some DNA, time and cause of death or some hits in the database for possible identification, they didn't have much to go on yet. They would need to identify the women to really start investigating. Even the witnesses who found the bodies didn't have much to say.

No one in the group could decide if the Brewer case was connected or not. There was a fifty-fifty divide. Maime was roughly the same age as the other women and same build as the first woman. That's all they had to go on, other than the women washing up near

George's office. Until Maime was found or they could identify the other women and the circumstances of their deaths, too many unknowns remained.

"The media seems to be right on these cases. We need to make some kind of official statement soon," Luke reminded them when the questions ended.

"Are we saying we have a serial killer on our hands?" Jenkins wanted to know. Ted Jenkins was the oldest of the old timers and the only white guy among the three senior detectives.

"I don't think we can make that jump at all until we have more information. It's certainly not a term we want the media to run with. No need to cause unnecessary alarm."

Luke barely got out his last word before Norwalk shot his mouth off.

"Of course it's a serial killer. What else could it be? Three victims, all women and all the same age. They died the same way and found in the same place. Don't be stupid."

Luke couldn't deal with a pissing match right now. Before he could respond though, Cap spoke up forcefully.

"Under no circumstance will anyone from this department mention anything about a serial killer to anyone. Not the Brewer family, no other law enforcement and most definitely not the media. We close all leaks from this office immediately. That is a direct order. Got it?"

Each detective nodded in agreement. Norwalk sulked but didn't say another word.

"Well, what are you waiting for? Go. Get to work," Cap barked loudly.

They filed out one by one from the conference room.

As Luke walked by, Norwalk muttered under his breath, "When you mess up the biggest case of your career, I'm going to have your job."

Luke didn't even respond. He just stopped and watched Norwalk walk away. He hated the guy. Luke didn't need more pressure right now, but that was typical Norwalk all the way. Norwalk had been gunning for Luke's position as the head of the violent crime's division since the day he started. Luke was going to make sure he'd never give him the chance.

CHAPTER 26

JUST AS I HEARD THE LOCK CLICK OPEN to Laura's front door, Cooper grabbed a hold of my hair and give me a tug backwards, probably more forcefully than he meant. I stumbled over my own feet, turned on him and yelled, "What are you doing?"

Cooper glared at me and took the keys out of my hand. He stood looking down at me with his hands on his hips. "What do you think you're doing?"

Truth was I didn't know exactly what I was doing. When Elaine showed us Laura's key, the only thing I wanted to do was get inside her house and find a photo of her. That's what I was thinking as I sprinted out of Elaine's house. I made it to Laura's porch before anyone else caught up.

"We have to know if it's her or not," I said. I stepped back and made room for Elaine as she joined us on the porch.

"You flew out of the house so fast I assumed you'd be in already. What are you doing out here?" Elaine inquired, a little out of breath from trying to keep up with us.

I turned to Cooper waiting for an answer since he was the one who was slowing this process down. "It's breaking and entering. We have no permission to go into her house," Cooper reminded me. "And we don't know..."

He didn't need to finish the sentence for me. I knew what he was going to say. We had no idea if Laura's house was going to be a crime scene or not. If she really was missing, trampling through her house could disturb possible evidence. Touching her phone, going through her purse would all be off limits, at least for now.

"Well what do you suppose we do? We can't just stand out here and wait," I said, starting to pace back and forth the distance of the porch.

Cooper had the key now. It seemed he was in charge. If I had been alone, I would have already been in and out of the house and known what I needed to know.

Cooper pulled his cellphone from his pocket, scrolled through numbers and placed a call. He left it on speaker, volume up so we could hear. When he got his neighbor Jenny on the phone, he asked when she had last spoken to Laura. She didn't remember the last time exactly, but Jenny told Cooper Laura had been a no show for her hospital shift that morning. Cooper didn't tell her we were standing on Laura's porch. He just let her know he'd look into it and be in touch. As he wrapped up the call, Elaine stood watching the both of us.

"I have permission to go in. I take in her mail when she's away," Elaine ventured.

Cooper shook his head no and called another number. No speaker phone this time, but I didn't have to hear the voice on the other end to know he was talking to Luke.

Cooper's voice shifted and he got straight to the point. He explained about George's alibi and then caught Luke up with recent developments. Elaine and I both waited for Cooper to get off the phone. I think Elaine was as frustrated as I was by the whole situation. Before either of us could stop her, she snatched the key out of Cooper's hand, and faster than I thought the woman could move, clicked open the front door lock and entered Laura's home.

Cooper looked too stunned to move. I knew him, he certainly wasn't going to tackle an old woman. Instead, he gave a blow by blow account to Luke. I waited eagerly. I definitely had a newfound appreciation for Elaine.

We watched her carefully move around the house not touching anything. She made her way through the living room and picked a silver picture frame off the end table and carried it back out to us, careful not to touch anything else.

She relocked the door, handed me the photo and said directly to Cooper, "Well one of us had to do something. We don't have all day if she is missing. I can't stand around while you two play cops and robbers."

Elaine turned to me, pointing to one of the girls in the photo, who seemed about my age, and said, "This one is Laura, such a pretty girl. The other is her sister."

I knew it wasn't either of the women they found last night in the river. I hadn't seen the woman today. I handed the photo over to Cooper.

He stared down looking at the photo for a few seconds. He looked up making steady eye contact with me and said to Luke who was still on the phone, "We've got another missing woman."

CHAPTER 27

LUKE AND HIS PARTNER TYLER showed up about fifteen minutes later. By then, Elaine was back at her house searching for Laura's parents' phone number. She said she had written it down in case of an emergency.

Cooper and I were sitting on Laura's front stoop, not talking. I was pretty sure Cooper was angry with me. I didn't care. This was all starting to feel like a nightmare that I couldn't wake up from. Not even a week ago I was home, safe and contained in my little world. The most I had to worry about was a late-night surveillance case that kept me from taking my dog out at a reasonable time or my younger sister who worked for me but did very little actual work. Now it seemed someone had turned the world upside down.

We watched Luke pull up and park at the curb in front of the house. He and Tyler made their way to where we were seated. Neither of them looked too happy.

"Just about twenty-four hours in town and we've got two missing women and three deceased. This has got to be a record for wreaking havoc if I ever saw one. You should go back to New York," Luke said sarcastically. His hands were shoved in his pockets.

"I think you had this going on way before I even boarded my plane. At least I can get someone to tell me their real alibi," I shot back.

He started to speak, but before he could get another word out of his mouth, Cooper glared at both of us and said angrily, "Knock it off. We've got more important things to focus on."

Luke and I eyed one another. I had to admit this was getting silly. He was better this morning and now his temper was flaring again. I was going to have to pull him aside and sort this out if we were going to be able to work together. We couldn't keep going at each other like this. I'd have to take the lead. I was, after all, the one that caused all this anger. But now, Cooper was right. We had more important things to focus on.

"Coop, what we got?" Tyler asked, moving past us on the porch, looking into the windows the same way we had. From his vantage point, I knew he could see Laura's purse and the other personal items I saw earlier.

Cooper gave them the full rundown. He motioned to the house next door and explained Elaine had retrieved a photo, which he handed to Luke. He mentioned Elaine was in the process of calling Laura's family. Cooper also explained his neighbor Jenny hadn't heard from Laura either, and she hadn't shown up for her hospital shift.

Tyler interrupted. Taking Cooper's seat next to me, he asked, "Miss Riley, George really tell you he was with this woman on Friday when his wife went missing? Don't you think that's something you should have called us about before y'all made your way over here?"

"George admitted he lied to you both and then told me about Laura," I said, making sure to get in the dig that the two of them wouldn't even be here if George hadn't confided in me. "Given he'd lied a few times, I wanted to ask her before I wasted any more of your time. I assumed you have enough to do sorting out the crimes that have recently occurred."

"You don't think it's strange that now we got two missing women both connected to George and three more that show up in the river behind his office?" Tyler pressed me.

"I think it's a little too obvious if you ask me. If you knew George, you'd know how smart he is. I don't think he'd be so obvious. Besides, we wouldn't have even known about Laura if he hadn't told me. I don't think he'd be dumb enough to hand us another missing woman he can't account for."

Cooper looked down at me. When I caught his eye, he shrugged like maybe I had finally struck some reason with him.

Tyler countered, "Maybe he knew someone saw him with Laura or that it would eventually come out. He was getting ahead of the game. Someone smart would see ten steps ahead of us. Maybe he's smarter than even you think."

"Why would he bring me down here then? Why get me involved? He knows once I start digging on something I dig and dig until I get to the truth."

"Maybe you're next," Luke blurted out. Then he looked at us like he hadn't meant to say the words out loud. Once they were out though, they hung in the air. I couldn't really respond. I didn't know what to say. What if George had some sort of psychotic break and was killing the women in his life? What if that is why he called me here? Maybe Luke was being jealous for no reason. I hoped that's all it was.

"Well that's a theory if I ever heard one. Coop, you'll have to keep an eye on her. We don't need her to be woman number six." Tyler looked at me sideways. "Then again, I think Miss Riley could probably handle her own."

Just then Elaine walked across the lawn with her cellphone in her hands. "I have Laura's father Steve on the phone. He wants to speak with the detective in charge. I figured one of you would be him."

Elaine stood with the phone outstretched waiting for one of them to take the call. Luke took the phone and walked away from the group of us.

"Have they spoken to her?" I asked Elaine.

"Not in days. Her mother Eva is on her cellphone right now calling other family and some friends to see if they have heard from her. When I told them she didn't show up at work, they knew something was wrong. Laura never misses work like that. Her father is going to catch the next flight here and make a missing person's report."

Luke walked back and explained pretty much what Elaine just told us. Luke turned to Tyler and said, "Let me call this in and get the crime scene folks ready on this. Laura's father gave us permission to go through the house and car and anything else we needed. While we wait for him to arrive tonight, let's pick up George and have a nice little chat at the station."

Turning to us he said, "In the meantime, can you two track down Dean? Don't let on that we know that he covered for George but see what you can get him to tell us. Maybe, like George, he'll be more honest with you."

"Stay out of trouble, Miss Riley," Tyler called over his shoulder as they walked off. Luke didn't even bother to say goodbye.

CHAPTER 28

LUKE WAS LIVID. Not only had Riley gotten the jump on him getting George's real alibi, she was still defending the worthless loser. He looked through the one-way mirror at George who was sitting at the small square metal table with his hands folded in his lap. Luke thought he looked entirely too calm and comfortable given the situation. He wanted to go into the room, pick him up by the shirt and shake the truth out of him. Or at least shake him until he pissed himself with fear.

Luke watched George a few more moments, calmed himself and then left his partner and a few other detectives who planned to observe the interview. Once he entered the interrogation room, Luke was completely back to normal. His rage had dissipated, and he was ready to get down to business. There was nothing in the room but the small table and two chairs. George sat farthest from the door while Luke sat arm's length from it. It wasn't a big room or comfortable in any way. It was designed like that.

"Do you have any idea why we called you back in here?" Luke asked, pulling out the chair and sitting down.

"You said earlier you wanted to go over some financials. I assumed you couldn't wait until tomorrow?" George replied, leaning on his forearms making steady eye contact with Luke.

"No, tell me about Laura Bisceglia," Luke demanded, cutting to the chase. He wanted answers now. He had played too many games already with George and was tired of wasting time. Luke believed wholeheartedly he was staring down a killer. He wanted justice, and he wanted it now. If he had anything, the slightest shred of evidence to tie to George, he'd arrest him on the spot.

"Riley told you already?" George said, exhaling loudly.

"No," Luke lied. He didn't want George to think he couldn't trust Riley. "We got a tip from a neighbor who had seen your car at Laura's place."

Over the course of the next thirty minutes, George detailed his entire relationship with Laura; how they met, kept in contact, met up, places they traveled and how they broke up – twice. Luke was a little surprised that George was giving him so much information. He bet money George was debating how much they knew. Luke didn't think George was going to take any chances at this point.

When George finally wound down, Luke looked at him and asked, "Anything else you think we should know?"

And then he waited. Luke was skilled at using silence to get what he wanted. He could sit and stare at a suspect for hours, neither talking. George didn't say anything. Five and then ten minutes.

Finally, George spoke.

He sat back and folded his arms over his chest and said, "I've told you it all. I don't have anything else. This is a waste of time. I cheated on my wife. I admit it. You need to be out there looking for her. I didn't do anything to her."

"Tell me where Laura is," Luke demanded calmly and evenly.

"What do you mean, where Laura is?" George asked clearly acting confused. "Work, home maybe. How should I know? I haven't seen her since I dropped her off on Friday night. I already told you that."

"Funny thing, George, nobody has seen Laura since you dropped her off. Actually, to be more accurate nobody but you can confirm that you even dropped her off at home on Friday night."

"What?" George gasped as his eyes widened.

Luke was impressed. George was a good actor. He looked thoroughly dumbfounded by the news.

"I'm telling you the truth. We went out, drove around talking, and I dropped her off. I broke it off for good. She was crying and upset with me and just wanted to go home so that's where I left her.

I swear to God, you have to believe me." George's voice was so high he was practically screeching.

Luke didn't say a word and instead got an idea. He got up and left the conference room. Returning, he slid two eight-by-ten crime scene photos of the women pulled from the river across to George.

"Look at these and tell me what you think," Luke said. He wanted to shock George. Make him sick or see if he had a reaction to his own handiwork.

George looked down at the photos, picked up each one for several seconds and then laid them back down on the table. He stared at Luke for several moments. He slammed his fist down on the conference room table and yelled, "Who is trying to ruin my life?"

Hiding his shock at George's outburst, Luke said all he could. "You tell me, George. You tell me."

CHAPTER 29

DEAN'S HOUSE was just off Country Club Road and four houses down from the club's entrance. He probably drove his golf cart from home right to the greens. The house was a massive two-story structure and landscaped perfectly. I had to admit it fit him and was a stark contrast to George and Maime's unkempt house.

I wanted to talk to Dean and see why he covered for George. Plus, he had reached out to Cooper so I was hoping he'd be willing to talk. Cooper and I approached, rang the bell and waited. Dean answered the door, looking like he had been asleep and startled awake by the doorbell.

"What can I do for you?" Dean asked as he leaned against the door and crossed his arms. He was barefoot and had on baggy jeans and a button down emerald green shirt with the top two buttons undone. His sleeves were rolled halfway up his forearms.

"We need to talk to you about George and Maime," Cooper explained.

We had agreed on the drive over that Cooper would take the lead on the interview. I wasn't really sure why as I could have done it myself, but Cooper felt that he might get Dean to open up. Some nonsense about good old boys, but Dean looked more ready to attend a polo match than sit in a duck blind.

"What do you want to know?" Dean asked.

"Can we come in and talk?" Cooper asked and started to step forward. Dean made no move to let us through the door. He didn't take the stance of a cooperative man.

"We'll be fine right here," Dean responded. He barely even blinked.

"George told us he was with you on Friday. What were you doing?" Cooper asked.

"Good try," Dean responded impatiently, shifting his weight from one foot to the other. "George already told me he told Riley that we weren't together."

"Well if you weren't with George, then what were you doing on Friday?" Cooper demanded.

"I see. Covering for George gave me an alibi, too. What am I your number one suspect?" Dean asked, smirking.

I wanted to smack the smirk right off his face. I really did not like this guy and something was gnawing at me that I couldn't quite place. "You said it. Where were you?"

"Well if you must know I was home alone. I was supposed to have a date, but she canceled last minute," Dean said. Then he looked at me and winked. "That time of the month."

I jumped in before Cooper could. "Let's just get down to it. What do you know about George and Maime? Where she might have gone? Your thoughts on George? Stop being such a pain in the ass. You get the drill. You know why we're here."

He put his hands up as if to say he was an open book and then said, "George is my best friend and has been for years. He didn't hurt Maime. He's not the reason she's missing. Yes, he had a couple of women on the side, but honestly, any man married to her would have too. She's not exactly compliant. I don't know anything more than that. I've always protected George, always have and always will. My business protects his business and his father-in-law's. That's the extent of my involvement."

I wanted to ask what he meant by compliant, but Cooper chimed in first. "You and Maime's father seem very focused on his law firm's reputation. I don't really understand why that would be the focus here. Don't you think finding his daughter should be more important than a business reputation? Care to educate me on that one?"

Dean sighed. "I don't expect you to understand. His firm handles a number of very wealthy, very important clients as does mine. Any type of scandal can have a damaging and lasting effect. Mr. LaRue cares about Maime's wellbeing, of course, but is well aware of George's dalliances and frankly how difficult his daughter can be. There are things that could come out that could have a negative effect on his business. That's why I'm here."

Cooper and I exchanged a look and then he inquired, "Care to share what those negative things could be?"

"No."

"Do you want us to find Maime? It was my understanding you were supportive of George hiring us. You seem to be stonewalling us now. What gives?" I asked.

"I don't think Maime's coming back. George will have to face that, and the police will have to realize that George had nothing to do with it. There's no evidence."

"You're so sure? Are you saying you think she just took off?" I wasn't really sure where he was going with this. But I could tell our window for getting information was closing. He was talking in a lot of circles and not really saying anything.

"I honestly don't know what happened to Maime. I think whatever did, she caused. The only thing I'll tell you is Maime was never the innocent victim to George's philandering. She had quite the roving eye herself."

Dean started to close the door on us, but turned back and added, "For what it's worth, Riley, George should have married you. Marrying Maime was the start of the destruction of a lot of lives. Now you'll have to excuse me, I have a business call I need to make."

That was it. He closed the door in our faces, and we were left standing on his porch. Dean just said a whole lot but very little at the same time.

CHAPTER 30

LUKE WANTED NOTHING MORE than to charge the scum with murder, but he had to let George leave. After George's outburst, he sat silently and didn't utter another word for almost fifteen minutes. Luke stayed just as quiet. Finally, George looked up and said he was leaving. He challenged Luke to either arrest him or to let him go. Luke didn't have enough evidence so George left.

Obviously, something in the photos of the dead women struck a chord with George. Whether it was the realization that they were connecting him to those crimes or the idea that maybe the dead women were connected to Maime and that maybe she really was dead, Luke couldn't be sure. Luke had watched George for any sign of recognition to indicate he knew the women, but other than the outburst, he didn't see any.

Luke didn't know why but he felt sure that George was connected to all of the cases and assumed Maime was probably the first. Why her body hadn't surfaced yet, Luke couldn't venture a guess.

George said he was going to retain Bard Epson who Luke knew was a solid attorney. He was licensed to practice law in a few states across the south and had won several major homicide cases for defendants in the last year in Memphis and New Orleans.

Luke had never been cross-examined by him in court or saw him in action, but his reputation was well-known. Luke found it telling that George didn't just call someone from his own firm or his father-in-law for that matter and instead hired out of his circle. George was threatening to get the best of the best. It was clear he wasn't going to be cooperating or making another statement anytime soon.

Luke knew to arrest George they would need more than speculation. They would need some hard evidence linking him to one or more of the crimes. They just didn't have it and so they had to let George go. Little Rock Police Department had already served a subpoena to search his home, but they would need to again. They hadn't been searching for connections to other women when they first searched. Luke knew he would have to get other subpoenas too. They might even put a GPS tracking device on George's Chevy Tahoe to track his every move.

If Bard Epson was involved, he'd have to connect with Cooper and Riley. Luke wondered how this attorney's involvement would affect Riley and Cooper's ability to share information. Typically, when the attorney hires a private investigator, any evidence they find falls under work product, and it would be unethical to share with the cops. But from what Luke understood, they were retained by George himself and so their cooperation walked a fine line at best.

As Luke sat at his desk, entertaining a fantasy of arresting and seeing George Brewer prosecuted to the fullest extent of the law, his partner came up behind him and slapped a manila folder in front of him, startling him out of his dream world.

Luke eyed the folder and then looked up to Tyler for explanation.

"We got a match on prints on the first woman. She's in the system," Tyler said with a big beaming smile.

Tyler picked up the folder and gave Luke the details. "Her name is Shannon McCarty, age thirty-eight. She lives in Little Rock. She was arrested on four separate occasions in New Orleans for prostitution over the last five years. Her father is our congressman."

Tyler went on to give Luke her address, background and conviction history.

Confused, Luke asked, "A hooker and a politician's daughter? She didn't look like a hooker."

"She's not a hooker. She's a high-end call girl. Madame and all," Tyler explained. "I called the New Orleans police department and talked to vice. They are familiar with her. Shannon worked for Madame Breaux. Breaux is known to the locals, been running her business for close to forty years. Her big mansion is in the Garden District. It's been in her family for generations. She caters to all the politicians and business clientele visiting the city. Detective I talked to said they all just look the other way. Some state senators are in her pocket. They can't touch her. They make arrests once in a while, but both the girls and the clients plead out and get right back at it."

"She lives here in Little Rock?" Luke asked, skimming through the file trying to fit all the pieces of the puzzle together.

"She must travel. From what the cop I talked to said, her girls are all over the south. Smart girls. Vanderbilt girls. Society girls. Apparently, she's not the only politician's kid working for Breaux."

"Anyone know she's missing?"

"Not that I'm aware of. I put a call into Breaux. Let's see if she calls back. No one else listed at Shannon's residence and no home phone listed either. She probably just has a cellphone. Her mom died when she was young and her father resides mostly in D.C. He's not back here in Little Rock too often."

"So, what's a high-end call girl working in New Orleans doing floating dead in the Arkansas River?"

Stacy M. Jones

CHAPTER 31

LUKE AND TYLER JUMPED at the sound of the ringing desk phone. Luke picked it up and heard a soft-voiced woman's New Orleans accent on the other end of the line.

"Detective, this is Ms. Breaux. Someone from your office called about Shannon McCarty."

"Yes, how do you know her?"

"She works for me," Breaux paused. When Luke didn't say anything, she continued her voice stronger and more direct. "Let's not play games, Detective. You and I both know you already know about my business and what Shannon does for me."

Luke appreciated her candor and met her with the same.

"I'm sorry to inform you of this, but yesterday morning, Shannon was found deceased in the Arkansas River. It hasn't officially been ruled a homicide, but we are fairly sure it was not accidental. Was she working in Little Rock?"

Several seconds passed before Breaux answered. When she did, she said, "No, she only took clients here a couple times a month. She missed an appointment two nights ago here at a local hotel with one of her regular clients. She would have been paid eight thousand for the night. She never showed up, which is unacceptable for my girls. She'd never done it before so I assumed something was amiss. I've been trying to locate her since."

"Before that, when was the last you had contact with her?"

"Tuesday of last week she came to collect her pay. Shannon said she was going to visit her brother in Baton Rouge but was to return by Sunday for her Monday evening client. Her brother was my first call. It seems she never arrived in Baton Rouge. He hasn't heard from her. Obviously, I can't call her father, although I'm sure he was aware. After her mother died, Shannon didn't have much of a relationship with him, just her brother."

"Does she ever take clients outside of your business?" Luke asked, straining at the word *business*. He hated prostitution as much as he hated drug dealers. Both crimes preyed off the weak. High-end or not, Luke knew many of the girls suffered from childhood issues.

"Not if she wanted to keep her job. To be candid with you, I run the business of my mother and my grandmother. It's a legitimate business that has no reason to be illegal, but it is. My girls are educated, sophisticated, and cater to some very wealthy and powerful clients. Shannon has worked for me since she was in college. When she graduated with a social work degree, she realized she made more money with me than she could ever as a social worker. Shannon was a smart girl. She wouldn't do anything risky. If someone killed her as you said, it was someone she knew and knew for a long time. Someone she trusted."

"Would you be willing to hand over Shannon's client list?"

"Not on your life," Breaux responded with a short incredulous snort.

"If it's someone she trusted and your other girls take over her client list, it could be someone on that list. We have two other women we found in the river not far from where we found Shannon. Do you have any other women missing?"

"No, all accounted for and interviewed. No one has seen or heard from Shannon. I will allow you to interview them if you send a detective down here. We'll be very kind to him, I assure you. Maybe you might want to pay us a visit yourself. Men quite enjoy the variety of what we have to offer."

"You do realize you're soliciting a cop?" Luke shook his head at her brazenness, but if the locals couldn't fight her, there wasn't much he was going to do out of his jurisdiction.

"You are also just a man, with needs," she said seductively, stressing the last part.

Luke ignored it. After that, he rushed her off the phone but not before getting Shannon's brother's contact information. It would be his first call, and hopefully, her brother could notify the father. That was not a call Luke wanted to make.

He'd check to see if a local New Orleans cop could handle some interviews. Luke didn't think it would do any good to send a detective all the way there. Breaux was also going to send Luke a recent photo they could use to put out to the media. Maybe friends or someone could help start filling in the timeline of Shannon's last days.

CHAPTER 32

COOPER AND I DECIDED to go our separate ways for the rest of the day. He wanted to interview Maime's parents, and given it was obvious that Maime's father didn't like me, we figured Cooper would have better luck on his own. Cooper was more intrigued than I was about the potential negative press that could befall the law firm. I just thought it was typical rich people nonsense. Cooper said he was going to dig a little more with the LaRues and see what he could find. Then he had a surveillance case.

I was on my own for the rest of the night, which I really didn't mind. I liked Cooper, but sometimes his slow southern pace drove me a little insane. Not to mention, he was such a stickler for the rules. Unfortunately, other than Maime's coworkers, who we planned to talk to first thing tomorrow morning, the only people we had left to interview were Maime's friends.

I stood in the road outside of my house, next to my Jeep, and scanned the list of names. I wanted to start first with the people who I knew absolutely hated me.

I took off and drove through the Heights and Hillcrest neighborhoods where they all lived. I didn't get very far though. The first six houses I went to, I was met with disgust, cursing and slammed doors. They all remembered me and not one of the women was willing to speak to me, even though technically I was hired to find Maime. They assumed I was there only to protect George and to steal him back. Nothing could be further from the truth, but I understood how they felt. Besides, back in the day, they had only ever heard one side of the story. To them, I was the woman trying to steal Maime's boyfriend. I'd probably hate me too.

The thing is, I never bothered to defend myself back then. I never told them I was just as duped as Maime. I don't think it would have mattered. I didn't really think they would have listened. Truthfully, and I hate to admit it, there was some sick twisted part of me that wanted to protect George even then. If I stayed the bad guy, George looked innocent. Let them think it was me contacting him, hitting on him and trying to lure him away. People only see what they want to believe anyway. I hated myself a little bit for that.

I couldn't blame those girls. I would have had the same response if this had been about Emma. I protect the people I care about. Right now, I had a job to do and it wasn't getting done.

Frustrated, I looked over the list again. There was one last name. Gina Young. She was Maime's roommate when all of it went down between the three of us. She was one of the women who called me, but she never seemed quite as angry as the rest. Gina was also with all of the girls on Friday when Maime didn't show up. I was hoping she might be my best chance at some information. She was married now, and I knew from Emma, she had a son close to Emma's daughter's age.

Gina lived only a couple of blocks away from me. She was standing in the doorway as I pulled up. My guess is one woman called the next, and they were all alerted I was on my way. I apprehensively approached but was pleasantly surprised that she greeted me warmly and invited me in.

"Sorry, the place is a wreck. My son Joshua is on a rampage today. Everything is torn apart," Gina said, showing me into the living room. "Can I get you something to drink?"

"No, thank you," I said as we were both seated on the couch. "Thanks for speaking to me. I know this is probably a little awkward. The others wouldn't even speak to me other than to cuss me out and slam the door in my face."

Gina shrugged sheepishly, folded her hands in her lap and said, "I'm a traitor, I guess, but you might have suspected that. I lived with Maime. I love her like a sister, and like a sister, I know her faults. A relationship is never all one-sided. George and Maime had problems from the start. You, you were just a symptom."

I don't know why but for the first time I felt compelled to tell someone in Maime's life the truth. Maybe finally I wanted to defend myself or maybe I really did want her to feel more at ease.

"Just so you know, I never knew about Maime until that day she found the email. George never told me, and once I knew, we broke it off. We might have called each other from time to time or kept in touch but nothing ever happened. I couldn't be someone's mistress. I don't share well."

"I suspected, but Maime just wouldn't hear of it. It was easier to blame you than him." She stopped and then went on, "But you aren't here to rehash old news. How can I help find her?"

"Just tell me what you know, anything and everything. Start as far back as you have to. We don't know at this point what detail could lead to finding her. Walk me right up to the night she didn't show, and how you came to know she was missing."

Gina leaned back on the couch and crossed her legs. She seemed to think for a few moments and said thoughtfully, "I know I'm supposed to think it but I just can't believe George killed her. My husband Mike and I have spent a lot of time with George and Maime. I just can't believe it and neither can he. I'm glad there's someone who thinks there might be another possibility. The more time they spend on George, the less they are looking for Maime."

I leaned toward her, shifting in my seat, surprised I wasn't the only one who thought that way. To hear it from Gina gave me a tiny glimmer of hope.

Gina continued over the next hour to fill me in completely on George and Maime's relationship and everything she knew about Maime. Most of it was mundane and routine, the things you expect to hear about someone's life. I wasn't prepared for the bomb she was about to drop though.

"No one knows this. I didn't tell the detectives yet either. When I first heard she was missing, I was worried Maime had just run away. I didn't want to create any more of a mess for her to come back to. With so much time passing, I'm worried. Maime doesn't even know I know. She was having an affair with Dean. It started back when she and George were dating."

I started to interject, but she held her hand up to stop me and continued.

"I don't know how they hid it this long. Also, last year, Maime developed quite the prescription drug habit. Dean tried to get her to rehab. When she wouldn't, he broke it off or at least that's what I've come to understand. I don't know if the affair or the drugs have anything to do with her disappearance, but it's something no one is looking into because they don't know."

Not even giving me a chance to speak, she got up, walked into the kitchen and came back with a slip of paper with an address on it. "That's where her dealer lived the last I knew. I followed her once. This is going back about three months. He might still be there. Be careful, it's a rough part of town."

CHAPTER 33

I KNEW I SHOULD have immediately called Luke about what Gina just told me, but my mind was reeling. I left Gina's, got in my Jeep, and drove directly to Dean's house. I wanted to confront Dean myself. Then call him out for being such an idiot. He told us Maime had a wandering eye. He would know best. He was screwing her.

I've done some terrible things in my life, but I don't know how someone could claim to be someone's best friend, be as close as brothers, and then screw his wife. I just didn't get it. I had no reason to believe that Gina was lying. She was believable and had no reason to lie.

I just couldn't wrap my head around Maime being addicted to drugs though. She never seemed all that stable, but I never suspected a drug habit. I wondered how it factored in. Where was she? It's like she just vanished. It was really starting to freak me out.

I handle crime all the time but rarely is the victim someone I know. Somewhere in the back of my mind, I wondered if I willed this to happen. Back when I was in the middle of all of it with George, I think I must have prayed night after night for Maime to get lost, to get out of George's life.

I bet Maime's drug habit was one of the reasons her father is so worried about his reputation. Dean mentioned negatives. That had to be one. That and screwing her behind everyone's back.

Given the possibility of drug addiction, Maime could be anywhere. She could be off on a binge. Or overdosed somewhere. Even taken off to get herself clean. I wondered if George knew about the drugs and which prescription drugs exactly. How could he not know? He lived with her.

The affair with Dean and a drug-addicted wife certainly gave George more motive. Not that he needed any. It was one thing to have an affair and want his freedom. It's another as a man to know your wife was involved with someone else. I had to guess that he didn't know. Otherwise, how could he still be so close and trusting of Dean?

I slammed my car into park in front of Dean's house and made my way to his front door. I pounded on the door several times and waited. No one answered. I stepped back off the porch and looked for any sign of life coming from the house. There was none. The garage didn't have windows so there was no telling if his car was there or not. I walked down the driveway and punched his number into my cellphone, hit send and listened to the phone ring. No answer. I didn't leave a message. I didn't want to tip him off. This required a face-to-face meeting.

I stood at the curb at the end of his driveway, watching his house for several more minutes, trying to determine my next move. He could be any number of places. I'd probably just waste my time driving around. I was too amped up to just go back home and wait.

I could at least try a few of the local spots and see if Dean was there. I wanted to call George, but that would have to wait. I didn't trust myself enough yet not to let on what I knew. I needed a plan for testing George on how much he knew. I started to mentally walk through the questions I needed to ask him when my cellphone rang.

"Ma, what's up? I'm kind of in the middle of stuff here," I said more impatiently than I meant to sound.

"You're alive? I'm sitting here watching the news about what's happening in that horrible place. Three dead women pulled from the river. Missing women. Is this why you're down there? To stir up trouble? You could have at least called your mother and told her you weren't dead," my mother Karen squawked into the phone, not kidding in the slightest.

My mother was a nurse. She divorced my father when I was very young. He went back to Ireland, where he was from. He came back once, long enough to get my mother pregnant with my younger sister Liv, and then left the final time. She raised us.

She came from a big Irish Catholic family herself, six sisters and one brother. They say it takes a village and that's what my family is. They all live in the same neighborhood. No one ever left, except me. My mother liked me under her thumb, which is why she hated Little Rock so much. She blamed the city for my departure years ago. Liv still lived at home and probably would until she found a suitable husband.

"Mom, it's work. I'm on a case. What are they saying on the news?"

"That George Brewer is a serial killer!" my mother yelled. Then she did what she always does, put me on hold to answer her call waiting.

She kept me stewing on hold for at least two minutes, which seemed like an eternity.

"You there?" her voice boomed into my ear as she clicked over.

"Yes. Mom, is that what they really said or just what you think?"

"Like I'm lying," she said clearly exasperated with me. "Well I'll tell you this, that man is no good. I said it from the beginning, but you don't listen to me. So really when you're dead - buried or cremated?"

My mother was obsessed with funeral arrangements. She already had her wake planned. I got the shock of my life one Christmas when I went to the cemetery to visit my grandparents. Right next to their headstone was my mother's, a small rose-colored stone with her name and date of birth engraved. A little warning would have been nice. But as she told me, it slipped her mind. I think she actually tended to her own grave when she visited the cemetery.

"I'll call you later," I said, ending the call and avoiding answering her ridiculous question. She was constantly trying to get me to plan my own wake and funeral. She acted as if I were two seconds from death all the time.

CHAPTER 34

I SLID INTO THE DRIVER'S SEAT of my Jeep and was just about to turn the key in the ignition when an older model black pickup truck pulled up next to me going in the opposite direction. Ben, the reporter from the other night, put down his window, leaned out and asked, "How's the case coming along?"

"On or off the record?" I wasn't sure what he knew about me but given his close relationship to Luke and the question, I'm guessing he at least knew I was an investigator.

"Off. I got something you might be able to use. Let me pull over and we can talk. I was going to try to get your number from Luke so this is good timing."

He pulled along the curb as I got out and stood next to my car. I hadn't really noticed the night before what he looked like. He had dark messy hair falling in his face, bright blue eyes and a disarming smile. He probably did well interviewing people for the paper. He was kind of a guy's guy. Men would trust him and women would be attracted so they'd naturally tell him what he wanted to know.

"Welcome back to Little Rock. I've been asking around about you. From what I hear you were a great journalist. Too bad you gave it up."

"This suits me better. You said you got something for me?"

"I do. I already told Luke so I'm pretty sure it's okay to share with you. George Brewer has had multiple affairs. He's got motive to kill Maime. You should probably look into that angle. I heard the rumors at the golf course. I was even able to get a couple of names. I can't share those with you but the police have them. I'm sure if you ask around you'll get them too."

Ben was a pretty good reporter. None of the news stations had run the story yet. I wondered why. This was a scoop if I ever heard one. I wasn't going to let on we already knew.

"If you're so sure about this, why haven't you run with the story yet? If it's true, this is a big break for you," I said, testing him.

"I haven't been able to confirm it yet with any of the women. It's all speculation right now. You know how that goes. Plus, I have a good thing going with the police department. I wouldn't want to piss off anyone by running a story too soon."

"You're playing both sides of the fence."

"What do you think about all this? Ever had a case like this?"

"A missing person's case?"

"A serial killer case. I mean, if it wasn't for people actually dying, they are kind of cool to write about and investigate. Don't you think?"

"I don't think anyone said there's a serial killer. But yes, they can be interesting cases." In some ways Ben reminded me of myself when I was a reporter. He was eager, making good connections with law enforcement, and really had an interest in crime reporting.

I wanted to know what else he knew and see if I could get any of the local gossip out of him so I asked, "Any chance you want to grab a beer and talk about the case? I got some time."

"Sorry, I can't. I'm covering the other missing woman story, too. Laura Bisceglia. You know about that, right?"

How did the media get a hold of this information so quickly? Cooper and I just left Laura's house at two-thirty this afternoon. It was only closing in on seven now. Her parents hadn't even arrived yet and no official report made. I couldn't see Elaine or her parents calling in the media yet. I was starting to wonder if there was a leak in the police department. Then thinking back, my mother did say missing women, not just one.

"How did you hear about that case already?" I asked cautiously.

"I guess you haven't been watching the news. It's gone national. We got a tip about an hour ago."

"Who was the tip from?" It was a stupid question. I knew he'd never reveal his source.

"I don't know. Like I told Luke earlier, my editor Cathy gets the information and sends me out," Ben explained as he turned to leave.

I watched him go, wondering what to make of him. He turned back, flashed me a smile, ran his hand through his hair and said, "Maybe some other time we can grab that beer. I'm sure you've got lots of interesting stories to tell."

CHAPTER 35

COOPER FOLLOWED THE GUY IN FRONT OF HIM desperately trying to keep up. He couldn't lose him. The guy drove like he was the lead car in the Daytona 500. After leaving the LaRue's house, where they didn't provide any new information other than insisting George was guilty, Cooper made his way back to downtown Little Rock and picked up his surveillance case. He watched the guy's condo until he left. Now he was flying over the streets of Little Rock. Cooper hated mobile surveillance like this. His truck wasn't equipped, especially not on the curvy streets of the city.

Together they climbed the hill on Cantrell, leaving downtown Little Rock behind. Cooper needed to stay close enough to catch all the green lights with the guy. But stay far enough back not to be suspicious. Luckily, it was dark out, and it would be harder for the driver to tell he was being tailed.

This was the third time Cooper attempted surveillance on him. He lost him twice before due to the guy's reckless driving. This time the guy was definitely working his way out of the city. Cooper had no idea where he was headed, but he was hoping it was to see his mistress. Cooper needed the evidence to give to his client, the guy's fiancée.

By the time they made their way out the Heights neighborhood and out to Highway 10, the guy was easily doing sixty-five, a good twenty-five over the speed limit. It seemed to Cooper, he was leaving the city limits of Little Rock and heading to more rural areas. When they hit a straightaway, Cooper dropped back to give the guy some space. As he drove, Cooper tried to recall if there were any motels out this far. He expected the guy to stay downtown so he really had no idea where they were headed. Sometimes this was the more interesting part of his job. He rarely knew when he headed out on a surveillance case where he'd end up. He had to be prepared for anything.

Several miles outside of the city the guy made a right onto a dirt road. Cooper flipped his lights off and followed a distance behind. The guy's brake lights cut through the dark, allowing Cooper to keep track of him. Not being able to see what was in front of his truck on the stretch of road without headlights wasn't the smartest plan, but Cooper knew it was a necessity. He slowed almost to a stop when the guy's car pulled off to the left at an older style motel.

Cooper pulled over to the side of the road just before reaching the motel. He parked and sat in total darkness with trees to the left and right of him. Just up to Cooper's left the motel's lights gave away the entire parking lot and the motel lobby. Through a big front window, Cooper saw one old guy sitting at the lobby desk, his legs outstretched and feet up on the desk while he watched a small television. A few cars littered the parking lot. Three of the ten rooms had lights on.

The guy Cooper had his eye on got out of his car and went to room number three and knocked. Someone answered. Cooper could only make out the bare arm of a woman. He wasn't going to get any photos or video evidence out here. Cooper would wait until they came out so he could get a good description on the woman. Now it was just a waiting game. At least Cooper remembered something to drink, and he had some pretty good tree coverage to take a leak.

The hours passed slowly. Cooper assumed they must be really going at it hot and heavy to be in there this long. His attention was starting to wane when suddenly a car zipped by him that looked like an unmarked police car. He sat up straighter to get a better look. The car pulled into the motel parking lot, joining a car that had just come in the opposite direction.

Cooper grabbed his binoculars and zeroed in on the unmarked car. He was so focused on checking out who the cop was and what he was doing, Cooper almost missed the guy stepping out of the

BMW parked next to the unmarked car. It was Dean. There was someone else in the passenger seat that Cooper strained to see. He couldn't really tell, but it almost looked like Maime's father Edwin. Edwin hadn't mentioned a meeting to Cooper when he was just with him, but then again, he hadn't said much at all.

Dean walked around his car and exchanged a few words with a guy Cooper had never seen before. They both looked around somewhat cautiously before Dean pulled a thick white envelope from the inside of his sport jacket and handed it to the guy. The other guy pulled out a stack of bills from the envelope and began to count. As he started, Dean laid his hand on top of the money and shook his head no. The guy put the money back in, looked around again and went to the passenger side of the BMW.

Cooper couldn't see what he was doing. He practically jumped out of his driver's seat and moved from side to side in an attempt to get a better angle. Cooper couldn't no matter how he tried. The other guy moved back towards Dean, shook his hand, slipped into his car and took off in the opposite direction of Cooper.

Dean stood for a few moments watching the car race off and then got in his car and turned out of the lot in Cooper's direction. There was nowhere for Cooper to hide. Dean was going to pass right by him. Cooper did the only thing he could think of. He slid himself down into his seat and ducked his head low and hoped that Dean didn't see anything more than an empty truck.

After Dean passed by, Cooper sat up and looked around again. All was quiet and the subject of his investigation was still tucked inside his hotel. Cooper debated leaving or calling Luke. He had no idea what he just witnessed or even who the guy was that took what Cooper could only imagine was a bribe in the dead of night.

CHAPTER 36

MY MOTHER AND BEN HAD BEEN RIGHT. The story had broken on all the national news stations. After leaving Dean's house, I came back to my own. Once inside, I started a fire in the fireplace, slipped off my shoes, threw on some comfortable clothes and sat down in front of the television. I ate the Chinese take-out I had picked up on the way home as I watched events unfold live on CNN. They were reporting from spots along the Arkansas River where the victims had been found.

Captain Meadows was giving a brief but effective rundown of everything that had happened over the last day and a half and what they had uncovered so far. I must have missed it, but at some point Luke had identified one of the women found in the river. They showed a recent photo of her, told the public she was from Little Rock but worked out of New Orleans. She was the daughter of well-known Congressman Mike McCarty. The media speculated that she was a high-end call girl but the police weren't confirming.

I flipped from station to station and they were all saying the same thing. Three women found in the river and two more missing. The only possible suspect was George Brewer. His connection with both Maime and now Laura sealed the deal in the media's mind that George must be a deranged serial killer. Law enforcement didn't connect George to the cases of the deceased women, but they also didn't say they weren't connected, which was enough for the media to make the assumption. If George Brewer had connections to the missing women, he must be connected to the dead ones, too. They speculated that it was just a matter of time until Laura and Maime were found in the river.

Maime's friends, who refused to speak to me, were interviewed. Each of them had George arrested, tried, convicted and sitting on death row. I really couldn't eat anymore. The whole thing made me sick to my stomach. I brought my dishes to the sink and debated when I was going to tell Luke about the bracelet. I should have done it today. I knew it would have been one more piece connecting George.

Could I really have loved a serial killer? I wonder the number of women that have had to answer yes to that question. It was a club to which I definitely didn't want to belong.

My phone rang just as I finished washing my dinner dishes. It was George. He needed to speak with me immediately and was coming over. I had to tell him I wasn't at the hotel. He was surprised that I still owned the house. He stood at my front door less than ten minutes later. While logic should have told me to be afraid of him, I just couldn't muster it up. The only thing I asked him was to dodge the media. I didn't want them following him over.

"You look awful. What's the matter?" Obvious answer but George looked twitchy even for the circumstance. He sat down on the couch. I took the chair opposite him.

"I have to tell you something. It's hard for me to say. I need your help. I think I'm being framed," George said, leaning back on the couch and closing his eyes.

"Framed? Why do you say that?"

He kept his eyes closed and said almost in a whisper, "I know one of the women they found in the river."

"I know," I deadpanned. I wanted this explanation. I was ready for it.

George sat up and looked at me like I had no idea what I was talking about. "You know? How could you possibly know?"

"Just explain. I told you before, I can't help you if I don't know the truth."

"I'm not proud of this, but when I travel to New Orleans for work, I hired her from time to time. I'd see her here in Little Rock, but we never meet here. It was just when I went there. It was too risky at home."

I tried to hide the shock I felt. I must have done a good enough job because George kept talking. He explained how he had been given Madame Breaux's number from a friend of his, one of her other clients. That was how Breaux worked, client referrals only. He explained that it was easier sometimes than meeting a woman. That hiring one meant no strings for sure. He paid what he paid, had a wonderful night and she never asked for more. George said it was worth the money to get what he needed and leave it behind until his next trip to the city.

"Did you hire her this week, George? Did you hire her to come screw you while your wife is missing?" The anger just bubbled up. I could feel myself close to losing my temper in a way I hadn't ever with him. I got up, walked to the kitchen and started washing my dishes again, slamming them around in the sink. I couldn't even control my temper enough to ask about the woman wearing the bracelet. This made four women he was connected to.

Shannon wasn't the woman wearing the bracelet.

He came up behind me, standing close enough to feel his breath on my neck. He reached out for me. I shrugged him off.

"Don't touch me. Don't ever touch me," I shouted.

Turning to him with my hands soapy and wet, I shoved a finger into his chest. "Tell me, did you sleep with prostitutes before we were together? While we were together?"

"No, I swear to you."

I didn't believe him.

"Did you kill her?"

"How can you ask me that? Don't you know me at all?"

"All I know for sure is you don't know what the truth is."

Out of sheer frustration, I knew I was going to cry, and I wasn't going to give him the satisfaction.

Pointing to the door, I yelled one last time, "Get out of my house. I can't even stand the sight of you right now."

CHAPTER 37

LUKE LOOKED AT HIS WATCH. Ten-thirty. He was exhausted. He wondered where Riley was. Probably home. He regretted having been so terrible to her all day. He needed her on his side. She could get information from George he clearly couldn't. If Luke was really going to be honest, he also missed her.

There was a time not too long ago that he and Riley would have ordered dinner in, sat up all night and discussed his investigations. When things ended, he missed that. He missed everything about their relationship. Luke hated to sound so cliché but she really was one of his best friends. He didn't want to admit it to himself but it had been the best relationship he had ever had. He still didn't even really understand why it hadn't worked out. He had too much to think about now to worry about it though.

Luke sat at his desk and flipped through case file after case file. He talked to Shannon McCarty's brother Devon. He knew even less than Breaux. A local New Orleans cop was working some local angles for them, interviewing some of the other girls to see if there was some way to use some political pressure to get the client list. Shannon's father, who had the clout, was playing the public relations game, saving his own reputation. He didn't seem to care his daughter was dead, just that his political career wasn't destroyed as a result. He'd be no help.

There was still no positive identification on the two other women. Nothing came up when they ran their prints, which just meant they weren't in the system.

Luke stretched at his desk. He felt the stress of the day settle into the muscles of his back and neck. It was hard to take in everything that had happened so far. He felt like weeks had passed since George Brewer had shown up at the police station saying his wife was missing. The only thing he really knew without question was that George was the center of this whole investigation. Luke just didn't have all the pieces to the puzzle yet, but he knew it was just a matter of time. That's just how it goes in most homicide investigations. Pieces of the puzzle start to fall into place and sometimes you have just enough to know what you're missing.

The cases were overwhelming the city. Residents were terrified. The tip line they had set up was being flooded with false leads and hysterical female residents who called for every strange looking car in their neighborhood and bump in the night. Luke understood. Nothing like this had happened in Little Rock for as long as he could remember. People were panicked. It's easier when the missing and dead don't look like you. They could still pacify themselves with the idea that it will never happen to them. But when the women appear to be the girls next door, the moms at the soccer games, it brings it just a little closer to home.

One thing did keep catching Luke's attention. Shannon was the first woman found, but she wasn't the one found with the word *whore* painted onto her body. He wondered if the third woman was also a prostitute. She hadn't been arrested as far as he could tell. Was there an angle there he was missing? If there was, then how did Maime and Laura connect? Clearly neither of them had been prostitutes. They were the kind of women most others envied, living in the best parts of town, running with the Junior League set. Maybe they didn't connect to the other cases, but then that would be one heck of a coincidence.

The medical examiner's office was swamped and lab tests were coming in far slower than they needed. In some ways, the investigation was really hinging on some major factors that Luke needed before they could do much else. Most importantly, they needed to know times and manner of death.

The media was breathing down their necks calling for interviews. So far Luke let Captain Meadows handle it. Luke was starting to believe there was a leak somewhere within the police department that he needed to close fast. Too much information was getting out. They hadn't released that Shannon was a prostitute, but it came out on CNN less than an hour after her identity was released.

Steve Bisceglia was due in at any time to make the official missing person's report on Laura. Luke continued to flip through the case files until his eyes started to close.

Luke decided to stop for the night. He looked up to the ceiling and began to say a silent prayer for a break in the case. He didn't get very far when his office phone began to ring. He picked it up and barely put it back on the receiver before he rushed out of his office.

When Luke made it to the main entrance of the police station, he was met with a white man in his early thirties who clearly had been crying.

Clutching Luke's hand, he said, "My wife, she's missing. I just went to the airport to pick her up from a business trip to Los Angeles, but she wasn't on the flight. I called the airlines and found out she never boarded in LA. I called her coworkers. They said she never made the trip. They hadn't been able to reach her all week. Now her cellphone is off. The last time I saw my wife was last Thursday morning when she left for the airport. Help me find her, please."

CHAPTER 38

I HEARD THE CRACK OF THUNDER and opened my eyes in time to see the lightning strike. The storm outside seemed to be right on top of me, flashes of light brightened the room and then left me in darkness. I pulled the covers around me and tried to close my eyes to sleep. Storms never scared me, but the rain was coming down hard on my roof. Thunder crashed again.

Then faintly, I heard a strange scraping noise that seemed to be coming from downstairs. I heard it again, more distinctive now, like a chair was being dragged across the floor. I bolted upright and strained to hear. I was alone in the house, and although this was a safe neighborhood, my mother's earlier conversation about my impending death quickened my pulse. Rain pounded on the roof loudly and the roar of thunder cracked again. I wondered if I could make it out and across to Joe and Emma's. I'd be safe there but stuck in the rain on their porch until they woke up and let me in.

I slid out of bed and planted my bare feet on the cold hardwood. I slowly crept toward my dresser and pulled my Glock out of the top drawer. It had been tossed in among satin and lace panties. I had pulled it out of my locked cabinet earlier that night. I never used it other than practice on the range. I didn't even like having it, but with the work I do, it was a necessity.

The gun felt like raw power in my hands. I still didn't feel safe. I stood in the middle of my room gun in hand and debated if I should pull on more clothes before heading downstairs. My pink tank top, no bra and gray shorts hugging my butt were not exactly the best attire to confront a prowler. No time to change though. The noise got progressively louder and then was accompanied by a crash that sounded like the chair slammed to the floor. My hands shook and my knees felt weak as I crept down one stair at a time. I flipped off the safety on my gun as I went.

I got to the fourth step from the bottom and looked over the banister into my living room. Empty. I could see out the front window to the driveway, my rental still parked where I left it. I moved one foot in front of the other down the stairs, through the living room, and to the threshold of my kitchen. The lightning brightened the rooms as I moved.

"Who's there? I've got a gun. I'll shoot if I have to." The words caught in my throat coming out barely above a whisper. My hands shook. I wasn't sure I could actually shoot, but whoever it was didn't know it was a hollow promise.

I could see part of my kitchen from where I stood; sink and cabinets with a straight shot to the back door that led onto a patio and then into my backyard. There was no sign of anyone but a quick flash of lightning illuminated the door. The bolt lock was turned in the open position. I knew I had locked it before I went to bed. I swallowed hard. I had hoped that my imagination was running away with me, but my imagination didn't unbolt that door.

I hesitated and debated for a few seconds whether to confront or run out the front door to my car. I didn't have my keys though and didn't know where I had left them. I wasn't even sure where my cellphone was. Probably in my bedroom. I never did have a house phone. I would have to confront whoever was there.

As I rounded the entry way into the kitchen, I reached inside against the wall, flipping the light switch upright. I moved quickly with both my hands wrapped around my Glock and my right index finger on the trigger. I pointed the gun into the kitchen toward my dining table and chairs where the noise grew louder. My eyes adjusted to the light. When I saw who was sitting at my kitchen table head in his hands, I nearly dropped the gun.

CHAPTER 39

"LUKE, WHAT ARE YOU doing here? I almost shot you." I lowered my Glock to my side. My pulse raced and confusion took over the intense fear I felt seconds earlier.

He looked up and slumped farther down in the chair. He kicked his long legs out in front of him. His eyes were bloodshot. The only time I saw his eyes look like that was when he had been drinking, which was rare. He was squinting. I assumed the bright kitchen light was bothering him. I flicked the light off and set my Glock on the counter.

I started to walk towards him, but he got up, stumbled, and took two or three long strides towards me. He closed the distance between us in mere seconds. Before I could speak, he pushed me against the wall, put his hands in my hair holding my head and kissed me hard. All I could breathe in was him; his tongue darted in my mouth, his lips sucked on mine. I lost myself.

He moved his body against mine suggestively and kissed me more passionately. A familiar feeling spread through my stomach and made my pulse race as much as it did moments earlier. My hands rested on his chest. I clutched at his wet white dress shirt. He was wet from the rain. I felt it against me, against my face and body.

Before I knew what was happening, he stopped kissing me and shoved me backwards. I stumbled, my head hitting the wall.

He moved back, pointing his finger in my face. "How could you get out of my bed, get dressed, walk out my front door and leave the state. Never calling me or returning my calls. You left me, with nothing. No word. I didn't even know if you were okay, if you were safe. You have no idea what you did to me."

I reached my hands towards him, but he shoved them away and stepped back out of my reach. Hot tears spilled down my face. "Luke, I was confused, scared. I never meant to hurt you. I thought it was better this way."

"Better for you." He moved back to the table, yanked out the chair and sat back down.

He was right. I left him without saying anything. Crawled out of his bed like a coward, a thief in the night. I packed my bags and went back to New York. He called and kept calling. I didn't know what to say, so I thought saying nothing was best. I had felt myself falling in love with him, and it terrified me. I wiped my tears on the back of my hand and looked at him unsure of what he wanted to hear.

"What are you doing here now? You're drunk. You hate me. You've made that obvious to anyone around us. Even Cooper is wondering what is wrong with you."

"I had to see you again. I don't know. You're like a drug. I hate you for that," he spat. "Go back to New York please, baby girl, you're killing me."

I moved towards him, pulled out the chair next to him and sat down. I half expected him to move away from me, but he didn't. "I can't. I'm in this now. I can't just walk away. George needs me."

"Screw George. I need you," he shouted, jabbing himself in the chest with his index finger. "Did that ever matter to you? Did I ever matter to you?"

I reached out and held his hand. He didn't push me away. "Of course, you mattered to me. You still matter to me," I quietly admitted. "You know that."

"But you left. Why? We'd been together for a year and then you just up and left. Just tell me why. Living not knowing has been killing me for two years now."

"I don't have an answer. I was scared."

"Scared? You don't think I was scared? I didn't walk out on you and never speak to you again, now did I?"

I looked down and shook my head ashamed. "What can I say, you're a better person."

"Yes, I am, and I deserve better," he said, staring at me. I couldn't meet his gaze.

He let go of my hand, got up abruptly and walked towards the back door.

"Luke, where are you going?"

"Now you care?"

"I've always cared. I just didn't know what to do. Please believe me. I didn't mean to hurt you."

"I'll never believe anything you tell me again."

I deserved that but still it stung. "You can't leave, you're drunk. You can't drive like that. How'd you get here?"

"Walked from Billy's," he called over his shoulder as he was about to turn the doorknob.

Billy's was a cop bar a few streets over from me tucked into the neighborhood. I've never really known Luke to drink and certainly not in the middle of an intense investigation. I couldn't imagine what he was going through.

I got up and walked towards him, rested a hand on his back and said, "It's storming out and too far for you to walk home. You can't drive. Stay here."

He turned to look at me, shook my hand off him and asked, "Where would I sleep?"

"You can have the spare room if you want it."

His cold smirk said all I needed to know.

I conceded and held my hands palms up to him in defeat. "You can sleep in my bed."

He stood still as if deciding between his options.

"How did you get in here anyway?"

He reached in his pants pocket and pulled out a familiar key, waving it. "You gave this to me once. You didn't stick around to take it back."

My spare house key. He reached his open palm out to me with the key in it. I thought for a minute. "Keep it," I said and shook my head, eyes lowered. "You never know when you might need it."

Luke put the key back in his pocket and reached for me. He pulled me into him and kissed me long and deep. We pulled apart. He looked down into my eyes and said somberly, "This doesn't mean you're forgiven. I'm drunk. I can't be responsible for my actions."

CHAPTER 40

LUKE WOKE UP IN AN UNFAMILIAR BED. He immediately reached his hands to his head, which felt like his brain was being slammed into his skull. He squinted his eyes hoping that would make it easier to see. It didn't. What he did last night was beyond stupid. He'd pay for it all day.

He stretched his arms across the bed and realized he wasn't alone. Memories of the previous night flashed in his mind. He groaned audibly at the thought that he had actually broken into Riley's house. Did he kiss her at some point? He couldn't quite remember.

Riley was curled on her side, her bottom against him. He resisted the urge to turn on his side and cuddle against her. He felt the anger he carried with him like a shield over the last two years bubble up in his chest and then dissipate. He was so tired, hungover and just worn out from regret. He felt defeated.

Luke sat up and swung his feet to the floor. He realized then he was naked except for his black boxer briefs. Did he undress himself? He looked over at Riley snug under the covers. He pulled them back slightly to look at her; tank top and shorts. She was dressed at least. Hopefully, that meant nothing had happened, but he couldn't remember. He was sure he had been too drunk to perform. He hoped he hadn't tried anyway. His head started to pound again, and he dropped his head into his hands. It was then he noticed on the nightstand next to him the bottle of water and two small white aspirin. Luke took them and drank half the bottle in a few gulps.

He picked up his cellphone that was sitting on the nightstand, too. Luke scrolled through his phone and was grateful at least there were no missed calls and no messages. He had stopped briefly into Billy's to unwind before attempting to sleep. A beer turned into more than he could remember. It was stupid.

He stood, stretched and looked around Riley's room. It had been years since he had been in here. Even when they were together, they mostly stayed at his place. His bed was bigger, a king-size compared to her queen. Neither of them were typically cuddly sleepers. He stood and watched her sleep.

He missed her. And there she slept. He had to admit it was a struggle to resist the urge to climb back into bed, wrap his arms around her and never let her go. He hated that his pain and anger at her could dissipate so quickly. That right there was the kicker. It didn't matter if he loved her or hated her, she consumed his thoughts. For some reason, he just couldn't walk away even after all this time.

Luke looked around the room for his clothes. He didn't see them and started to make his way across her room to her bedroom door when a silver object on her dresser caught his attention. Luke knew he'd seen this somewhere before. He picked up the silver bracelet and held it in his hand.

Where had he'd seen this before? Maybe it was something that Riley had worn when she was with him. The nagging feeling was still present. He couldn't let it go. He held it up, turned it around and that's when he noticed the design. Celtic trinity knots.

The hair on his body stood up and a wave of understanding took hold. This was the very bracelet they found on the second woman they pulled from the river. What was Riley doing with the same bracelet?

"Riley," he yelled, forgetting all about his pounding head. "What is this? Where did you get it?"

Riley opened her eyes, blinked twice and closed them again. Luke closed the distance to her bed and sat on the edge. He nudged her awake.

She sat upright, anger in her eyes. "Luke, what are you doing?"

He waved the bracelet in her face. He knew by her look, she'd been caught.

"I was going to tell you. I was just trying to figure out what it means," Riley explained as she climbed out of bed and took the bracelet from his hands.

"There are some things I have to tell you. Can we get some coffee first and talk? George gave me this a long time ago. It's the same as the one you pulled off the woman in the river."

"What do you mean George gave you this bracelet? I know it's the same as the one we pulled off the dead woman," Luke barked. "Why do you think I'm so angry off right now? How long have you known?

Riley shrugged, "Maybe they make a lot of these."

"They make a lot of them? That's your explanation? Nice try. At the very least, his wife and mistress are missing and now this connection to a dead woman. So, I'll ask again, what are you doing with this?"

"This bracelet doesn't necessarily mean anything," Riley said just as a loud knock at the front door caused them both to jump.

Luke stood arms out to his sides and asked her accusingly. "Who is that? Where are my clothes?"

"Probably Cooper, I forgot he was supposed to come over this morning," Riley explained to him with a dismissive wave of her hand. "I washed your clothes last night and threw them in the dryer. They were wet and muddy. I thought you would appreciate having clean clothes this morning."

"Thanks," Luke said softly and ran his hand over his head and let out a sigh. He needed a shower and a shave. "I appreciate that, but how am I going to explain being here?"

"I don't know but give me a minute," Riley said as she stood in the middle of her room and looked around as if some explanation would occur to her from the thin air.

"We don't have a minute," Luke said more impatiently as there was another loud knock.

"I'll call Cooper and tell him to go and pick up coffee. Wait until he leaves, then get dressed and wait at the table. I'll shower up here. We'll just tell him you came over to talk about the case. I guess I can tell you both about the bracelet."

Luke shrugged. He guessed that was as good a plan as any. He waited as Riley called Cooper. She told him she was about to shower and that Luke was on his way over. She asked him to head to the Starbucks on Kavanaugh to pick up coffee and breakfast for three.

Luke shook his head at how easily she could get men to do her bidding. "You just snap those little fingers and get men to jump, don't you?"

Riley shot him an annoyed look and growled, "Don't go back to being a jerk so quickly. We were doing okay for a little bit."

She turned her back to him, pulled her top over her head and threw it to the floor. Then she pushed her shorts down her legs and revealed her naked supple backside. She walked down the hall and into the bathroom naked without even turning to see if he looked. Luke was momentarily stunned. This woman was going to be the death of him, but he was pretty sure he was going to die with a smile on his face.

CHAPTER 41

ALMOST AN HOUR LATER, the three of us sat around my kitchen table and enjoyed hot coffee and breakfast sandwiches. Luke told us about Sam Bloomfield, the guy who showed up at the police station the previous night and reported his wife missing.

When Sam pulled out a photo of his wife, Luke had the horrible job of explaining that Sam's wife's body had been pulled from the river the night before. Sara was the second victim the police found in the river. Luke and another officer drove Sam to the morgue to identify his wife. Luke explained to us that Sam was devastated, as most anyone would be, and barely kept himself together.

Luke said he didn't stick around for long. He assigned another detective to question Sam well into the night. Luke thought Sam was nothing more than a grieving husband and didn't think they'd get very far. But everyone had to be treated like a suspect until ruled out.

It seemed, or at least from the story Luke heard last night, that Sara was supposed to be on a business trip. She was a local real estate agent with an upscale firm headed to a big yearly conference in Los Angeles. Sam had left town last Thursday, the same day as his wife. He had gone with friends on their yearly duck hunt. His cell didn't get any service at their cabin so he didn't think it was unusual not to hear from her. They rarely spoke while he was on a hunt.

When Sam returned a week later, he saw her car in the driveway but no Sara. She usually took a cab to the airport so he thought he'd surprise her and pick her up when she returned. Only she wasn't on the return flight. As Sam learned later, Sara never made it to her business trip at all. No one had heard from her since Sam had seen her the Thursday morning before he left. Luke asked Sam if he or his wife had any connection to George or Maime. Sam knew of no connection at all. He had been gone all week and hadn't even been following the news.

At least there was only one woman left to identify. When you can't even identify the victims, cases rarely get solved. As hard as it was for Sam, this was a step forward for the case.

Luke finished explaining and then said, "Even though Sam didn't know of a connection to George there must be." Turning to me he demanded, "Now tell us about the bracelet."

I showed them both the bracelet and explained that George had given it to me as a gift. I fingered the clasp and showed them where it had been broken. I explained that when I took it in to be fixed, the jeweler mentioned that the piece was not one carried in the store but had been specially made. That was all I really knew. Seeing it on Sara Bloomfield confirmed for me that there was a connection to George.

"You've known this the whole time? You couldn't be bothered to tell us?" Cooper asked his arms crossed. "What are you doing? You lied about details of your relationship with him and now you hide evidence?"

Cooper threw his hands up and walked away from the table, standing on the other side of the room. "I can't work like this."

"I know. I'm sorry," I conceded and meant it. "I don't have an explanation. I was shocked when I saw it on her wrist. I wasn't sure until I came home and confirmed it was the same one. I haven't said anything to George about it. My gut says he gave it to her. We'd have to check the jewelry store to see how many were made and who they were sold to."

I looked at them both trying to give them my most contrite face, "I really am sorry."

Cooper was still angry. I couldn't blame him. If he did this to me, I'd probably quit working with him. If you couldn't trust your partner, who could you trust? My reasons for withholding now seemed stupid.

Luke leaned across the table, put his hand on my arm, and said, "You are just going to have to start trusting me and Cooper. We're in this together."

Cooper eyed us suspiciously. He pointed an accusatory finger between the two of us as he asked, "You two want to tell me what is happening here? First you hate each other and now suddenly we're in this together?"

Without going into too much detail, I explained to Cooper how badly I had ended things with Luke, and added that now that we had talked, I hoped we could work together.

"I can't if you continue to hold things back from me," Luke said in response.

"Me either," Cooper echoed.

They had me. I wasn't a team player. I never had been, but if I wanted information from Luke, I'd have to give it in return. I wasn't ready, but I let the other shoe come crashing to the ground.

"George told me last night he knew Shannon McCarty. He hired her a few times on business trips to New Orleans."

"You have got to be kidding me?" Cooper said in an exasperated sigh.

"He said he's being framed."

"Him and every other dirtbag I've arrested. We're screwed regardless. I can't interview him now. He left the station yesterday and said he was getting a lawyer. Did he tell you?" Luke asked, directing the question to both of us. We shook our heads no.

"I brought him in to ask about his alibi and Laura's disappearance. I showed him the photos of the other women. He looked agitated and asked me who was trying to ruin his life. Then, he asked for a lawyer."

"You still think he's innocent?" Cooper asked me sarcastically.

"Actually, as strange as it sounds, yes I do."

CHAPTER 42

COOPER AND LUKE GROANED IN UNISON at my admission. I knew I was in the minority of probably everyone on the police force, all of Little Rock and probably most of the U.S., but yes, the more I heard, the more I thought George was innocent. Luke and Cooper spent the next twenty minutes debating with me, laying out the evidence. I held firm.

"The package is too neat. The case has been handed to you on a platter with a pretty red bow. George is not an idiot. He's not going to leave a trail of evidence to his door this deep," I said, trying to drive home my point.

I could tell they were both disappointed in me. I wasn't letting it go. "There's more though," I added. "I found out some information about Maime."

I told them all about my meeting with Gina Young. I filled them in on the drugs and the affair with Dean. Neither one of them seemed as shocked as I was when I heard. They didn't think the lead was too promising. Both remained zeroed in on George. They reminded me it was just more motive.

While we were on the subject, Cooper had his own strange tale about Dean. Cooper described what he saw the night before on his surveillance case. "I don't know who the guy was or even if he was a cop, but we should look into it. It was weird. They definitely wanted whatever they were doing to remain hidden. It could be related to Maime's drug use."

"You'll have to come down to the station. We'll walk around to see if you can identify who you saw. He could be from the Sheriff's office or even North Little Rock police department. We'll check it out though," Luke said.

"Luke, last night when George saw the photos of the missing women, did he notice their jewelry?" I asked, rolling the bracelet in my hand.

"I don't know about the bracelet or ring, but yes, he had to have seen the earrings."

"We should focus on that. Maybe like Cooper said, it might be some kind of signature the killer is using. If you could do that, I want to run down the drug angle on Maime."

I started picking up the table, carrying dishes to the sink from breakfast. I just wanted to get moving. I didn't like how they were looking at me. Cooper looked at me with pity, like I was blinded by the facts and still strung out over George. It was Luke who finally spoke up.

"Run with the drug angle if you want. You need to be safe, Riley. I know you think you can trust George, but promise me you won't be alone with him anymore."

Then he turned to Cooper and said forcefully, "Don't leave her alone with him."

"Riley, I agree with Luke. All the evidence right now, even though I admit it's circumstantial, is pointing at George. I know he's our client, but we have to take precautions just in case," Cooper reiterated.

Luke got up to leave. He gave me the cellphone numbers of the detectives who worked over on the southside regularly in case I needed some backup. I had my own contacts over there from my reporting days. I figured I'd be fine, but I kept the detectives' numbers just in case. Cooper left first. As Luke was leaving, I remembered something.

"You know I ran into that reporter, Ben, last night. He said he heard some gossip about George's affairs. He said he gave you some names."

"You weren't on the list if that's what you're worried about," Luke said and then continued. "It was some women we hadn't heard about so two of the detectives are running down some leads to locate them. I don't remember their names. I can let you know later."

"You're not worried about him running the story?"

"Nope, he's around the station a lot. He hears things. We trust him. He hasn't screwed us over yet," Luke explained.

"The media seems to know an awful lot. Do you have it under control? There's probably a leak. You want me to call my old editor and see if I can find out?"

"I got it covered, but thanks," Luke said. He started to go but turned back, leaned down, and kissed me on the cheek before he left.

CHAPTER 43

LUKE LEFT RILEY'S HOUSE thinking about the potential media leak. Both Cooper and Riley had mentioned how odd it was that the media was showing up so quickly. He had thought earlier there might be a leak. Now that Riley mentioned it, Luke realized he should take it more seriously. One of the uniformed cops had mentioned that at all three crime scenes, two of the news stations had arrived before the police did. Someone from the crowd could have called it in. Now Luke was wondering if they did have an inside leak trying to derail the investigation. He immediately thought of Norwalk.

For now, it would have to go on the back burner, Luke had more important work to focus on. He was on his way to the jeweler, J.T. Roth & Sons, where Riley said her bracelet was from. Luke was hoping he could get the jeweler to tell him a little more about the bracelet, how many were made and who purchased them. Luke knew they might be overlooking something when it came to the jewelry. As Riley had reminded him, some killers leave a signature and the jewelry could be it.

Luke would never admit it in front of Riley, but she made a few good points about George being framed. She was right that the evidence was too neat. The killings had a lot of the markings of a serial killer. As much as he wanted to, Luke just couldn't see George fitting that mold. Then again, Luke reminded himself, the evidence all pointed to George and no one else. That was the problem, if not George, then who? No one else had any motive to kill these women, and the women's only connection so far was George. Luke was lost in thought as he entered the jewelry store.

"How can I help you?" asked a man dressed in a fine tailored suit. "Looking to buy something pretty for your wife?"

Luke thought of Riley. Then immediately put that thought aside and wondered where on earth it had come from. They had never even talked marriage.

"Not today. Hoping you can help with a case," Luke said, showing his badge. The man took a good look and then ushered him into a side room. He motioned for a younger woman to take his place behind the display case positioned directly in front of the shop's entrance.

"I'm Jeb Roth, the owner. What's this about?"

"I have some photos. I need you to tell me if these are pieces you made. It's related to an ongoing investigation. We have reason to believe they came from your store." Luke put the three photos of the jewelry in front of him. He also had Riley's bracelet in his pocket.

Luke watched Roth pick up the photos one by one, saw the recognition in his eyes, and was not the least bit surprised to hear what the man had to say.

"We don't make a habit of discussing a client's private purchases."

"I understand. I can leave and come back with a search warrant, if you prefer. That will open you up to discussing a lot more than what I asked. Up to you," Luke said, shrugging like it didn't matter to him one way or the other. He picked up the photos and turned to leave.

"Wait," Roth called to him and then let out a sigh and said, "George Brewer. I've made a few of the bracelets for him as well as other pieces like the earrings for his wife. George designed and ordered the bracelet. The earrings and ring I can only tell you came from this shop."

"You're sure? It's strange a man would order more than one of the same bracelet. How many has he ordered? Have you made these for any other client?"

"No, this is exclusive to Mr. Brewer. I'll need to check the records." Roth went to a large filing cabinet against the wall and riffled through files. He pulled out a manila file folder and flipped through the pages inside. "He's ordered four of the same bracelet over the last five years."

Luke pulled out Riley's bracelet and handed it to Roth, "This is the same as the photo. How would we tell this particular bracelet from other designers?"

Roth pulled out a magnifying glass and held it close to the bracelet so both he and Luke could see. There on the inside of the bracelet, Roth pointed out two very small letters G.B. – George's initials.

"That's how you'll be able to tell. He initials each of his orders. I can't tell if the earrings and ring are uniquely from George, but they do come from our collection. If George purchased them, he initialed them."

"Any women come in with these bracelets that need to be fixed?"

"Just one a few years back. We don't keep that kind of information. I just remember she was a pretty girl with auburn hair. We fixed it while she waited. I don't even think we took her name."

CHAPTER 44

I COULDN'T HELP BUT THINK about Luke as I drove to the southeast part of Little Rock. A part of me was glad that we made up, but I worried Luke would get ahead of himself. There was still a part of me that didn't know if I was willing, or even ready, to give anything another try. Besides, I was only supposed to be in Little Rock until we found Maime. I had a life back in New York that was waiting for me.

As I drove, my thoughts stayed focused on Luke and our kiss last night. I would have thought the passion might have died between us over the years. That kiss proved it hadn't. In that moment, we were right back to where we had left off. There was a time when I thought George was going to be the only person I ever felt that overwhelming feeling of familiarity with. Luke quickly proved that I had it with him, too, and more. If I was willing to admit it, the connection was always stronger with Luke right from the beginning.

Of course, thinking about Luke right now was probably natural given where I was headed. Right back to the spot where Luke and I first met. I had been a reporter in Little Rock for just a few months when I was called to cover a shooting. The tip came into the newsroom hotline. They had sent me immediately. Unfortunately, I got there even before some of the cops did. What I saw has stayed with me to this day. It is a memory I wish I could forget.

Alexander Baltazar was just eleven years old when he was gunned down in his grandmother's front yard. His body still laid uncovered in the grass when I pulled up. He was just a fifth grader. By all accounts I'd come to learn, he was an excellent student. His parents had left him with his grandmother for the week while they went to Memphis to the St. Jude's Children's Research Hospital where his seven-year-old sister was having a lifesaving operation to remove a brain tumor.

Up to that point, I'd seen a lot of death and violence but never had I witnessed a sight like that. Alexander was just a child, a total innocent life taken for reasons I couldn't even possibly fathom.

When I arrived at the scene, his grandmother was being held back by two uniformed cops. She was wailing in misery, and at the sounds of her screams, the reporter in me ceased to exist. I walked over to her, wrapped my arms around her and tried to comfort her the best I could. Soon after, a tall black detective pulled up to the scene. I noticed him right away and the grief on his face.

The witness reports from the neighbors came pouring in. It was a truck with three white men who drove through the neighborhood shooting. No specific target. It just seemed any person they came across. Given the makeup of the neighborhood, all of the victims were black. A man had been shot in the leg and a woman shot in the arm. Then they came upon Alexander. It was a shot to the chest that killed him.

When I saw his body that day, it made me physically ill. I had walked three houses away and thrown up on the neighbor's front lawn. The local pastor, Bishop Charles Moore from Mt Moriah Church put his hand on my back as I threw up and then sat me on the curb. I quickly shooed him back to Mrs. Cecelia Baltazar, Alexander's grandmother. I sat alone unmoving for what seemed like hours.

Arkansas had more than its share of racial violence and tension in its history. In some areas, there was still deep-rooted racism that persisted, but it was still a shock to me. Eventually the cops took witness statements, the medical examiner came and went, the forensics team did their job and other reporters left.

The community rallied around Mrs. Baltazar. She told police that when she heard the gunshot, she ran to the front yard from the back yard where she was hanging the wash, but by then, Alexander was dead. She couldn't see anything but the back of the pickup truck.

As residents returned home and the cops cleared the scene, I was still sitting on the curb at the side of the road. Luke had walked over to me and checked to see if I was okay. I don't even remember the conversation we had. He tossed my keys to one of the other officers and drove me directly to Billy's Tavern. There, we sat and talked about what occurred and how enraged and sickened we both were feeling.

I didn't realize then why he was being so nice to me, but he gave me the only quote law enforcement gave on the story that night. There would be many more exclusives after that on that case and others. It was the start for Luke and me.

My story ran in the morning edition of the paper. It was a story I covered until the three defendants – three white teens from a neighboring county – were all convicted of first degree murder and sent away for life. It was little vindication for Alex's family and friends, but at least some justice had been served.

Through the case, I became friends with Bishop Moore and Alex's grandmother, Cecilia, who I came to love as my own family. They grew to trust me through my compassion for the case and fair reporting.

My insistence on covering the drug angle of Maime's case was a little self-serving. I had grown to know the neighborhood and had sources that would give me the truth. And I wanted to see people I cared about while back in town.

CHAPTER 45

I PULLED UP IN FRONT OF MS. CECELIA'S house just as she was walking, with a watering can in hand, to water the flowers in her front yard. After Alex's death, for the longest time, she couldn't bear to be in the yard, but she said she grew tired of that. As she put it, she decided to reclaim her home. She made a lovely garden around a beautiful white stone with Alexander's name on it. Since then, she tended to the garden in the way she would have tended to him, with grandmotherly love and compassion. She definitely had a green thumb, something I definitely didn't. I couldn't keep a cactus alive.

During the criminal case, she was at the courthouse every day. She wasn't allowed in for the proceedings because she was a key witness for the prosecutor's case. But each day she came to court and each day we had lunch together. Conversations moved from reminiscing about Alexander as a little baby, to her son and daughter-in-law and my work to more personal stories about each of us. She grew up poor in the segregated south. She told me stories that I knew were true but still found hard to fully grasp.

Eventually, I told her about George, the move to Little Rock and even a little bit about Luke. She adored Luke, and I think really hoped things would work out for us. After the case, we would visit weekly. She'd feed me like I'd never eaten before. When she was feeling up to it, I'd take her shopping or to the movies, and occasionally, I'd even be able to pry her out of the kitchen and take her out to dinner. She was one of the people I didn't mean to hurt when I left so abruptly. We still talked by phone, but this was the first I would see her in almost two years.

As soon as she saw me standing on the edge of her lawn, she dropped her watering can and moved down the yard with her arms outstretched with a smile full of joy.

"There's my girl," she called to me. "You've been away for far too long."

After a long hug, she pulled back and looked me over and said, "You're too thin. Haven't you been eating?"

I loved this woman.

She ushered me into the house, placed a quick call to Bishop Moore and went about fixing me lunch. I filled her in on my family, my business and coming back to Little Rock. She had been following the news and was as shocked and saddened by the dead and the missing as everyone else.

Bishop Moore arrived, and trailing in behind him was a sullen looking boy who made his way into the kitchen. Dressed in jeans, a tee-shirt and old ballcap, I guessed he was about fifteen years old. He got a look at me and said, "You're white."

Cecelia flipped his hat off his head. Bishop Moore rolled his eyes at him as he wrapped me in a hug.

I stuck out my hand to the kid and said, "Really, I hadn't noticed. I'm Riley."

"Bobby," was all he said in response.

"Nice to meet you," I said, sitting down at the table.

"Bobby works down at the church after school and helps out Cecelia with chores now and then. He lives with his dad down the street. He's a good kid, usually," Bishop Moore explained with a smile. "What brings you back to town?"

I caught all of them up with the information I could share about the case and my part in the investigation. I explained the possible drug connection and that I was trying to find Orlando Knight, the drug dealer.

"You don't want to mess with him. He's bad news round here," Bobby said in between bites of Cecelia's chicken salad sandwich.

"What can you tell me about him?" I asked.

Bobby looked down. I suspected he was afraid of talking in front of Bishop Moore and Cecelia.

"It's okay, you can tell us. You won't get in trouble. In fact, what you know will probably help me."

He looked to Cecelia and then to Bishop Moore, and they both nodded in agreement to what I said. Bobby looked back to me and said, "He's always trying to sell us drugs. He talked my friend Marcus into stealing stuff out of a car last week. I don't like him."

"Ever see a white lady come to buy drugs from him?"

Bobby seemed to think for a minute. I didn't know if he was debating telling me or what, but then he dropped a bombshell right at the table. "Nope, not to buy drugs, but last week a white lady drove her truck down the alley on the side of my house. Then got into a car with some white guy and left."

"When did she drop the car off? Was it during the day or at night?"

"It was at night. I was waiting for my friends who come to the window. I was waiting on them and heard a noise and looked out. But it wasn't them. Just some lady parking her car," Bobby said and then went on. "I remember it was Friday night. I only remember cause my dad always has friends over to play cards on Fridays. You're not going to tell anyone that I told, are you?"

"I don't know if I have to tell anyone or not. But this might be real important to what I'm working on. It's really good that you told me. Could you take me to see the car?"

"I can show you, sure. I don't know what you want to see it for - it's all burned up."

CHAPTER 46

AFTER A FEW MORNING ERRANDS, Cooper made his way to Maime's office. He hoped they were working. It was Veteran's Day and some places were closed. If they were working, his plan was to sweet talk her coworkers into telling him more than they told Luke when he interviewed them.

Luke said they hadn't told him much, just that Maime's work was slacking off and that she left Friday afternoon around three. Everyone in the office assumed Maime took her car, but when they closed shop around five in the afternoon, her SUV was still there. Her vehicle had not been recovered so the assumption was Maime went back to work sometime after five.

Maime worked for a pharmaceutical company that had its headquarters in North Carolina. Maime shared an office in West Little Rock with three female coworkers. It wasn't a large building, only one floor, but it looked like they were the only occupants. The other office spaces were dark and no names were on the glass doors.

"Good mornin', ladies," Cooper said, grinning as he strode through the front door of their office. The office was one big open space with four desks, some filing cabinets and a room to the side Cooper guessed was used for meetings. Three of the four desks were occupied. The fourth he guessed was Maime's. All of the women looked exactly like Cooper imagined female pharmaceuticals reps looked – blonde, big-breasted and wearing short skirts. Cooper's kind of woman.

"Mornin," the three of them chimed in unison.

"I was hoping you'd be able to help me out. I'm looking to find some information about your coworker Maime Brewer. I know y'all talked to the police, but I thought maybe there were some other things you could share with me."

"You a cop?" asked Linelle.

"No, ma'am. A private investigator," Cooper explained with a smile.

The ladies returned the smile, shared a look with one another and over the course of the next ninety minutes spilled everything they knew. By the time Cooper left, he'd had two cups of coffee, got a little dirt on Maime and even landed the only single woman's phone number.

The women explained that Maime had grown quite erratic in the weeks leading up to her disappearance. Her work had slacked off, her sales plummeted, and she was about to be fired. Some suspected a drug problem, although they couldn't be sure what. The drug samples she had access to at the office were mostly women's drugs, treating everything from prenatal care to menopause symptoms. There was nothing she sold that would really be the kind of prescription pill she'd get hooked on.

They also shared that Maime took late lunches at least a few times a week with a man they didn't know. He would often pull up right to the front office door. She would leave with him, and as the women said, return later in the day looking "like that cat that ate the canary."

The more they described him, Cooper thought it sounded a lot like Dean.

The Friday of her disappearance the women said Maime skipped her usual lunch and left late in the afternoon for a sales appointment or at least that's what she told them. No one really bothered to watch her leave but were all surprised when they left at five that Maime's SUV was still there. They assumed she would have taken her own car for a sales meeting. They suspected then that she had lied, but no one really thought much of it until the news report that she was missing. It really hit home Monday when she didn't show up for work.

By the time Cooper left, he was feeling pretty good as he walked across the parking lot to his truck. He got a pretty girl's number and good confirmation that Maime was definitely having an affair. As Cooper got to his truck, he noticed there was a car wash just across the side street. He wondered if the car wash employees ever paid attention to the pretty girls from Maime's office. He made his way across the street, and to Cooper's delight, they were more than willing to talk. The cops had never bothered.

They told Cooper that they noticed all the girls. They'd have to be blind not to. Maime, they said, left most days with a dark-haired guy in a silver BMW 5-series sedan. The Friday she went missing one of the guys noticed she walked to her SUV, climbed in and waited a few minutes. He noticed because she sat there and talked on her cellphone. The same BMW pulled up, Maime climbed in, kissed the driver and they left together. They never saw her return. Her SUV was still in the lot when the car wash closed up at seven that night.

It was all Cooper needed to hear. He was almost a little excited about his next stop.

Deadly Sins

CHAPTER 47

COOPER PULLED THROUGH the wrought iron gates of the Little Rock Country Club. He made his way up the tree-lined hill to the Georgian style main house with its huge, white round columns lining the front veranda. The house looked like it belonged on a true southern plantation rather than as the main building for the club. The house was built in 1917, made especially for the club and never served as anything else. Cooper was sure it was the replica of some plantation house somewhere, but he never did pay that much attention to history.

He drove his truck through the main parking lot and parked his truck among brand-new BMWs, a few Jags and even more luxury SUVs. Cooper paid a pretty penny for his club membership, but it was the only advertising money he needed to spend. Anyone who was anyone belonged to the club. He picked up most of his clients, especially the law firms, right on the club's greens, golf club in hand.

Walking through the main house had a way of making you feel more important than you really were. It was the only time Cooper had that feeling – other than solving a case.

Cooper said hello to the trophy wives and their husbands as he headed straight back to the bar area. There he found just who he came to see. Cooper walked up to the bar, ordered a Jack and Coke and took a seat right next to Dean.

"Who let you in?" Dean asked without turning to look at Cooper. They made eye contact through their reflections in the mirror in front of them. Dean had a cigar in hand and brandy in front of him. "This club is for members only."

"Funny thing, I'm a member and you know that because you've seen me here before. Let's cut through the bull," Cooper said, watching Dean straight ahead while rolling the ice around in his glass.

"I told you everything I had to say last night. Don't you have anyone better to question?"

"Nope. See, I think there are a lot of secrets you have rolling around in your head. I think you really want to tell someone. I thought I'd give you that chance."

Dean didn't speak for several minutes. Then he turned to Cooper and said aggressively, "I'm not someone you want to mess with. Whatever you think you have, you don't."

Cooper knew he'd gotten to Dean for him to come off so defensively. They certainly weren't going to have a friendly chat. Cooper hadn't thought he would get the information so easily. He was just willing to give Dean the chance. He also enjoyed screwing with him. Innocent men were usually willing to cooperate. Cooper got the distinct impression that Dean was guilty of more than just an affair.

Cooper put his drink back on the bar and threw down a twenty that more than covered his tab. He got up close to Dean, leaned over him, and said in a low tone, nearly a growl, right in his ear, "Screwing your best friend's wife and being too dumb to realize that there are at least four witnesses willing to testify that you picked Maime up Friday afternoon — making you the last person to see her alive — isn't what I would call nothing."

Undeterred, Cooper went on, "You might want to consider who you're messing with. When you get done playing whatever game you're playing, you might want to let all of us know where Maime is before we start to think you've killed her and a few other women, too. Wanting George's life and his wife seems like strong motive to me."

Dean didn't say a word. Cooper strutted out happy he'd made his point. He didn't look back. He was pretty sure he left that smug fool sitting there with his jaw hanging open. Right now, Cooper held all the cards. He wanted to keep it that way awhile longer.

More than an hour ticked by as Cooper waited in his truck for Dean to leave the country club. His plan was to follow Dean and see where he was headed now that he was spooked. That was exactly why Cooper hadn't let on that he'd seen him and the cop the night before. He was giving Dean more rope to hang himself. Cooper wanted solid evidence of them meeting first. He thought the confrontation at the club would be enough to get them back together. He hoped he was right.

Cooper moved his truck far from any BMWs and waited. At least Cooper would be able to confirm what Dean drove, if he drove instead of walked. That was also a possibility, but Cooper was betting Dean was lazy. It was dark the other night, and Cooper couldn't make out anything other than Dean's car was a BMW. He didn't know the model.

Cooper wasn't really sure what to make of Dean yet. While he confirmed the affair, he wasn't really sure Dean could kill Maime. Not to mention how the other women would factor in. He had to agree with Luke that it wasn't just a coincidence that all the women seemed to be connected in some way or another to George. If it wasn't George, and Cooper couldn't get past how strongly Riley felt it wasn't, then it had to be someone close to him. He didn't like George, but Riley seemed to know him better than all of them so he couldn't totally rule out her feelings on the situation, even as naïve as he thought she was being.

Cooper watched Dean leave the club's main house and walk through the parking lot to the silver BMW 5-series sedan in the corner that Cooper suspected was Dean's. It was. Cooper gave him enough distance as he drove down the driveway and out to Country Club Road. Cooper was quick to follow behind. They snaked through the streets of the wealthy Heights neighborhood. Dean went straight back to his house. As they approached Dean's house, Cooper pulled over to the curb blocks from the house and waited.

Almost a half hour ticked by and the same unmarked car pulled up. The guy parked in the road almost two doors down from Dean's house. It was mid-day. With the angle of the sun, Cooper was able to use his telephoto lens to get a clear shot of the man as he exited his vehicle and walked up Dean's driveway. From where Cooper was sitting, he could still get a clear shot of Dean opening the door and letting the man inside. Cooper clicked off a series of photos in rapid succession. Cooper decided to wait and follow the guy after he left Dean's house. In the meantime, Cooper used the telephoto lens again to zoom in on the car tags. He copied the letters and numbers down and sent a quick text to Luke with the information.

Cooper didn't like this whole situation. This wasn't the simple missing person's case he thought when he started. The more he followed Dean and interacted with him, the less he liked him. He was shady, too secretive, and what kind of man has an affair with his best friend's wife. That right there in Cooper's mind made Dean capable of just about anything. Several scenarios of what could be happening ran through his mind, but nothing seemed to stick.

Just then, Dean's front door opened and the guy hurried out and down the driveway. He got to his car, pulled a quick U-turn and headed out towards Kavanaugh Boulevard. Cooper closed the gap between them in a matter of seconds and continued to follow.

Eventually, they both ended up at the police station. Cooper held back, watching him, and only pulled fully into the lot once the cop had gone into the building. Cooper watched him speak to everyone he passed. The guy looked every bit like he belonged there. If there was any doubt left in Cooper's mind that Dean and this cop were up to no good, whatever just went down at Dean's house confirmed it. Cooper had the photos to prove the connection. Like playing cards, you never wanted to show your hand too soon.

CHAPTER 48

LUKE RUSHED BACK TO HIS OFFICE after leaving the jewelry store. He wanted to look at the earrings they pulled off the third victim. She still hadn't been identified. Luke hoped he could identify the earrings. That would at least be a start and another possible connection to George, if the initials were there. If not, it would be back to the drawing board.

As Luke pulled into the police station's parking lot, he noticed Cooper's truck. Before he could walk over to him, Luke saw several officers coming out of the building all racing towards their vehicles. Luke had his door open and one foot on the pavement when his partner slid into the passenger seat.

Tyler said breathlessly, "They found another woman. Murray Park again. Almost the same spot just down river a little. This is getting out of control."

Luke slammed his door and sped off out of the lot, heading through downtown Little Rock. He went across side streets to connect to Cantrell and then Rebsamen Park Road. He drove with a steady eye on the road and complete silence in the car. He wasn't even sure what to ask first.

Once they hit the straightaway on Rebsamen Road, Luke finally asked his partner, "What do we know so far?"

"Not much. Like yesterday, a guy out on his boat coming in for the day spotted a woman's body and called 911. A couple of uniformed guys on patrol got over there as quickly as they could. At least the scene is secured. We asked them to start taking statements from the few people around. That's about all we know. No identification or anything yet. We only got the call about ten minutes before you got back. Purvis and his team should be there already. I was going to call you but saw you pulling up."

"I was at a jewelry store. We got a lead on the jewelry and a few other things. I was just coming back to look at the earrings. The bracelet found on Sara Bloomfield is connected to George without question," Luke explained. Then he turned to his partner and said with satisfaction, "George Brewer hired Shannon on business trips in New Orleans. We've got another connection."

Tyler looked at Luke, his eyes wide and mouth open but didn't say a word. He sat there silent, probably feeling what Luke felt when Riley first told him.

"We get any identification on the third woman from the river?" Luke asked, pulling into the park.

Tyler had spent the better part of the day working to get identification on the third victim.

"None at all. She's not in any system and so far no missing person's reports matching her description. Prints didn't come back either. We got nothing," Tyler said, shaking his head. He added, "You know we have to make another statement to the media. We have to get out in front of this."

"I know. I don't even want to think about that right now, but the media will be swarming. Call Cap and get our public information officer down here too."

Luke parked and headed right to where Purvis and his team were moving her from the water. Luke pulled on latex gloves from his back pocket as he walked. He passed two uniformed cops who had already sectioned off a perimeter with yellow crime scene tape. He raised it and walked directly to the body. Luke was anxious to see if it was Maime or Laura. Not that he was hoping for either, but he was hoping it wasn't another victim.

"What do we have?" Luke called out as he approached.

"Same as the others. I'd guess she's mid-thirties, definite petechiae present. No writing this time but wearing a silver chain with an emerald pendant."

Then Purvis added thoughtfully, "Her body seems to be in better condition than the last. I finally got some details back on the others. We need to talk. Let me finish here, and then I'll fill you in."

Luke barely heard him. He was too focused on wanting to know if it was Maime or Laura. As the medical examiner's team got her out of the water and into the black body bag on a stretcher, Luke looked over the woman wearing only a bra and underwear like the others. Her hair covered her face. Luke reached over to her and gently brushed back the tangled, wet blonde hair to get a look at her face. Then let out a string of curses. Not Maime or Laura.

Luke felt like his head was spinning. Drips of sweat dampened his neck. Little Rock was being torn inside out by a monster he couldn't get a handle on.

He looked down again at the victim. Tangled in her blonde hair was the thin silver chain. Carefully, Luke felt around and found the emerald pendant Purvis mentioned. He turned it over. Barely legible, right there on the back, were the initials G.B.

CHAPTER 49

LUKE WALKED BACK TO HIS CAR to update Tyler. Tyler was still on the phone talking to their Captain about making an official statement. Luke stood impatiently before finally interrupting and taking the phone out of Tyler's hands.

"Cap, it's not Maime or Laura. We've got another victim. Purvis is going to do the autopsy immediately and hopefully get us some answers tomorrow. We have to make another statement. They are already camped out down here at the scene. We're going to look like idiots if we don't get out in front of this."

Captain Meadows agreed. They'd have to play it by ear, but soon if they weren't informed, the public was going to lose confidence in the police. This was the way it always happened. The police department walked a fine line with what was too much information to share and what wasn't. The news leaks weren't helping either. The nightly news was running coverage on all of the women found in the river and Maime's and Laura's disappearances. It was all the national news was playing, every channel, and every broadcast. Speculation was raging on social media.

Luke was handing the phone back to Tyler when he saw Cooper approaching. He motioned for the uniformed guys to let Cooper through.

"Luke, what is going on?" Cooper asked, looking as shell shocked as Luke felt. "I was parked at the station and saw everyone pull out of there, so I followed."

"Another woman's body washed up. It's not Maime or Laura. You find out anything?"

Before Cooper could answer, Purvis made his way over to them, motioning Luke out of the line of sight of the media. Luke asked Tyler and Cooper to join them. The four of them walked down closer to the river away from the other cops and prying eyes.

"This is as bad as it gets, four women in three days," Purvis said obviously shaken. "We deal with a lot of homicide cases in this city but nothing like this in all my years at the medical examiner's office. The women all seem to be around the same age. The three we already examined seem to have been strangled with the same instrument, some kind of heavy wire. That's my preliminary for this woman, too. The marks on their necks all look the same. It's cutting their skin as it's closing off their air supply. All the women were bound. We can plainly see the marks on their wrists and ankles. No water in their lungs. They had undigested food in their stomachs. My best guess is they are being held for a period of time before they are killed."

"Any signs of sexual assault?" Luke asked.

"None. Because they are in the water for a period of time, we aren't getting much on fibers or anything else to test. Somebody knows what they are doing. I'm going to go back to the morgue and work on this victim. Let's meet tomorrow. I'll give you an official report of what I know to date. I got potential time of deaths for you. We can sketch out a timeline."

"Sounds good. Thanks for the rush," Luke said.

"No problem. Wouldn't have it any other way. The victims are too similar and manner of death the same. Whether we want to admit it or not we've got a pattern killer here. You need to warn potential victims and you need answers from me to do it. We've got to stop this and fast," Purvis said. He turned and walked back to the white medical examiner's van.

Luke wasn't sure what else to say. Hopefully they'd get some identification on the two unknown victims. It was happening so fast it was hard to get a handle on it. Most of the police department resources were going into these cases, but it still felt like they were spinning their wheels. They were all overwhelmed. Luke played a potential statement to the media over and over in his head while Tyler and Cooper talked about the cases.

So much had been leaked already, he'd have to confirm and then give enough facts to keep them at bay for now. This was the worst part of his work. He hated dealing with the media. Law enforcement was never doing enough no matter how hard they were trying. People didn't understand they weren't some kind of superheroes. He had a hard enough time accepting he wasn't. Luke sure didn't need the public to remind him.

CHAPTER 50

BISHOP MOORE, BOBBY AND I STOOD in the alley next to Bobby's house looking at what remained of the SUV. It was obvious someone had intentionally set fire to it. Its tags were missing, and its VIN number scratched off. Overall, it was pretty much destroyed. You could still tell it had been a SUV and that the fire started in the front. It hadn't burned all the way to the gas tank. I could still make out the charred Land Rover detail on the back. I would have bet money this was Maime's missing vehicle.

After a few more attempts to pry information out of Bobby, he explained that they smelled smoke right away. Once his dad saw the flames, they all ran out of the house, grabbed anything they could, and put the fire out. Someone called the fire department and then the police. Bobby said they were still waiting for someone to come out and take a report. The fire department never showed up that night.

I looked to Bishop Moore for an explanation. He explained that the neighborhood had become so rough, particularly at night, that the emergency response system was getting a lot of false reports, and that, coupled with the gang activity, sometimes the responders chose not to come out of fear for their own lives. "Forgotten neighborhood" is how Bishop Moore described it.

It made me sad to think any neighborhood could be considered forgotten, even with the prevalence of drugs and gangs and violence.

"What time do you think the car was dropped off?" I asked over my shoulder to Bobby as I walked around what was left of the Land Rover, looking for any identifying clues.

"It was about nine-thirty. My friends were supposed to be at my house by then so I was waiting. I kept looking out the window. When I saw her, I was gonna tell my dad, but he don't like to be bothered when he's playing cards."

"How soon after the lady left did the fire start?"

"I don't know exactly, but it was pretty soon after they left. There was all the smoke. I didn't need to tell my dad then. He saw it for himself."

"Did you see who started it? Was the lady still around when the fire started?"

"I don't know who started it. She got out of her car, got in the guy's car and then a few minutes later the fire started. When she got in his car, I stopped looking out the window. Then I smelled smoke and looked out again and saw the fire."

I pulled my phone out and handed it to Bobby and then Bishop Moore. They each took a few seconds to look at Maime's photo. She didn't look familiar to either of them. Bobby said it was too dark to really get a good look at her. He just knew it was a woman.

"When did you hear about this?" I asked Bishop Moore, pointing to the charred SUV. I knew he lived several blocks away.

"Not until the next day when the kids in the neighborhood were talking about it. I called the police. This isn't our first abandoned vehicle in these parts, and not the first fire we had to put out ourselves."

"Did you see what kind of car the lady got in?" I asked Bobby.

Bobby shook his head no. I excused myself, walked halfway down the alley and called Luke. I got his voicemail but didn't leave a message. I tried Cooper next. When he answered, he didn't even say hello. He launched into the details of another woman's body found in the river. I swallowed hard. My mouth went dry. Cooper said he was still with Luke at the scene. Then he was quick to get off the phone.

I shouted and caught him just before he ended the call. "I think I found Maime's car. You have to tell Luke. You'll need to send down a team. It's been torched."

Cooper promised as soon as they were done at the river, he'd tell Luke and head my way. Hanging up, I walked back to Bobby and

Bishop Moore. We walked around to the front of Bobby's house. I noticed a few blocks ahead of me was a group of black men huddled together walking across the road. They seemed to be right in the area of the address I had for Orlando Knight.

I turned to Bishop Moore and Bobby and, pointing up the road, I asked, "Is that Knight?"

They both looked, but it was Bobby who responded, "That's him. I wouldn't go up there, Ms. Riley. He's dangerous."

CHAPTER 51

I HEARD BOBBY'S WARNING but didn't listen. I headed directly to Knight and the group of six men where they stood. Based on their appearance, I don't think it would be hard to guess some gang affiliation. I needed an answer. Knight's appearance and reputation wasn't going to dissuade me.

The group of men eyed me as I approached. I got a few whistles and overheard a few derogatory sexual comments. They weren't the first I'd heard in my life. They weren't going to be the last. I didn't give them the satisfaction of a response or any kind of reaction.

Instead, as I approached the group, I asked, "Which one of you is Orlando Knight?"

Not one of them responded, but all of them turned to look at one man standing in the middle back of the group. Everyone's eyes were on him and soon mine were as well. I didn't quite know where to look though. He was completely bald and had tattoos covering almost every inch of showing skin. His face, his bald head, up his arms and even across his knuckles. Names, dates, and words I'd never heard before were scattered across him. I wanted to make eye contact, but my eyes darted over him on overload.

After a few seconds, I pulled myself together and moved forward, parting the men around him. Knight was about my height, so I stood toe to toe with him. Finally, I looked him right in the eyes and said, "I'm Riley, a private investigator. I need to speak with you privately."

That drew more whistles and jeers from the crowd. Knight smirked. He eyed me up and down and said, "Okay, baby, how bout we head inside. I'll give you all the time you need."

I shifted my weight from one foot to the other but didn't flinch. Boys were always trying to play up for the crowd. It didn't seem to matter what age they were. Knight was no exception. He had a reputation to protect.

"Nice try. But, no. Out here will be just fine," I said without a trace of fear in my voice.

"Isn't a pretty thing like you worried you might get hurt in this neighborhood?" Knight asked, reaching out and running his index and middle finger down a strand of my hair.

I didn't budge. I didn't want to show any fear at all, but I was terrified. These did not look like men I wanted to mess with. I stared him down for several more seconds.

Knight gave in first. "What you want?"

He took me by the arm and moved me out of the crowd and down the road out of earshot of the others. When he stopped walking, I shook free from his grasp.

I pulled out my phone and pulled up Maime's photo. "What do you know about her?"

He took my phone from me and brought the photo up to his face. I couldn't really tell from his reaction if he recognized her or not. His expression didn't give much away. He handed my phone back to me.

"What you paying for the information?"

I slid a fifty from my pocket to his outstretched hand. Right or wrong, sometimes you just had to play it the way it went on the streets.

Knight took my phone back, eyeing the photo for a few more seconds. He handed it back to me and said, "I ain't never dealt with her, but pretty little girls like her usually want the prescription kind. Just a little to make her feel good. How about you, you interested in a little something?"

"Only information."

He laughed.

"What else you got for me because I know that's not all. You don't want me to come back, do you? You know I will. I'll keep coming back bothering you until I get what I want. I'm a pain in the butt like that."

That brought a little smile to his face. He dropped some of his posturing and gave it to me straight. "I bet you are."

After a moment, he cocked his head to the side and asked, "Truth?"

I nodded.

"I ain't talked to her, but I know her. She got a man come pick up her stuff about every two weeks. White dude, we call him GQ – practically wearing plaid pants. Nice car, too. Thought of jacking it once or twice, but he's a real good paying customer. We wanted him to keep coming back. She usually in the car with him but doesn't get out. But she missing, right? We don't want nothing to do with no missing white chick."

"Good plan. Who's the guy? Do you know his name or hear her call him anything?"

"Nope, first time he came to us he said his name was Smith and that's what we call him. But most people coming into this part of town don't go by their real names. We don't require identification," Knight added with a smirk.

"How about a tag number or description of the car and the guy?"

"No tag number, but he GQ all the way, baby. We gave him the nickname for a reason. He's about my height, bulky and dark hair. Drives a BMW 5-series. Real sweet ride."

CHAPTER 52

I LEFT KNIGHT STANDING on the side of the road. As I walked back, I could feel his eyes on me. I turned back once, he nodded his head at me and turned back to his crowd. Bishop Moore stood with Bobby in front of the house.

"You're crazy," Bobby said to me as I approached. Then he walked back into his house, waving to Bishop Moore as he slammed the front door and disappeared from sight.

Bishop Moore reached out and put his hand on my shoulder. "You know he's right. But so crazy you might get more done than the cops."

"If you always let fear stop you from doing what's right, nothing will ever get done."

"You okay here waiting? I'm going to head back to Ms. Cecelia's if you don't need anything else," Bishop Moore inquired. I always had the feeling he had a little crush on Ms. Cecelia, but at their age I didn't know if either would entertain it. They should.

"I'm fine," I reassured. "The cops and my friend Cooper should be here any minute. I've got some calls to make anyway while I wait. Plus, I think Bobby is going to keep an eye on me," I said, pointing to the house where Bobby peered out at me from the front window. We both waved to him. He slipped back, disappearing from sight.

After Bishop Moore left, I sat down on the curb and tried George's lawyer for the first time. I had missed a few calls from

George. He left me a message with Bard Epson's office and cellphone numbers. I tried both. I had to leave a message with his secretary at his office and left a voicemail message on his cell. I tried to sound urgent in both and hoped for a prompt return call. Now that George hired a lawyer, a lot was pending on how we'd move forward with the case.

I tried George but had to leave a message when he didn't answer. George was technically my client. I hadn't been updating him on our progress or what exactly I had been doing. Some clients want the full report while others don't care and just want the outcome at the end of the investigation. Given how much George had paid us and how crazy this all had become, no matter what Luke and Cooper said, I felt I owed George at least an update.

Cooper pulled his truck up to the curb, and we walked together down the alley.

"What did they do?" Cooper asked, walking around the SUV.

"You know, the usual. Destroyed all evidence and hoped no one would find it here," I said sarcastically.

"Do you know who set it on fire?" Cooper asked.

"No, but I suspect it was whoever was with Maime. By what the neighbor said, she went willingly."

Cooper went back to his truck to grab his camera and walked back to me.

"This case gets stranger and stranger. I want to show you a photo I took today. I didn't get the chance to show Luke. Maybe you'll know him. I don't."

Cooper showed me several photos of Dean's car and the guy who Cooper saw meeting with him the night prior. I didn't recognize the guy either. I had been gone from Little Rock long enough that there was a decent amount of turnover at the police department.

"Got any more details from the scene today?" I asked. So much had happened it almost slipped my mind that Cooper was coming back from the scene of another victim.

While we waited for the cops, Cooper filled me in on the new developments, including Luke's confirmation about the jewelry. I had never noticed George's initials on the bracelet. I was surprised to hear what Luke had found. I was also glad to hear that Luke planned to hold a press conference.

The details were flowing out about these cases fast and loose. There was a lot of misinformation out there and even more that was potentially true but remained unconfirmed. I knew how much Luke hated making formal statements to the media especially on camera so I hoped the crime scene guys would hurry up and get here so I could be there at the press conference.

After about a ninety-minute wait, an entire crime scene crew finally pulled up. They got down to their work quickly after some preliminary questions.

Luke's partner Tyler pulled up alone a few minutes later.

"Well, well, well look who showing us up," Tyler said, appraising the damage. "What do you think? Is it Maime's?"

"I can't say for sure. There's a pretty good witness who saw a woman fitting her description dropping it off on Friday night right before the fire started. You know they called this in and the fire department couldn't be bothered to show up. Neither could your colleagues. It's been here since her disappearance," I scolded him.

"Not my department. Make a formal complaint to your boyfriend," Tyler said, smiling at me.

CHAPTER 53

LUKE WAS AS READY as he was ever going to be. He stood in front of the police station with his arms resting on the podium that was set up for the press conference. He had the official statement typed out in front of him.

There were a sea of reporters, cameras, and bystanders filling the parking lot waiting for him to speak. His captain and other city officials stood behind him. Tyler was still at what was potentially the scene where Maime's car was found. Luke would much rather have been there.

Little beads of sweat formed on his bald head and were starting to roll down his back. He wanted to get this done and over with. Luke was meeting with the medical examiner first thing the next morning. He had called right before the press conference to tell Luke he had made some interesting finds and similarities between the victims. They debated putting off the press conference until they had that information. Purvis advised that what he had to say was definitely not media ready.

Luke stood there under the hot lights and waited for the press to get their cameras ready and the cue to begin. He would give his statement, short and sweet and then take a few questions. He looked out into the crowd and felt a little relief to see Ben, Cooper and Riley amid the reporters. At least there were a few friendly faces.

Luke raised his hand to silence the crowd and indicate he was about to begin.

"Good evening," Luke said, his voice a little unsteady but gaining more confidence as he continued. "As you know, four women have been recovered from the Arkansas River in the last three days. We have been able to identify two of the victims so far. The first woman found was Shannon McCarty, Congressman Mike McCarty's daughter. Sara Bloomfield, a thirty-two-year-old woman from Little Rock was the second to be found Wednesday evening. We are still working to identify two victims, one found on Thursday and the other earlier today. The women are in their late thirties to early forties.

"We encourage cities and towns around Little Rock to bring any missing person's reports fitting this description to our attention. We believe the women are killed at a another location and then dumped into the river. At this time, we also have reason to believe that these deaths are connected to one another and to the missing person's cases of Maime LaRue Brewer and Laura Bisceglia.

"Finally, we are diligently tracking down leads to identify these victims, locate the two missing women and find the person responsible for these heinous acts. They will be held accountable. Little Rock Police Department has named Maime LaRue Brewer's husband George Brewer as a person of interest in the missing women's cases at this time. We encourage all of our residents to act with safety in mind and to report any information to our tip line. Even the smallest details can be the break needed in these cases. I will now take questions."

"Are you saying George Brewer is a serial killer?" the local NBC news reporter shouted out first.

"We have not made a determination that these homicides are the result of a serial killer. The deaths may be connected. George Brewer is simply a person of interest in the missing person's cases," Luke said matter of fact. He had to walk a fine line with what he said about George given they had no solid evidence to even make an arrest.

"Shannon McCarty was a known prostitute in New Orleans. Was she meeting clients here?" a reporter shouted from the back.

"We don't know. Regardless of her profession, Ms. McCarty did not deserve to die," Luke said. He hoped that subject would drop.

"What about the jewelry found on the victims? We heard it was connected back to George Brewer," a male reporter shouted.

Luke tried to contain the shock he felt. This hadn't even been discussed widely around the police department.

"Yes, each woman was found wearing one item of jewelry. However, we are not going to comment on that at this time."

Another reporter asked, "What can you tell us about the allegation that George Brewer was having an affair that led to Maime's disappearance?"

"What we know right now is that George Brewer was having an affair with Laura Bisceglia. We cannot release any more information than that at this time."

Over the next several minutes, Luke handled more general and routine questions. Most he would not confirm the information they wanted. He watched the reporters jockeying for position, each taking a turn and jotting down notes with each answer.

Luke was just about to wrap up when a female reporter who asked the first question stepped up in front of the crowd, holding her microphone toward Luke and asked, "How do you respond to the information that the women were all held for several days after they were taken and drugged with succinylcholine to render them totally helpless?"

Luke immediately turned and looked back to his captain. They made eye contact. Cap made the signal to wrap it up. Turning back to the crowd, lights flashed in Luke's eyes and the journalists erupted in follow-up questions. Beads of sweat started to form on his brow even though there was a chill in the air. Luke gripped the sides of the podium and responded one last time. "We have no information on that allegation at this time."

In between flashes of light, Luke looked for Riley and Cooper. He caught Riley's eye and jerked his head back to let her know she should follow him into the station. She nodded, tugged on Cooper's sleeve and then whispered in his ear. Luke turned and walked back into the police station followed by the other officers and his captain.

As they rounded the corner into the building out of earshot from the reporters, Luke asked no one in particular, "Who is leaking information?"

CHAPTER 54

"WE GET ANY TOXICOLOGY REPORTS BACK?" Luke asked Purvis over the phone as he rounded the flight of stairs, heading back to his desk. He knew Purvis wasn't going to be able to make it to the police station. He was still finishing the autopsy on the victim found earlier that day.

Luke wanted to know what that reporter was talking about so he had immediately called Purvis. When his assistant balked at pulling him out of the autopsy suite, Luke insisted.

"Not yet. We've got it on rush though," Purvis explained impatiently.

"Do you routinely test for something called," Luke paused and looked down at his notes to remember the name of the drug the reporter mention, "succinylcholine?"

"No, it's an anesthesia adjunct. Why would we test for that?" Purvis asked. Luke detected a note of concern in Purvis' voice that he hadn't heard before.

"We had a reporter ask us if the victims were given this to render them helpless before they were killed. We have absolutely no information, evidence or knowledge on this. Obviously, we have to see if it's true."

Purvis agreed to run the test for it. He said he'd pull some notes about past cases he was familiar with where this drug was used. He suggested Luke do some research himself. Luke had no idea what this drug was, where it was available, and what it would do to a victim's body. He also wanted to know how a reporter had received that information.

Luke reached under his desk to an evidence box and pulled out the bagged ring and earrings pulled from the victims. He carefully moved the items around inside their respective bags to get a better look. Sure enough the initials G.B. were on both.

Luke was gathering his files as Riley and Cooper made their way into the row of detective cubicles. Luke motioned for them to go into the conference room. He quickly picked up the phone to buzz his captain to join them.

Once seated around the table, Luke asked Riley to give them the run down on the SUV she found as well as anything related to the drugs. Riley explained her brief interview with the neighbor kid Bobby and drug dealer Orlando Knight.

Luke was impressed. He was honestly surprised she got Knight to talk so easily. At this point, he didn't really care how she did it, Luke felt they were running out of time and any help they had the better. That's why he asked Riley and Cooper to join them. He wanted to ask Riley and Cooper to follow up on a few things for him. He'd need his captain to approve it.

Riley continued filling them in on everything she found that day including Bobby's eyewitness account of the SUV and Knight's confirmation of Maime's drug use. Luke wondered who the guy was that was seen purchasing her drugs. Luke knew he'd never get Knight to go on record as he was notorious for not speaking to police, but he trusted the information that Riley was able to gather.

After Riley was done, Cooper updated him on what he found out about Dean. Cooper said he finally had a clear shot of the guy that was seen meeting with Dean and accepting money from him. Cooper said the photo was in his truck. Luke asked him to hold off getting it until he could explain why he called them in.

"I know this is unorthodox." Luke paused and turned to his captain. "I should have asked for your approval first, but I'm hoping Riley and Cooper will conduct some interviews for us that I think they will get further on than we will."

Captain Meadows started to protest.

Luke interrupted him. "Just hear me out. They obviously uncovered some things we missed anyway. We are in over our heads with work. Our guys are working around the clock and still can't keep up. Let's use the resources we have."

Captain Meadows sighed but let Luke continue.

"Cooper, I want you to go back to Sam Bloomfield and start digging around about any connection Sara may have had to George. I don't know how the media already knew, but all of the jewelry pulled from the victims has the initials G.B. I talked to George's jeweler this morning. He told me George engraved his initials on all the pieces he had designed or purchased there. There's a connection. We need to find it. Sam might be more forthcoming with you."

Cooper agreed and said he'd head over there after they finished meeting.

Turning to Riley, Luke said, "The media obviously knows things we don't. At first I suspected a leak inside this office, but they were asking things today about the jewelry and the drug that I wasn't even aware of. It's not in any file, and it certainly hadn't been discussed. I know the media won't give up their sources, but you were one of them. Would you be willing to see what you can get from them?"

"What are you thinking?" Riley asked with hesitation in her voice.

Luke was happy she hadn't said no. He'd been anticipating a fight about how it was impossible, that a reporter never gave up their sources.

"Sometimes you get a killer who wants to communicate with the media. Maybe he's letting some details slip to show he's ahead of us. We need to beat him at his own game."

"Have you asked Ben about the calls to his paper?" Cooper interjected.

"I did the other day. Ben doesn't ever take the calls. He said his editor does, and then assigns him the work. He's checking for me to see if there has been anything unusual. Today it seemed it was the television reporters not the newspaper reporters asking the questions about information they shouldn't have even known about yet."

"You know they won't give up their sources," Riley reminded them. "But, I'll see what I can do."

Luke turned to Captain Meadows to see if he had any objections. He didn't. Right before they were all about the leave, Cooper asked Luke to walk down to his truck with him to take a look at the photo he had taken of the guy meeting with Dean to see if Luke knew the guy.

The three of them walked to Cooper's truck. Cooper pulled out his camera and handed it to Luke. When Luke saw the photo of Dean and who he was with, he wished he could say he was surprised, but he wasn't. Norwalk had some serious explaining to do.

CHAPTER 55

WHEN RILEY ASKED COOPER to help her with this case, he jumped at the chance. Now he was barely able to keep his head above water with how fast everything had happened. They still lacked the key details to connect the dots. Sitting around the table at the police station earlier, he saw how tired and frustrated both Riley and Luke looked. He felt the same.

Now that Riley and Luke were getting along better, it made the work so much easier. Cooper had known they had dated but didn't know until this morning how serious it had been or how badly Riley had ended things. Luke always kept things close to the vest.

Cooper knew back when Riley left something was wrong with Luke, he just wasn't sure exactly what it was. Luke hadn't wanted to talk no matter how many times Cooper tried. Cooper remembered that time like it was yesterday. Luke banged around his office, skipped golfing and football games, and all but became a recluse outside of work. At work, Luke threw himself into each case like a man possessed.

Cooper didn't think Luke had really dated since, but then again what did he know, Luke obviously could keep a secret. The only thing Cooper hoped was that Luke didn't get hurt again. He hated to see one of his best friends go through such a hard time. Luke already had tragedy in his life. He didn't need more. Cooper knew he should pull Riley aside and see what her plan was, but he was sure this wasn't the time. Everything but these cases would have to be put on hold.

Pulling up in front of the Bloomfield residence, Cooper realized he didn't know much about Sam Bloomfield. He also hadn't had too much time to prepare for the interview. Luke filled him in on a few details before he left the police station. All Cooper really knew was Sam and his wife Sara had been married for four years, both in their thirties and had no kids. They just bought this house about a year ago.

Sam was high up in finance at a bank. Sara was a local real estate agent at one of the higher-end national real estate companies handling the Heights and Hillcrest. In the interviews the cops had already conducted, there was no reason to suspect that Sam Bloomfield had anything to do with his wife's death. He was a distraught husband. Nothing in his background had come up to make anyone suspicious. He also had a rock-solid alibi. And other than the jewelry, there seemed to be no real connection to George.

Sam greeted Cooper at the door, and Cooper explained why he was there. Sam wasn't alone he explained. By the number of cars in front of the house, Cooper hadn't thought so. Purvis had yet to release Sara's body so no funeral arrangements had been made yet. Cooper was pretty sure everyone there was eager to hear some news and find some justice.

"I don't really have any updates," Cooper said as he walked through the door. "I'm a private investigator who was hired to find Maime LaRue Brewer. Detective Morgan asked if I'd come to speak with you about any connection she might have to George Brewer."

"There's none that I know of. I already told the cops this," Sam explained, guiding Cooper into the living room. Sam made introductions to some of the family and friends sitting around the living room. Their faces were red, eyes searching and tear-filled. Cooper was sure he wouldn't remember their names. It was a blur but brothers, sisters, aunts, uncles and parents were all there together, consoling one another and offering support to Sam.

Cooper took a seat on a low chair at the end of the living room. To no one in particular, he began asking a series of questions trying to assess what kind of life they led and where Sara might have come into contact with George. There really was nothing that anyone could pinpoint. By all accounts Sam and Sara had a normal and happy life. Sam played on neighborhood baseball and football leagues. Sara went to every game she could. They were looking forward to starting a family but were trying to get some travel out of the way first and save more money.

Both of them were great at their jobs and respected by their peers. Sam woke up on the last day he saw his wife alive, had breakfast with her, and kissed her goodbye as they both headed to their respective trips. That was the last he spoke to her or saw her again. There in his life one moment and gone the next. Cooper couldn't wrap his head around how unfair life was at times.

Sitting between his mother and mother-in-law, Sam explained that in the days and months leading up to the day Sara disappeared, no one was bothering either of them. Sara was her usual upbeat self. There was nothing to indicate that the unthinkable was going to happen.

Cooper couldn't even begin to imagine what Sam was going through. He had never lost someone he loved that much. If Cooper was going to be honest, he was pretty sure he had never loved someone to that extent.

Cooper asked the last of his questions. He gave his condolences and stood to leave when Sam said hopefully, "Sara worked from home a lot. I asked the detectives if they wanted to go through any of her work files before her boss came and picked them up. They said no. I can let you look if you have the time."

Sam walked Cooper down a small hallway to Sara's office. It was painted a soft yellow. Sara kept her office spotless. All her files were arranged in the filing cabinet and her desk was neatly arranged with everything in its place.

Sitting down at Sara's desk, Cooper started a thorough search. He was pretty sure some of what he was looking at was confidential, but he wasn't going to turn down the access.

Cooper had only been searching for about an hour when he came across a client file with George's name in it. Sara and George may not have known each other personally, but she had definitely met him.

By the document Cooper held in his hands, it seemed George was one of Sara's clients. She was helping him search for a new house.

Cooper took out his cellphone, snapped several pictures of the documents and returned the file to its place in the filing cabinet. Cooper spent a few minutes returning the office to the way he found it and thanked Sam on his way out. He promised Sam they'd be hearing from the police soon.

CHAPTER 56

BY THE TIME I LEFT THE POLICE STATION, it was already seven-thirty. I was hungry and tired and didn't feel like doing much of anything. It had been an incredibly long day and even my bones were starting to ache. Not wanting to disappoint Luke, I dragged my tired self over to Channel 5 News to poke around for Janelle Brady. She had been the reporter who asked Luke about the drug.

Once inside the studio building, I didn't get past the front desk. I was able to get into the front lobby, but no one was there. A phone on the desk directed me to place a call to be directed to the extension I needed. I went through the automated system until I reached Janelle's extension. I left a message. There was a door that led farther into the studio. A quick tug told me it was locked. I didn't seem to have much of an option. I didn't know anyone else who worked there. I'd have to go home and do some research. I'd come back tomorrow.

I arrived home about twenty minutes later. As I was putting my key in the front door, Emma walked across the lawn towards me. She had a foil-wrapped pan in hand. Greeting me with a quick peck on the cheek, she thrust the pan into my hands. "I made lasagna for you. I figured you wouldn't cook. You look tired."

Leave it to your best friend to tell you the truth.

Emma followed me into the house. I put the pan and my things on the kitchen counter. Emma pulled a plate out of my cabinet and set it on my table along with a glass and silverware. I stood leaning against the sink, watching her. She set everything on the kitchen table, reminded me to eat and to get some sleep. Then she headed for the door.

As Emma walked out, she said, "That was a good press conference Luke gave. The reporters are making it seem like George is a serial killer. If he's not guilty, his reputation is shot."

About an hour and a half later, I was curled up on the couch, blanket over me and a half-eaten plate of lasagna on the coffee table in front of me. I cringed when I heard a knock on the front door. I thought it might be George. He had called me several times since I had been home. We'd already talked for over an hour. I didn't update him on finding what I thought was Maime's car or the drugs or the affair. I was saving that for morning. I was far too exhausted to go into it all this evening.

Instead of being focused on our investigation, George complained about the very thing Emma said. That no matter what happened from this point on, his reputation was destroyed. The one thing I couldn't stand about George, and still couldn't, was his ability to play the victim. He acted as if he had absolutely no part in what was happening to him. I couldn't listen to the whining anymore.

I pulled open the front door prepared to be a real witch. I was pleasantly surprised to see Luke standing there. He had changed from his work clothes and had on jeans and a long sleeve tee-shirt. He stood there looking sheepish with a container of milk and a box of soft batch chocolate chip cookies in his hands.

I couldn't help myself, I let him in. We bumped around the kitchen together as I heated a plate of lasagna for him. He sat at the kitchen table, watching me. I didn't set the plate down in front of him though. I walked it into the living room and set it on the coffee table. He sat next to me on the couch. We arranged ourselves comfortably under my blanket, my toes tucked under his thighs.

I watched him eat deliberate bite after deliberate bite. That was one of the nicest things about being with Luke. We could do something as simple as sit on a couch together with no pressure to fill the silence.

After he ate and put his plate down, I stretched my legs across his lap. Luke ran his hands softly over my legs, looked over at me and said with raised eyebrows, "Do we talk about us now or later?"

"Later," I said definitively. "Right now, tell me how you're doing with this case. It's got to be awful on you. I can't even imagine the stress you're under."

"I feel like it's a make-or-break my career kind of case. I know it's not, but Little Rock has never had something like this happen at least not as far back as I can remember. I just don't know which way to turn. Nothing makes any sense. We've got all circumstantial evidence to work with and now this weird drug. Not to mention, one of my detectives is meeting up with the main suspect's best friend. With the strange tips to the media, I feel like I'm missing something right under my nose."

He sounded as exhausted as I felt.

"There will be a break. There always is. It just seems bad right now because it's happened all so suddenly. A week ago, there was no case and now there have been six victims. You're behind the curve, anyone would be," I said, hoping to comfort him and really hoping he saw the reality of what he was dealing with. Luke had always been a perfectionist. I knew how much pressure he was putting on himself.

"Laura's parents came to the station after the press conference. They want me to arrest George. Maime's parents want me to arrest George. I want to arrest George. I don't have enough. I talked to the prosecutor's office tonight. We just don't have a case on him," Luke explained with resignation in his voice.

"What do you have on him?" I asked.

Luke eyed me.

"I promise this will stay between us."

With only a slight hesitation, Luke explained, "No real physical evidence other than the jewelry connecting him to the victims. Cooper called me on my way over here. He said he found documents in some of Sara Bloomfield's work files with George's signature. George hired her to help him buy a house. It was dated two months ago. George knew her, and obviously, he was connected to Maime, Laura and Shannon. But a connection just isn't enough. We can't even say he was the last one with the deceased victims. The thing that bothers me the most is why would George search for a new house if he planned to kill his wife?"

"I have no idea. That doesn't make sense. Are you doing any surveillance on him?"

"Some and we're also going to put a GPS tracker on his truck. We're just waiting for clearance on that. Maybe he'll lead us to them. At least if we're watching him and more bodies are dumped in the river, we might be able to rule him out. We've got guys watching the river now, too. I don't know what else we can do. We are running down every lead, trying to identify the unknown victims. I'm just at a loss of what else we could be doing. Everything we do have is connected to George. Just not enough yet to arrest him."

I knew there were no words I could say to make it better. Instead, I sat up, turned his face to mine and kissed him. Luke kissed me back and ran his fingers through my hair. All at once we found our old rhythm, like no time had passed at all. This was all I could offer him right now. I hoped it was enough. He waited on the couch while I put his dishes in the kitchen and walked through the house, shutting off lights and locking doors.

When I returned to him in the living room, he stood waiting. I sunk into his body, my arms around him tight and kissed him again. We broke apart long enough for me to lead him by the hand up the stairs and into my bed.

CHAPTER 57

"**WE NEED TO TALK,**" **I DEMANDED**, brushing past
George and stepping into his house. It was clear he was surprised to
see me so early on a Saturday morning. Luke had to be back into the
station by six that morning so I woke up with him and decided to
start my day. It was now just after nine.

I smiled as I thought back to last night with Luke. Turns out, we
were too tired to make love. Instead, we crawled into my bed,
snuggled against one another, and fell fast asleep.

This morning, Luke was in a rush. We shared a hug and quick
goodbye kiss with the promise of finishing what we started the night
before. Before he left, he asked me to go through all of the victim's
cellphone bills to see if there were any numbers that matched. I
walked him out. He pulled the files from his SUV, handed them to
me, and then was gone.

George's house looked like he hadn't picked up in days. Several
newspapers were spread around the living room and a broadcast
from CNN blared on the television. It was deafening. Coffee mugs
and dirty plates littered the end tables. Clothes were thrown on the
floor. George didn't look much better. His eyes were bloodshot and
his hair was sticking up all over the place.

"Go shower and pull yourself together. I'll clean up in here," I
ordered. I knew what I had to tell him was going to be difficult to

hear. I wanted him in a better frame of mind. He stood for a moment in the middle of the living room just watching me.

I didn't wait for him. I started picking up and moving the dirty dishes to the kitchen and into the dishwasher. The kitchen was even messier. I think George realized I was serious and he went to shower. I moved through the house picking up and cleaning as if it were my own. I'm a lot like my mother in this regard. I clean when I'm stressed. A total neat freak anyway so it's hard for me to focus in cluttered environments.

By the time George showered and changed, the house had been thoroughly straightened and was back in order. The dishwasher and the washing machine both were going through their wash cycles. I was sitting on the couch waiting for George and watching Luke's interview being played again and again on CNN.

"They think I'm a serial killer," George said as he walked into the living room and took a seat next to me.

"You keep saying that. Nobody said you were a serial killer. They asked the question because a lot has been happening around you. Whether you like it or not, you've become the eye of the storm." I wasn't going to sugarcoat it. It all had become too serious for that.

"I'm not a serial killer, Riley," George stressed again, his eyes level with mine. He folded his arms over his chest and looked to the ceiling.

"Obviously," I reassured. "I found out some things you need to know, and you need to tell me what you know."

George didn't say anything. He turned to look at me.

"Why were you looking for a new house?" I asked directly. No point beating around the bush. If I asked him if he knew Sara, he'd deny it. I didn't feel like playing games.

"I only saw a few houses. Things were really bad with Maime. If I divorced, I lost everything. This is her house. She owned it before we married. She'd fight me for it and win in a divorce. I didn't know if I could do it, but I was at least looking for another place to live if I needed it. Maime threatened a couple of times to kick me out."

"Were you involved with Sara Bloomfield?"

George vigorously shook his head no. "Never. Not once. I had only met her a few times. I swear to you."

I believed him. Not that I trusted George not to try, but by all accounts, Sara's marriage was happy and stable.

"Did you know Maime was taking drugs?" I asked

George let out a sigh. "Yes, but I only realized it maybe a month ago. I tried to talk to her about it. She wouldn't listen. I never did find out what she was taking. I never found the drugs in the house or in her purse or anything. The more I asked her about it, the more she hid it from me."

I waited to see if he had more. I wasn't going to tell him about the Land Rover I found. Luke hadn't confirmed it was Maime's yet.

George looked at me, eyebrows raised. "What did you find out?"

"She was getting drugs from a drug dealer named Orlando Knight in the southeast part of the city. I'm still not really clear on what drugs specifically, but it was pills, the prescription kind. But George, she didn't buy them directly. A guy bought them for her."

George looked at me like I was crazy. "Who, who would buy her drugs? What guy?"

"Do you know if Maime was having an affair?"

George pulled the remote control off the coffee table and shut off the TV. He turned to me and explained, "I never knew for sure, but yes, I suspected. But so was I, so I couldn't really say anything to her."

"I know this is going to be hard to hear. I have reason to believe it was with Dean. Knight said…"

I didn't get out the rest of my sentence. George forcefully threw the television remote across the room, smashing it into the wall. It shattered, breaking into pieces.

He turned to me, his face contorted in anger in a way I've never seen. He grabbed me by my shoulders shaking me. His fingers dug into my skin hurting me. His eyes were unfocused.

"Stop! Let me go," I yelled, grabbing at his hands and trying to pry them off of me.

He stopped but didn't let me go. His face was red, his pupils dilated.

He shouted in my face, "Why, why would you lie like this? What is wrong with you? Isn't my life enough of a mess? Is this your way of getting me back? How could you believe some drug dealer?"

I finally shook him off me and stood, "Get yourself together. I have no reason to lie to you. I didn't do this to you, but you have to face the truth. This could be relevant. How do we really know what Dean is up to?"

George got up, grabbed his keys from the coffee table, and stormed out of the house. He was out the door before I could even catch up. I raced after him and barely got out of the way as he pulled out of the driveway. I ran to my car hoping I could catch him.

CHAPTER 58

I SQUEALED MY SUV TO A STOP in front of Dean's house in just enough time to see Dean open the front door. George grabbed him by the shirt and shoved him backwards into the house. The door closed. Then it bounced back open. I called Luke and told him that he needed to get to Dean's house or get a squad car there immediately. I rattled off the address.

By the time I made it through the open door and into the house, George was on top of Dean, both of them splayed out on the hardwood floor in the foyer. George was straddling Dean, one hand clutching his shirt and the other pulled back ready to punch Dean in the face. George must have already landed a punch, blood trickled down from Dean's nose.

"George!" I screamed. "Get off of him." I stood there helpless as George hit him again.

Dean must have gotten some strength from somewhere because even though he took another shot to the face, he fought back, shoving George off of him. They rolled around the floor, punching and kicking at one another. It was hard to tell if either was landing their punches. They knocked over a foyer table. Keys, mail and a lamp crashed to the floor.

There was no way I could pry them apart. They both outweighed me, and there was a good chance I would take a hit in the crossfire. I didn't know what to do so I tried to stay out of the way.

"What is wrong with you? Stop it!" Dean yelled out in between breaths, dodging George's fists.

"You screwed my wife, you backstabbing…I'm going to kill you," George shouted back, taking swing after swing.

"You were screwing everyone in town," Dean retorted, not denying it, landing a shot to George's gut.

Blow after blow they landed. It seemed to take forever for the cops to get there. Finally, I heard sirens off in the distance. Two cop cars squealed their brakes in front of the house and officers ran towards the door guns drawn.

After a bit of struggle, the uniformed cops pulled George and Dean apart and shoved them in opposite directions. That was when Luke walked in and saw the messy scene.

"What is going on here?" Luke demanded. He looked at them and then over to me.

They both sat on the floor. Both out of breath. George's face was red. He was still enraged. I think he knew better than to continue with the cops there. Dean wiped his bloody face on his shirt. Neither of them responded to Luke.

"I told George about the drugs and the affair," I said as way of explanation.

Luke furrowed his brow at me and shook his head. It was clear he wasn't happy with that decision. I never thought George would lose his temper like this. I knew he'd be upset, but this wasn't a response I expected.

"You never loved her. Did you kill her?" Dean shouted at George from across the room. They both slumped against opposite walls.

"No, why are you trying to ruin my life?" George asked resigned. "How could you do this to me? How could you buy her drugs?"

Blood continued to drip down Dean's face. His nose was clearly broken. He leaned back against the wall in obvious defeat. I couldn't tell, but it seemed as if Dean was crying.

We all just stood there looking at him. The minutes ticked by. It was getting more and more uncomfortable. The tension was high. The cops seemed ready to arrest. I was just on edge waiting to see what would happen next.

Dean finally stood up, pulled himself together and arranged his clothing back into place. He looked down at George and said evenly,

"I didn't just screw your wife. I loved her. We loved each other. I never bought her drugs. I took her to rehab the day she disappeared. I haven't seen her since."

CHAPTER 59

TO SAY I WAS SPEECHLESS was probably an understatement. I wasn't sure how Dean could know where Maime was this whole time and not tell us.

Luke stuck his hand out and helped George off the floor. Dean left, walking into a back room of the house. We stood there in silence. He returned with ice and a towel for his nose and a baggie of ice and towel for George.

Luke waved off the uniformed cops. Dean guided the four of us to the formal dining room to the left of the foyer. We all took seats around a large oak table. Once settled, without too much prompting, Dean finally started to give us some details.

Dean explained that he had been having an affair with Maime for years. She had turned to him when she suspected George was having yet another affair. Maime showed up at his place late one night. She had been crying and wondering what she had done to deserve it. She couldn't take the sleepless nights anymore, wondering where her husband was going.

She told Dean that George wouldn't answer his cellphone when he was away from home and lied to her all the time about where he was and who he was with. Maime confided in Dean that she knew there was another woman. There were phone calls George wouldn't answer when she was around. Late at night when George thought she was asleep, she found him whispering into his cellphone. She came to Dean looking for comfort and guidance and had even talked divorce. Dean told us one night turned into a few lunch meetings. Lunches turned to dinners. When one thing led to another, their affair started. As the months wore on, Dean said he suspected Maime was seeing someone else, too.

He had no idea who, but it was shortly after her drug habit became apparent. She always seemed out of it, manic one moment and depressed the next. Dean said he thought maybe Maime was having a mental breakdown. She was twitchy at times, her eyes dilated, and her words slurred like she was drunk. Dean never smelled alcohol on her, never saw her drink so he started to suspect drugs.

The breaking point, Dean said, was a night a few weeks back. Maime came to Dean's place late in the evening. She passed out on his bed and didn't fully wake for two days. George was on a business trip, Dean explained. He didn't know what else to do so he called Maime's father. Dean said he didn't feel like he had much of an option. Edwin came to his house. Dean admitted the affair. Together, they made a plan to get her into rehab.

"I was just oblivious to this whole thing. No one thought to clue me in?" George asked, the shock in his voice apparent.

"You were the cause. I've talked to you before about your affairs. There wasn't any stopping you," Dean explained with an obvious anger in his voice. "And anyway, Edwin wasn't convinced you weren't the one drugging her to keep her oblivious and occupied so you could continue running around."

I really thought George was going to leap across the table and hit him again. He didn't. He didn't say anything. He sat looking disgusted like Dean was possibly the most idiotic person alive.

Before Dean clammed up and stopped talking, Luke encouraged him to talk about what happened the day Maime went missing.

Dean said he picked Maime up from work that Friday and drove her to the rehab in Maumelle, a suburb just across the river from Little Rock. Dean said Maime was crying and didn't want to go. Edwin had threatened to financially cut her off the night before if she didn't follow through with treatment.

The three of them met, and Edwin told Maime that her behavior was out of control, and he couldn't have her embarrassing him or his law firm. Dean said the speech was harsh. He felt bad for Maime that Edwin was being so cold, but she finally agreed to go.

Dean said he dropped Maime off at the rehab and then went straight to his office. He worked for several hours. He explained that right about the time he came home about nine that night, the intake nurse at the rehab called him and said that Maime had left the facility. They said they had finished the intake process and she was put in her room. When it came time for lights out, she was gone. They searched the facility and the grounds but there was no sign of her. The nurse assured him this happened all the time when people voluntarily checked themselves in. Other than calling Dean, they didn't think much of it.

Dean said he debated between going back to the rehab to search or to her office to see if her SUV was there. Dean said he and Edwin planned to pick her SUV up in the morning and bring it to her house. When George got back from his trip, they would explain.

With her missing, Dean decided to try her office first. He had raced back to her office assuming she'd get her car as quickly as she could. By the time he made it there, her SUV was gone. He assumed she took off and was in hiding someplace, avoiding going back to rehab.

Dean confided he and Edwin had been searching for Maime ever since. They had hoped she would turn up, but then women's bodies were found in the river. Maime hadn't made contact with anyone. There was no trace of her after leaving the rehab. Dean said he talked to everyone at the rehab he could and no one saw her leave. He assumed someone picked her up. He didn't know who. No one seemed to know anything.

Luke and I shared a look. Luke asked, "Well that's certainly some story. Dean, if this is true why haven't you told us this prior to today?"

"Because we honestly thought that George found out about the affair and killed her."

CHAPTER 60

DEAN'S CONFESSION HUNG IN THE AIR. For several seconds, no one spoke. Dean shifted in his seat, his eyes darting back and forth between us.

"When George asked me to say I was with him Friday night, I was pretty sure he had killed her. I thought it was his way of telling me he knew what I had done. I didn't know what to do. Then bodies started piling up. I've been as confused as everyone else. I really do love Maime though. I really do."

George's eyes were zeroed in on Dean, and for a moment, I thought he was going to take a few more swings at him. He didn't. Resting his head in his hands, he said resigned, "I didn't kill her. I didn't kill anyone."

Turning to Dean, Luke demanded, "I need you to come to the station and give a formal statement. I need to see if there is anything else you remember. We need the details of the rehab and your contact there. I have one question you can answer right now."

"Okay, what?" Dean asked cautiously.

"Why have you and Edwin been meeting and paying Detective David Norwalk?"

Dean looked down, but didn't speak. We waited. The seconds felt like hours.

Finally, he explained, "He was moonlighting for me. I had him follow Maime a few times, trying to find out about the drugs. Instead he followed me and took photos of Maime and me together. He was blackmailing me."

I was sure neither George nor Dean noticed the slight twitch in Luke's eyes. Heads were going to roll when he got back to the station. Luke stood, reminded Dean to meet him back at the station later today, and then motioned for me to walk him to the door. Once out of earshot, he asked me if I'd be okay alone with them. I said I would be. He told me he'd call me later and then left.

Dean stood quietly in the dining room waiting for us to leave. George didn't say anything to him as he walked towards the door and walked out of the house. Before I could follow, Dean reached out, putting a hand on my arm and pulling me back. He ran his hand down his bruised face, a trail of dried blood under his nose.

"I really love her, Riley. I was only trying to help her. Make him understand."

I nodded but didn't say anything. What could you say in a situation like that?

Stepping out of Dean's house, I saw George's Chevy Tahoe pull around the corner and out of sight. I went to my Jeep, turned the ignition and clicked off the radio. My head was starting to pound. I made a quick trip to Starbucks, loaded up on some caffeine, and headed back to George's house.

When I got there, his truck was parked in the driveway and his front door was wide open. I walked in to find him lying on the couch, arm thrown over his eyes and an ice pack on his cheek.

"Here," I said angrily, handing him a cup of coffee. "We need to talk, George. Now."

Stretching my legs out in front of me, crossing them at the ankles, I leaned my back up against the couch on the far end from where George was lying.

"My life is falling apart. I keep making it worse. I don't even know how to help myself anymore," George pleaded.

"Stop feeling sorry for yourself. You keep making poor decisions and then expecting everyone else to clean up after you. It stops now," I said. Then I really laid into him.

"If you ever lay a hand on me again, I'll kill you without thinking twice. Trust me, Luke probably wouldn't even charge me. I'm going to ask this only once. Have you ever hit or laid a hand on Maime or any other woman in anger?"

George sat up. He didn't look at me. "No, not once. I'm sorry. I didn't mean it. It's just what you said, I just couldn't. I lost control."

"Save the excuses. It never happens again," I said forcefully. "Luke said he interviewed you the other night. Your lawyer hasn't returned my call. He needs to call me. Tell him that. Luke said he showed you photos of the other women and you reacted strangely. You knew Sara and Shannon. Did you know the other woman?"

George shook his head no. "I don't think so. I thought maybe the other looked familiar, but I couldn't place her. Riley, I didn't kill anyone. I don't know where Laura and Maime are. I don't have anything to do with it. You have to believe me."

I sat watching him, taking slow sips of my coffee. I was exhausted, thoroughly sickened by everything and everyone. I could feel the anger starting to bubble up in my chest. I was mad at myself for ever loving and trusting George. I was livid at him for everything he'd ever done to me, Maime and every other woman in his life.

I knew I couldn't sit with my anger anymore. I got up and walked to the door to leave. Before I left, I turned to him one last time. "George, I think right now I might be the only one that believes you. You've got so many secrets though. You've got to help yourself. If you know something that can help this investigation, you have got to start cooperating with me and with the police. Otherwise, you are going to be arrested for the murders of all these women. Right now, you do look like a serial killer. The affairs, all the lies, and that little stunt you pulled grabbing me and shaking me – you've got something going on and you need some serious professional help."

George didn't say anything at first. He eyed me and then a sarcastic smirk spread across his face. "How long have you been sleeping with Detective Morgan? He spent the night at your house last night."

I stepped out the front door without looking at him or saying another word. The idea that George was spying on me shook me to my core, but there was no way I was giving him the satisfaction of a response or a reaction.

CHAPTER 61

LUKE WAS HALFWAY BACK to the police station when Purvis called him. Luke answered on the second ring. "Talk to me."

"I'm standing in your office waiting for you. I've got the results you wanted. I had to make the guys at the lab work overnight." Purvis paused and took an audible breath. "Luke, all four victims are positive for succinylcholine."

"Be right there." Luke hung up. He called Riley to give her the confirmation that the media definitely had the information first. Luke knew she was planning to speak with the reporter. Armed with this, she might get further.

Arriving back at the station, Luke found Captain Meadows, Tyler and some of the other detectives including Norwalk gathered around the conference table. Purvis was at the end of the table with files in hand. Luke took a seat next to his captain.

Purvis started immediately, "As I just told Luke, I found traces of succinylcholine in all of the victims' blood."

"What kind of effect does this have on a person?" Tyler asked before Luke had the chance.

Purvis explained, "It's basically a short-term muscle relaxant used in anesthesia. It can render a person unable to move but leave them conscious, for at least a few moments, depending on the dosage. Even though you can't move, you are still aware of what's happening. Eventually, it will kill you by shutting down your diaphragm and cutting off oxygen to your brain."

"Why the overkill?" Luke asked confused. "The victims were tied up, which we see by the ligature marks, so why drug them? Is this a common drug?"

"Just to terrorize them. Maybe the killer gets off on it," suggested Captain Meadows.

Luke shrugged and shook his head, not sure.

Purvis continued. "I can't answer why. You'd all know that better. But no, it's not common at all outside of hospitals and horse farms. They use it frequently to put down horses. I found a few cases in California where this was used in criminal cases. It could be used more than we realize. It's not something a medical examiner will commonly test for as part of a regular toxicology screen."

Purvis paused for other questions. When there weren't any, he continued on. "I noticed other than the restraint marks on their wrists and ankles, the women didn't show other signs of struggle. That would be consistent with this drug and being restrained. I also found small shallow puncture wounds that could be consistent with administering the drug. They were definitely held for a few days, killed, and then dumped. We'll have to go over the timeframes but it looks like the third victim you found yesterday received the worst of it. She was clearly beaten before she was strangled. It was pink nail polish that was used to write the word *whore* across her body."

Nobody said anything for a few moments. Luke then got up and started drawing a timeline on the chalk board, connecting victims and the dates they were recovered. Purvis laid out time of death for each of the victims in relation to when they were found.

All of the victims, oddly enough, had been dead about seventy-two hours give or take. Purvis couldn't be absolutely sure how long they had been in the water before they were found in relation to their time of death but basically three days on each from time of death to recovery.

The only case they really could draw a full timeframe on was Sara Bloomfield. They knew Sara went missing on a Thursday morning and was found the following Wednesday night. Purvis said she had been dead approximately seventy-two hours. That would put her murder right about Sunday. What exactly was the killer doing with her from Thursday to Sunday? Then another thought hit Luke. Both Maime and Laura were kidnapped on Friday. If the cases were connected, where was Sara being held while the killer was out kidnapping two women in one night? Was that even logistically possible? Luke posed the scenario to his team.

"He kidnaps them, keeps them tied up and drugged or keeps them in a remote place so he doesn't have to worry about anyone hearing them or seeing them," Captain Meadows suggested.

Tyler added, "I think we also have to consider that he knows his victims. It doesn't sound like Maime put up much of a fight. Riley told me the kid she interviewed said the woman dropped off her car and then willingly got into the other guy's car. Remember, Luke, there was no sign of struggle at Laura's house either."

He was correct. Neither, it seemed, fought their abductor, which did make it seem like it was someone they knew and trusted. Again, Luke thought of George.

The thing that puzzled Luke the most was, that if it was George, where was he hiding the women? How did he get Maime to voluntarily leave her car in the worst part of the city and what was he doing with these women while he held them before death? Why the fake outrage with Dean? Was it just for show? Each new bit of evidence only yielded more questions.

The detectives started running theories with each other and then Norwalk spoke out louder than the rest. "Luke, are you going to face the facts now or when we have twelve more bodies? There's a serial killer killing these women. Purvis here just said it. I can head up this investigation if you don't think you are up for it, you know given your history and all."

"Luke can handle this case just fine," Detective Jenkins yelled, pointing his finger at Norwalk. "And another thing. Don't be running your mouth off to reporters. They have enough inside information. Maybe we should be wondering where it's coming from."

Captain Meadows slammed his fist into the table. "Okay, okay enough. Norwalk, you have enough cases waiting on you. You all have enough work to do without all this fighting. Now go and do it."

The detectives filed out. Purvis promised he'd call when he had additional information.

"You okay?" Cap asked Luke once the room was cleared.

"Yeah, fine," Luke said, trying to shrug off Norwalk's comment.

"You know this case better than anyone. You got this. I have faith in you," Cap reassured as he walked out of the room leaving Luke standing alone in front of the evidence board.

CHAPTER 62

LUKE SPENT ANOTHER HOUR poring over all the evidence and then went back to his desk. He spent the next few hours with two other detectives hunting down surveillance video at the airport to see if Sara Bloomfield even made it there to catch her morning flight. Then they spent time calling the Bloomfields' neighbors and tracking databases, trying to hunt down the identities of the other two victims.

They weren't making much progress. Luke wanted to get George back into the interview room and have another crack at him. That wasn't going to happen. Under no certain terms could Luke interview George again. George was not forthcoming with information, and his attorney was blocking another interview. They didn't have enough to arrest, either. Luke did the next best thing, he called Cooper and asked to meet with him.

While he waited for Cooper to arrive, Luke made a quick call to Riley who said she was headed to the news station. Luke needed to know who was calling in those tips. He knew the leaks couldn't be from the police department. They all just found out about the drug. Luke's only thought was that the killer himself was making the calls. He suggested that to Riley.

When Cooper arrived, Luke filled him in on the medical examiner's findings. The biggest lead they had right now was that the killer was holding his victims for a period of time and drugging them before killing them. Luke needed to know and know now if there was a place George could have Maime and Laura stashed away.

"You need to pay your client a visit and dig a little deeper," Luke demanded. "You know George lawyered up and won't talk to me. Maybe you'll get further. He's still your client."

Luke looked around to see who was listening. He pulled Cooper close, and barely above a whisper said, "It would be unethical for me to tell you to act as an arm of law enforcement, but I think your client is withholding information from you. There are a lot of unanswered questions, most specifically how jewelry with his initials ended up on each victim and if he's got a place to keep Maime and Laura and the other victims stashed. You have to get him to talk. Time is running out."

Cooper got the message and got up to leave.

"You can tell him we found his wife's car, too. Maybe that will rattle him and shake some information loose," Luke added as Cooper headed for the door.

"It's confirmed?" Cooper asked surprised.

"The crime scene tech supervisor paid me a visit this morning. He said while they were going through it, they located a wallet and cellphone under the driver's side seat. The wallet and cell belonged to Maime. Even though some of the car was badly burned, they were able to confirm the make and model was the same as Maime's. The findings left little doubt it was her car. He guessed whoever did it planned for the car to be totally torched but didn't stick around and make sure. Maybe, they wanted it found."

"We'll get him," Cooper assured.

"I hope so."

Luke went back into the conference room to go over Maime's case just one more time. With the new information about the car and other leads, they had a better timeline of her disappearance.

Luke now knew Maime left work at approximately two in the afternoon. Dean confirmed he picked her up then. They drove around the city for about an hour arguing about whether she was really going to rehab or not. Then Dean said he brought her to the rehab at three-thirty and never saw her again.

Tyler had already confirmed the story with the rehab. The nurses confirmed that Maime was finished with check-in and was shown her room by six in the evening. She had refused dinner. The last time anyone saw her was around seven. The next bit of evidence they had was that by nine-thirty that night Maime's car was being dropped off on the southside by an unknown man and woman. Dean had told Luke he thought Maime had a spare key. Dean had informed Luke he had taken Maime's main set of car and house keys when he dropped her off at the rehab, but she was known to keep spare keys around.

Luke had called Maime's father who quickly confirmed Dean's story. Luke still couldn't wrap his head around why they never told the police this information from the start. Edwin wouldn't answer that question. Luke guessed it had more to do with protecting his own reputation. Luke wasn't a parent, but he couldn't imagine being more concerned about his reputation than the life of his child. No matter how much grief and embarrassment she might cause.

Luke wasn't positive if Maime dropped her car off herself or whether it was a man and woman who had kidnapped her. He had no reason to believe she didn't do it herself and then left with an unknown male. Clearly, she was familiar with the neighborhood, having purchased drugs from there.

If it was Maime, Luke knew identifying the man who was with her that night was going to be critical. Riley didn't think anyone got enough to get a description. Luke was going to ask her to take some photos of George and Dean back to Orlando Knight and his crew to see if he could at least identify which of them bought her drugs. Luke had no reason to believe it was anyone other than one of them, even though they both denied it. They were both caught in one lie after another.

Luke had no way to account for Dean either that night and most specifically from the time he left work around seven. Dean allowed the cops to go through his phone records, and after a quick search, Dean had placed only one call that night and that was to Maime's father.

Luke was still waiting for Verizon to provide the report on the victims' and George's cellphone locations. Luke stared hard at his notes, trying to connect the dots. Constructing timelines allowed Luke to step back to see the pieces of evidence that were missing. He knew that like a puzzle, it would just take a few more bits of evidence for some of it to start making sense. He just hoped it came before there was another victim.

CHAPTER 63

I DECIDED TO CALL FIRST before going over to the news station because I didn't want a repeat of being locked out like the day before. I had three people to interview – Janelle, her news director and whoever took the initial tip. When I called ahead, I explained some basic information about who I was and that I wanted to make sure the right people would be available. I didn't give enough away that they'd refuse a meeting though.

On my drive to the station, Luke confirmed the news tips were accurate and his suspicion was that maybe the killer was calling in the tips. That was a clear sign to me that the killer wanted all of us to know what he was doing. Maybe he wanted recognition or maybe he just wanted to show us he was more in control than we were.

When I arrived, I was met by Janelle and Dave Brockton, the news director. I didn't like Janelle on sight. She came from money and it was fairly obvious from the Jimmy Choo stilettos to the way she walked. Not my kind of journalist. They weren't gritty enough and often would just buy the story instead of dig for it. Before I could say a word, Janelle struck the first blow.

"We know that you are George Brewer's ex-girlfriend. Are you willing to give us an exclusive interview?" Janelle asked eagerly as she ushered me into Dave's office.

I was not surprised. Although this was not information that had been made public, people knew, of course. I did wonder where they got this information. If it was information that came from the same tipster, it meant the killer was close enough to me or others closely linked to the investigation to know that information. Between what happened with George earlier today, and now this, my nerves were shot.

Janelle and Dave stood side by side waiting for my answer. They seemed quite eager to interview me. I quickly corrected their assumption without confirming or denying their information.

"I think there's been some confusion. I'm only here to discuss some news tips you've been provided. We can start with where you heard about a relationship between George and me."

"News tips?" Dave asked, cocking his head to the side reminding me in some ways of my yellow lab Dusty when he is listening intently to what I'm saying.

"Yes, you've been at crime scenes very early. At the police press conference yesterday, Janelle asked Detective Morgan about the victims being held and drugged with succinylcholine. Now this assumption I've had a previous relationship with George. It's important to know where this information is coming from," I explained, remaining calm and professional.

"We can't give out our sources. You should know that," Janelle said with a condescending tone I wanted to smack out of her mouth.

"I understand that in a normal circumstance you cannot share that information. We have reason to believe the information you were provided may have come directly from someone with prior knowledge of the victims and this case."

Dave got up and closed the door. I was hoping he would be more willing to share information than Janelle. He sat back down and explained again that they couldn't share that information. Janelle launched into a diatribe about journalistic ethics, and how if they reveal their sources, no one will share with the media. She seemed to like hearing herself talk.

I wasn't really a fan. I wanted to explain to her that I knew all about journalistic ethics, but I held my tongue and took a different approach.

"You understand that by withholding this information you are putting the case in jeopardy, and therefore, the missing victims more at risk. We still have two missing women. You might be able to help save their lives. Withholding this information to keep your ratings up is putting people's lives at risk."

"How so?" Dave asked.

"Can you at least provide me with how the tips came in?"

"We've had both emails and calls," Dave explained.

"Are they from the same source? Do you have a name?"

"Yes, it appears they are the same person. They never gave a name," Dave said. He waved me off. "We are really on shaky ground here. I don't think we can share further."

He got up as if to end the meeting.

I didn't budge. "Have you found anything odd about these tips?"

Janelle turned to Dave. He nodded and sat back down probably realizing I wasn't letting them out of the conversation that easily.

Janelle explained, "They came from the same phone number and email address. We seem to be the only one getting this information. As you stated, we are often the first one at the crime scenes."

She paused for a moment and seemed unsure if she should go further. Then with uncertainty in her voice, she said, "We're there even before the police."

"Have you given any consideration as to why that is?"

"We thought at first there was a leak in the police department. Then yesterday at the press conference, when Detective Morgan acted like he didn't know what I was talking about, we decided the tips probably weren't coming from the cops. Detective Morgan obviously didn't know the information. He's not that good of an actor," Janelle detailed.

That much was true. Luke had a hard time with his poker face in situations like that. Get him in the room with a suspect, he can lie, but for some reason, any other time, he wears everything on his face. When Luke called earlier, he gave me enough leeway to share whatever I needed to get the information. I decided I wasn't getting anywhere fast with these two and needed to throw down my ace.

"I'm going to share something with you. This information must remain off the record for now. Detective Morgan said he'd give you the exclusive to run it when he is ready to release the information if you agree. Agreed?"

Janelle and Dave looked at each other. Then both nodded in unison.

"Janelle, when you asked Detective Morgan about the victims being held and drugged with succinylcholine, he was surprised because they had not uncovered that information yet. It was confirmed this morning from the medical examiner's office. That means that there is a very good chance that whoever is providing you with the tips is involved in the case. It may even be the killer."

CHAPTER 64

I WATCHED AS JANELLE SWALLOWED VISIBLY at that realization. Dave looked distressed. Nobody, even a seasoned journalist, wanted to harbor a killer. There were possible legal implications, but broader than that, it was a moral issue. I'd been faced with similar situations in the past. Many journalists had and some even went as far as to sit in jail to protect their sources. I was hoping this wouldn't be the case here.

"If this is true, why aren't the police here?" Dave asked.

"This goes beyond source confidentiality. We are trying to close ranks and keep this quiet even within the police department. We won't share the information you disclose to us. But we need to know it. Please call Detective Morgan if you don't feel comfortable sharing it with me. He'll confirm he asked me to be here."

Right in front of me, they openly debated for several more moments whether to trust me or not. Then Dave got up, walked over to his desk and pulled a manila folder out of the top drawer. He came back to the table and handed it to me.

"It's all in there. We got the first one the day Maime LaRue Brewer went missing. Then several more calls and emails came in. The number isn't blocked. From what we can figure, they come from a prepaid cellphone. When we call it back, there is no voicemail or anything. It just rings and rings. We even tried to trace the IP address on the email, but they are routed all over the place. One message said it came from China, another from Russia and several others from New York and California."

"Is it a male or female that calls in the tips?" I asked.

"Male," Janelle interjected. "It's the same voice. You can tell it's not a real voice. I mean it sounds almost mechanical, but you can tell it's male."

"I'm going to need copies of this," I said, patting the contents of the file. "Is there anything else you can tell me?"

Dave looked to Janelle and then explained, "The calls and the emails are directed to Janelle. When he calls in, he won't speak to anyone but her. We noticed that she is similar in age to some of the victims."

"It's creepy," Janelle said, wrapping her arms around herself. "It's my job so what am I going to do?"

A thought occurred to me just then so I asked, "Does the caller sound like anyone you know? Think about how this person talks, the sound of their voice and words they use."

Janelle thought for a few moments and then shook her head no.

I went on, "I know you interviewed George Brewer when Maime first went missing. Did you get any feeling or any sense it was him that was calling?"

"Not at all," Janelle said confidently. "It's not someone who is familiar to me. He doesn't remind me of anyone. It took us a few tips before we even realized it was serious. The caller continued to ask for me. Then as we kept getting to crime scenes first, we knew it was real. We just didn't know what to do."

I got up to leave taking the folder with me. I cautioned them to call Luke the minute they got another call or email.

CHAPTER 65

THE LAST THING COOPER WANTED was to be alone with George. He had really grown to hate the man. While Cooper wasn't known for his temper, he really wanted a chance to beat George to a pulp. He was pretty sure Luke did, too.

Earlier that day, he had called Riley to get an update and see when they'd meet up. Riley didn't sound like herself at all so Cooper pressed for a reason why. Finally, Riley gave him the full update of everything that had happened, adding reluctantly that George had grabbed her in anger and hurt her.

Riley also confided that George's parting remark about Luke was what had her freaked out the most. She couldn't understand why George would be spying on her or driving past her house late at night. Riley said the way George said it was not casual and friendly or even inquisitive. She said George sounded hostile. Riley said it was the first time she'd ever seen him like that.

The idea that any man would put his hands on a woman angered Cooper. Knowing it had been Riley enraged him. George had no idea what he had in Riley, but he was going to make sure he found out. Without Riley still supporting his innocence, George had nothing.

Cooper knocked loudly three times on the front door before George answered.

"I need to ask you some questions." Cooper spat out each word as he moved past George into the house.

George guided them to the dining room where they had sat only days earlier for their initial interview. Cooper felt like months had passed since then.

"I'm going to ask you one last time. Do you know where your wife is?"

"No, I have no idea," George said defensively. "I've told you that. I don't know why I bothered hiring you, and paying you all that money if you can't be bothered to believe me."

"We found your wife's Land Rover. Her wallet and phone were inside," Cooper told him, watching for any shock or surprise on George's face. Cooper didn't see any.

"What does this mean?"

Cooper noted right away that George didn't immediately ask where they found it.

"It means we found her vehicle but no trace of her inside. No clues to where she might be. Aren't you even curious where it was found?"

George shifted in his seat, then said dramatically, "Yes. Where? Who found it?"

"Riley found it in the southeast part of the city. There is a witness who said he saw a woman dropping it off there at about nine-thirty the night Maime went missing. The woman then left with a man. Do you have any idea who that man might be?"

"No, of course not. I haven't even been to that side of town in years. I can't even remember when the last time was now that I think about it. Could the witness identify who it was? Are they sure it's even Maime?"

"We have some basics, but we are keeping that confidential for now. No, we aren't positive it's Maime. The timing fits from when she left the rehab. We know she's gone to that neighborhood to buy drugs. It would be a crazy coincidence if it wasn't."

Cooper didn't wait for George to comment. He continued undeterred. "The car was badly burned. Several minutes after the woman walked away from the car, it caught on fire. The cops think whoever did it was trying to get rid of it. Neighbors saw the fire and put it out."

"Are you saying she left on her own? That Maime just took off? Is that the new theory?" George asked, leaning forward resting his arms on the table. "I'm sure you know by now she was having an affair with Dean and possibly someone else. Obviously, given that and the drug addiction, I guess I didn't know my wife very well at all."

"What's obvious is that you are more concerned about getting laid than your wife's safety," Cooper snapped back.

He couldn't help it. George did this to him. He was smug, and as Riley mentioned earlier, too eager to play the victim.

George didn't respond, just shot Cooper a disgusted look. Cooper walked George through timeframes again from when they suspected the women were dumped into the river. Although the timeframes were a best guess, Cooper was hoping to snag George in more lies. Cooper also walked him through the timelines of the Sara Bloomfield case.

George didn't seem to have an alibi for any of it, other than being at home alone or with Dean. As far as Cooper was concerned, George looked guiltier by the minute.

"Is that it? Are we done?" George asked during a lull in conversation.

"Not even close," Cooper said with a smile. "Care to explain to me why each of the victims found in the Arkansas River had jewelry with your initials on them?"

CHAPTER 66

"IS THIS YOUR IDEA OF SOME SICK JOKE?" George asked incredulously. He got up and walked around his kitchen. His face was getting redder by the second. Cooper wondered if he was trying to keep from losing his temper.

"No, no joke at all, unfortunately for you. The police can connect you with the jewelry on each of the victims, and of course, you are aware of your connection to the missing women. Then there is your added connection to Sara Bloomfield and Shannon McCarty."

Cooper waited for several moments, hoping George would offer up some reasonable explanation. When he didn't, Cooper continued, "George, the police are closing in on you. I'm giving you a chance to explain. As your investigator, I can't help you if you don't tell me what the deal is here."

"I don't have any idea what you are talking about. I heard that on the news about jewelry. I thought it was misinformation."

"It's not. It's fact. Did you engrave jewelry you bought with your initials?"

"Yes, I did," George said angrily. George walked back over to the table, pointed at Cooper and said, "I never gave Sara or Shannon jewelry. I've never killed anyone."

"Then how do you explain the jewelry with your initials on each of the victims?"

"I'm being framed. Someone is trying to ruin my life."

"That's your theory. Who would do this to you?"

"If I knew who, I wouldn't be standing around here waiting to be arrested for crimes I didn't commit. This is why I hired you. It seems you're in bed with the cops just like Riley. I didn't realize she turned into such a traitor."

It took everything Cooper had not to get up and slam George into a wall.

Cooper knew the whole neighborhood could probably hear him, but he snapped back loudly with a raised voice, "That traitor, as you call her, has been working hard to keep you out of jail. You wouldn't see that because you're too selfish. You have no idea the kind of person Riley is. You don't even deserve to breathe the same air."

George didn't offer a rebuttal or response. He kept his head down, not meeting Cooper's eyes.

Cooper demanded, "Show me where your wife keeps her jewelry. I need to know if anything is missing."

Cooper followed George to the master bedroom. Once inside, George went to the walk-in closet to a row of drawers and pulled open the third from the top and took out a heavy jewelry case. George sat the case on a low closet shelf and went through the jewelry piece by piece. Cooper saw expensive looking earrings, emerald and diamond necklaces and intricately designed bracelets.

George looked up at Cooper and then back down to the case. "Maime didn't wear this stuff often. She wore cheaper pieces usually made of beads and stones. Stuff you can find at some of the women's specialty shops around town. I don't know what she had on the day she went missing, but there are definitely pieces of jewelry that should be here that aren't."

"What's missing?" Cooper inquired as he watched George sort through the jewelry again.

"A bracelet, two rings, pair of earrings, an emerald pendant and the ruby and diamond necklace that I just gave Maime for our anniversary. She never wore it unless it was a special night out."

Four of those items had already turned up on the victims. There were still two missing women. Cooper was surprised George told him anything was missing. Cooper wouldn't have known if he was lying or not. George could have told Cooper nothing was missing, but he didn't. He implicated himself further. If he was guilty, he knew which victims were found and what jewelry he had placed on them. Cooper wondered why if he did do it, he'd just admitted it.

"Do you know how long all this has been missing?"

"No, I never go through this case. I can't even tell you the last time I looked in here."

Cooper waited for a better explanation.

George stood his ground. "Look, I told you, I'm being framed. Are you going to help me or not?"

"Who else had access to this case?"

"Maime obviously and her parents. A few friends knew she had expensive jewelry."

"You really have no explanation for what's missing?" Cooper asked sarcastically. He was testing George to see how far he could push him.

George didn't take the bait. He just shook his head no. George put the jewelry case away and walked back to the kitchen. Cooper followed.

They spent the next hour going over properties George had access to. It was a short list. His father's hunting cabin and his parents' home. That's all. All had been searched. If George was keeping victims at any of these places, the police would have found them.

Cooper was frustrated he hadn't found out more. He wasn't sure what he expected. That George was just going to confess, say he was a killer and lead him to his wife and Laura. George still looked guilty, but Cooper agreed with Luke. There just wasn't much connecting George other than a missing wife and mistress and the jewelry. No real physical evidence, no witnesses, and no murder weapon.

Cooper thought he'd try one last thing. Walking towards the living room, Cooper turned to George. "I'm sure you heard on the news the other night, the victims may have been drugged. Do you know anything about the drug succinylcholine?"

"No, nothing," George replied. "What is it?"

Cooper didn't bother to explain. George lied so often and so well, Cooper couldn't tell if he had just told him the truth. He only told him to see George's reaction, but Cooper saw no recognition in his expression.

Cooper left through the front door, made it a few steps, but turned back to George with fire in his eyes. "Riley told me you put your hands on her and that you are driving by her house at night. There are more people than you realize who care about her. If any harm should come to her, there's a good chance that person who did it is going to end up floating in the river with the rest of the victims. Understand me?"

Cooper didn't wait for George's response. He walked to his truck knowing his anger just got the best of him. He'd technically just made a threat against the life of his client – a first in his career.

Then again, Cooper thought as he drove away, George's life wasn't worth much anymore anyway.

CHAPTER 67

LUKE WRAPPED UP HIS WORK and was just about to leave the office to hunt down a few more leads when Tyler motioned Luke over to his desk. Luke stood behind him waiting, catching just bits of conversation.

"How long has she been missing?" Tyler asked into the phone. He jotted down notes on the pad in front of him and motioned for Luke to take a look.

Luke read the notes in anticipation. He was hoping it wasn't another body found. It wasn't. Hot Springs Police Department was calling about a missing woman from their area they felt might fit the description of one of the victims found in Little Rock.

Tyler continued with the call gathering a basic description of the woman, and then requested Hot Springs police fax over the missing woman's photo.

Tyler ended the call and turned to Luke. "Sounds like this last victim we found. Her name is Lisa Cramer."

"How long has she been missing?"

"Since last Saturday night. She came to Little Rock to see a band playing at a bar downtown and hasn't been seen since," Tyler explained.

"Who called in the report?"

"A friend of hers called it in initially when she didn't return on Sunday. Hot Springs police assumed she'd met someone up here and just stayed for a few days. They didn't take the report seriously. By Friday morning, when she still wasn't back, her coworkers called the police. Then they took it seriously. After seeing the press conference, they thought they should give us a call."

"Who did she meet up here?" Luke asked, leaning against Tyler's desk reading over the notes from the call.

"No one seemed to know. Her friend said she drove up alone but was going to meet friends. They said Lisa was a private person, really independent, and if she didn't offer details, friends knew not to ask," Tyler explained just as the fax machine came to life.

Luke pulled the fax page from the machine. He looked at the photo of the woman. He couldn't be absolutely certain, of course, but he was pretty sure Lisa was the last woman they pulled from the river.

"Call them back and tell them to get up here with someone who can identify her," Luke demanded. "I'll call Purvis and meet them at the morgue. Tell them to meet us in two hours. That should give them enough time. This can't wait."

Luke quickly walked over to his desk and placed a call to the medical examiner's office.

At just about six-thirty that evening, Luke walked Mark Klein, the detective from Hot Springs, accompanied by Lisa's sister, Amy, and friend, Sharon, into the morgue. Luke had prepped them that there was a possibility this was Lisa and asked both women if they were okay. They said they were about as good as the circumstance would allow.

Amy explained to Luke that she just wanted to get this over with. She was very concerned if it was Lisa how she'd break the news to their aging parents who had recently moved to Florida.

Purvis met them at the front door, and then walked them through a series of stark white hallways with blinding fluorescent lighting. He pushed open two swinging double doors that led into the room that held the bodies in the stacked metal freezers. One of the drawers was already pulled out, the outline of a body visible under the white sheet.

Purvis walked over. Luke, the detective, and the women followed. Purvis asked if they were ready. When both women nodded yes, Purvis pulled the sheet back from the victim's face. Looking down at the victim, both women began to softly sob. Luke motioned with his head for Purvis to pull the sheet back. Luke guided them back to the front office.

"That's her. That's my sister," Amy informed them through sobs. "What happened to her? When did you find her?"

"Her body was found yesterday in the river by a fisherman. She was strangled," Luke explained softly with as much compassion as he could. He remembered what it was like to be them when his sister was found.

"Who does she know up here that she would be meeting?"

Sharon responded, "Lisa lived in Little Rock in the Heights until three years ago. She had many friends in the area still and drove up often, at least a few times a month."

"Why did she move to Hot Springs?" Luke inquired.

"She had ended a relationship just about three years ago and when her ex-boyfriend got a new girlfriend, she started harassing Lisa all the time. It was unbearable so she moved to get away from it all. The break up was hard enough for her. The other woman just added to the pain. She wanted a fresh start."

"Why was the guy's new girlfriend harassing her?" Detective Mark Klein asked.

Luke was pretty sure where this was going. The story sounded eerily similar to Riley's.

"Lisa's ex had cheated on her with this woman and she was doing everything to make sure they had no more contact. Not that Lisa wanted anything to do with either of them, but the woman wouldn't stop. She made such a nuisance of herself; it was even putting Lisa's job in jeopardy."

Sharon described some of the calls and interactions the two women had.

Luke asked, "Any chance you remember the ex-boyfriend's name or the girlfriend's name?"

"I could never forget it. You should know them though. They are all over the news — George and Maime Brewer. Lisa was far too good for the whole situation. Seems he went and married the tramp."

CHAPTER 68

"**DO YOU THINK** people get what they deserve?" Luke asked, sitting down at his desk across from Tyler. He had spent the last two hours taking a formal statement from Sharon and Amy. Then he connected Amy with the police department's victim advocate who would help her make the call to their parents.

"What do you mean, like karma?" Tyler asked, shifting through the pile of paperwork on his desk.

"I guess. I don't know," Luke sighed. He kicked his legs up and reclined his desk chair. He laced his fingers together over his taut stomach and thought about the meaning of it all.

"I don't mean these victims but George and Maime. I haven't heard one good thing about these people since we started this case. You hate to ever say anything bad about a victim, but Maime seemed like she was one screwed up chick. George is no better. They seem perfect for each other actually. I mean nobody deserves to die, but these two seemed to have created all the negativity and hate they got back in their lives. It's hard for me to feel bad for either one of them," Luke explained. His thoughts were on Riley.

He wondered if she knew how lucky she was that it hadn't worked out with George. Sometimes you just have to be thankful for the road not taken.

"What's gotten into you? You don't talk like this," Tyler chided, looking over at Luke.

Luke waved him off. "I don't know, man, tired, I guess. It's just Sara Bloomfield and Lisa Cramer seemed like really good people. Even Shannon McCarty may not have had the most appropriate job, but everyone we talked to said she was a really good person. No one seems to have anything good to say about George and Maime."

"Where you going with this?"

"Just hear me out. Let's take Riley. She's great. She's this amazing woman and got all snared up with George. Same thing happened to her that happened to Lisa. She dated George. George cheated on Maime with Riley. Riley didn't know. Once they found out about each other, Riley backed off and went about her life. Maime harassed her and literally drove her out of town the same way it happened with Lisa. Sara is connected to George, too. Laura, his current mistress, is also missing and so is Maime. All these people are connected not just to George but to Maime, too."

"What are you saying?" Tyler asked, now standing by Luke's desk looking down at him.

Luke shrugged trying to get the picture clearer in his head.

"Not to diminish your theory," Tyler countered. "Sara was nothing more than his real estate agent. We don't even know if Maime knew about her. Riley is perfectly safe. We don't even know who the third victim is. Are you starting to believe that it's about revenge and someone is framing George? That's his theory. I think it's crazy. He's got means, motive and opportunity. Nobody else."

"I don't know what I'm saying," Luke said, sitting up straight in his chair, rubbing his tired eyes. There were still too many missing pieces for it to make any sense.

Turning to Tyler, Luke said, "Go home to your wife tonight. I'm going to get Lisa's picture out to the media and go downtown and canvass the bars with her photo and see if anyone recognizes her. We can get back at this in the morning."

CHAPTER 69

AFTER TYLER LEFT FOR THE NIGHT, Luke took Lisa's photo and made some copies of it. He called Ben from the newspaper and asked if they could run a story in the morning edition. Ben explained it was a little late, but he'd see what he could do. Luke faxed him over the photo and a short statement.

"You don't know where she went missing?" Ben asked Luke after he received the photo.

"No. She was headed to a bar downtown and that is as far as we know right now. I'm going tonight to try to track down some leads," Luke explained.

"We'll run it. If you get more details keep me updated. We can add to the story," Ben said, ending the call.

Luke made a few more calls to some of the news stations. Hopefully, by the ten o'clock news, Lisa's picture would be all over the city and people with any information could call into the tip line at the police department. There was a growing reward in this case. Families had put up most of the money. Luke wasn't sure about the last total, but he thought it was around $45,000.

After faxing Lisa's photo to the last couple news stations, Luke got into his car and drove to the River Market. Luke knew there were at least eight places that had live music on a Saturday night that Lisa could have gone.

Luke found a parking spot near where they had found the first victim. One by one he canvassed the bars showing Lisa's photo to the bar staff and the managers. No luck. No one had seen her or at least remembered her. Luke knew it was a long shot.

He hoped someone would remember seeing her. Little Rock wasn't a very big town when it got right down to it. People got to know faces if not names after a while.

Finally, he hit pay dirt on his last stop. It was at Stickyz that he found the information he needed. Luke had been there himself to see a few bands. It was still early enough that the band for the night wasn't on yet. Most people there were early drinkers or having dinner. Luke walked in, headed straight to the bar, and showed Lisa's photo to the guy tending bar.

The bartender barely looked at the photo as he waited on customers. He didn't say much of anything. Luke encouraged him to take another look.

The guy finally stopped, walked over to Luke and looked at the photo. "Yeah I know her. She's been in here on the weekends to see some bands. I don't know her name. She's a good tipper and nice so I remember her."

"Was she here last Saturday night?"

"Maybe. There were a lot of people in here so I'm not sure. What she do?" he asked dismissively, lining clean glasses on the bar shelf.

"It's not what she's done. It's what was done to her. She's one of the women we pulled from the river. She's dead," Luke said matter of fact.

The bartender stopped, wiped his hand on a bar towel, and extended his hand out to Luke. "That's awful. She was really nice. I'm Mike, I'm the manager just covering for my bartender until he gets here."

Mike pointed to a line of tickets on the bar and said, "Let me get through these orders. Then I'll go back and pull some receipts from last Saturday. She usually paid by credit card. I'll see if we have the receipt. It will show what time she paid. You can at least maybe see what time she left here."

Luke took a seat and waited. Mike finished up his work and walked into a back room. When he came out, he was carrying a credit card slip.

"She paid her tab just after one in the morning. It was a pretty hefty bill though. Eighty-eight dollars. It looks like she was buying drinks for someone else, too. She couldn't have racked up this high of a bar bill alone and still walk out of the place."

"Do you know who was with her?"

Mike nodded. "Yeah, she came in with the same guy a few times. I don't know if they are an item or what. But same guy, no one else. Actually, you probably know him. He's a cop. I think his name is Norwalk. He goes to my gym so I've seen him around. Just my opinion, but I always thought she could do a lot better than him."

CHAPTER 70

"I'M SORRY MOM IS WORRIED. I can't just quit in the middle of an investigation and come home," I grumbled to my sister Liv. Cradling the phone between my ear and shoulder, I carried groceries from my car into the house. I couldn't stand not having any edible food in the house. After my interview with the news station, I hit the Heights Kroger. As far as I was concerned, I was in for the night. I had the massive list of cell numbers to go through for Luke anyway.

Liv, my little sister by two years, continued to grouch at me. I continued to protest. We were about as different as two sisters could get. She was blonde where I was auburn. She was flighty. I was far more serious. After getting fired from several jobs she attempted, I gave her a job as my assistant. All that really meant was she showed up to my office and read magazines, flirted with my clients and never bothered to answer the phone. She still lived at home, and for all intents and purposes, was my mother's spy. Too bad she couldn't put those skills to work on actual paying cases.

"Women are dying all around you. Why are you making us worry, Riley? You're being really selfish," Liv said, laying on the guilt. She had a flare for the dramatic.

"Tell Mom I'm fine. It will be a little more time. Then I'll be home like I never even left. How's my dog?"

"Perfect. Come home, Riley. We need to talk. I have a new boyfriend. I don't know if you're going to be happy about it," Liv said with hesitation in her voice.

I knew she didn't really care if I was home or not. She liked it when she was the favorite and our mother was angry with me. It took the heat off of her.

"Yeah, I'm sure I'll like him. Does Mom?"

"Mom thinks we are great together. Oh hey, another call. I have to go," Liv sing-songed and then hung up. I didn't even get to say goodbye.

I pulled the phone away from my ear, staring at the screen wondering if I should call her back. I thought better of it and called my ex-husband Jeff who had been calling me every few hours for the last few days. It's not that I was ignoring him. I just didn't feel like explaining why I was in Little Rock. He, my mother and sister were as thick as thieves. It hadn't mattered that we had been divorced for eight years.

"Finally. So good of you to call," Jeff said sarcastically.

"What's up? All your message said was you had something important to tell me," I said impatiently. I moved around my kitchen putting my groceries away, hoping he'd just get to the point.

"I'm seeing someone," Jeff said matter of fact.

"Well good for you. It's about time you started dating again."

"It's your sister."

I set my bag of apples down on the counter. I wasn't sure I heard him right. "What's my sister?"

"The woman I'm dating. Don't get angry," Jeff said quickly. "We've been spending time together. Over the last few months, it just developed."

I couldn't immediately respond. I wasn't sure what to say. My ex-husband was dating my little sister. I didn't really get the connection. Jeff was extremely intelligent, almost nerdy, and my sister, well she was my sister. Intelligent was not really a word I would use to describe her. Bubbly, brainless and buxom usually came to mind.

"Hey, you there?" Jeff asked cautiously.

"Yeah, I'm here. Well if you're happy, go for it," I said and actually meant it. I was over Jeff. I had been for years. While I couldn't actually see him with my sister, if it worked for them, who was I to stand in the way. I had no idea my sister was attracted to Jeff. Hopefully, they'd be good for each other.

"You mean that?" Jeff asked. I could hear the hope in his voice.

"Yes, definitely. Have fun, but tell them I'm not coming home yet. I know that's what you wanted, too. Take care of them for me."

He said he would, didn't even argue with me, and we ended the call.

I had just finished making chicken marsala and a salad when Emma called my name as she walked in the back door.

"Did you hear they identified the last victim?" Emma asked, hugging me. Then she poured herself some tea from the fridge and sat down at the kitchen table.

"No, I've been out all day. Tell me."

"Lisa Cramer. Doesn't that sound familiar? Sounds familiar to me. She's from Hot Springs."

It did sound familiar. I couldn't quite place where I heard that name before. Lisa Cramer. I said it over and over again in my head, trying to retrieve how her name was connected. Then it hit me.

"I think Lisa Cramer was the name of the woman George dated right before Maime. I remember him telling me about her when Maime was harassing me. He said it wasn't the first time Maime had harassed someone. She had done it to his previous girlfriend."

"Oh, that's right," Emma said dramatically. "I remember you telling me that but couldn't place it."

I fixed my plate and made one for Emma. I carried both to the table and slid it in front of her. I didn't ask her if she wanted food. Emma always looked hungry. I assumed she'd eat.

I talked in between bites, updating her about where things were going with Luke and the case. The case itself was clearer than what was happening with Luke. The case still made no sense at all so that was saying something.

Emma filled me in on the neighborhood gossip. It seemed everyone thought George was guilty and a serial killer. The neighborhood was alive with gossip. All the older ladies were talking about the last time they saw George. They shared stories of seeing him at Kroger and how charming he was. Even how he had been sweet and flirted with them. George didn't care how old they were.

Nobody was happy women were dying, but gossip and speculation were commonplace in our Heights neighborhood. They were more than excited for the national news stations that were camped out on the streets, taking photos and live shots, interviewing the locals and making our little neighborhood famous. They acted put off, but you could tell they loved the attention.

"If I wasn't stressed enough, Jeff just called me and told me he's dating my sister," I said, finally taking the last bite.

Emma looked up from her plate with a wide toothy grin. Then she laughed. We both did.

CHAPTER 71

AFTER EMMA LEFT, I poured more sweet tea and pulled all the cellphone records out from the folder Luke had given me. Sitting down on my couch, I went to work. Carefully, line by line, I went through Shannon's, Sara's, Maime's and Laura's cellphone records.

Several numbers were repeated throughout each person's records. I checked them against some of the numbers that detectives had called or looked up and confirmed. There was a master list of phone numbers with names and addresses for each that I could use as a reference.

Sara's were mostly clients. Maime's and Laura's were a mix of work and personal. Shannon's were hard to tell. I guessed a mix of personal and her clients. I wasn't sure what Luke was hoping I'd find that his detectives hadn't already. All he said was he hoped a fresh set of eyes looking over all four at once might show something.

The task was tedious. The numbers started to blur together one indistinguishable from the next. There was a knock at the door just as my eyes glazed over. I was grateful for the interruption.

It was Cooper. I had forgotten he planned to come over that night to go over the case again. We weren't getting a chance to work together as much as we thought so spending some time comparing notes was important.

Like Emma who never gets to relax over a meal because she's always taking care of her husband and daughter, Cooper always looked hungry to me. I assumed it was because he was a bachelor whose dining was the equivalent of take-out. My mother never had the ability to cook for less than a brood of people. I realized I was the same way. If I'm just cooking for myself, I have leftovers for days.

Serving him a plate of food in the living room, I encouraged him to update me.

"George still insists he's being framed," Cooper said, devouring his dinner. "I had him go through Maime's jewelry to see if anything was missing. There is just enough jewelry missing for all the victims including Maime and Laura. Hardly a coincidence."

"Do you think Maime and Laura are dead? We just haven't found them yet?" I inquired, pulling the blanket around me. It was cold. I thought about starting a fire in the fireplace, but it was too late.

"I don't know. I can't really say for sure. Sara Bloomfield was missing for about a week before she was found. I just heard on the news they identified the last victim recovered. The report said she'd been missing since last Saturday. Luke said the medical examiner thought the victims were being held, which is probably true given what we know. Maime and Laura have been missing for longer than Sara and this other victim. Maybe there's a reason they are being held longer than the other victims. Maybe we just haven't found them yet," Cooper explained.

Earlier that day, I had told Cooper about what happened with George. Cooper was furious, so I was glad he spoke to George without a major fight. Not that I thought Cooper would but anything seemed possible these days. When Cooper was done with the details that he deemed important and relevant, I filled him in on what I had found.

"I talked to Janelle, the reporter who asked the drug question at the press conference. I got a little information that I need to share with Luke. I think the killer is definitely calling in tips to the news."

"That's weird. Why would he tip us off to the drug and the victims being held? That doesn't make any sense," Cooper said, looking thoroughly perplexed.

"Maybe he really wants to be stopped. Some killers have a compulsion to kill, and calling in is a cry for help. For others, it's a way to keep the media telling their story. They feed off the kill and then the notoriety that follows. Others it's a cat and mouse game. It shows they are smarter than the cops. Maybe they didn't think the cops would test for that drug, and for whatever reason, the killer wanted us to know it's being used."

"That's true. Purvis said it's not common and definitely not something he would have tested for," Cooper reminded me.

"That drug is a pretty big detail to not know about in these cases. It would seem to me the killer wanted us to know exactly how he worked. I can't imagine what the victims went through. It's one thing to be strangled and at least be able to fight back. But to be totally immobilized, awake and not be able to do a thing to try to save your own life, that's the stuff of nightmares," I said, shuddering.

Even when I tried to imagine what the victims went through; it was too terrifying to picture. To know you are going to die and not be able to do anything to help yourself. It would be my worst nightmare.

CHAPTER 72

COOPER WAS GETTING READY TO HEAD HOME
just as Luke arrived. Cooper sat back down on the couch and gave
Luke the full update about the jewelry. When Cooper was done, I
filled Luke in on the news tips.

"There's a good chance the killer is using the media to give us
information," I said. "They have a phone number and email address.
Maybe someone in computer forensics can trace the emails."

Luke agreed it could be possible. Stifling a yawn, Cooper
excused himself and headed home. Before he left, Cooper reminded
us he had a full day of surveillance on another case that would take
up most of the next day so we probably wouldn't see him. We made
a plan to catch up Monday. Then he left.

Luke followed behind Cooper and locked the front door. He
watched me as I moved over to the couch with my blanket and
snuggled up. Luke flipped off the overhead living room light, leaving
us just in the soft glow of the hallway table lamp. Luke watched me
for a few seconds. Then he kicked off his shoes and emptied the
contents of his pockets on the table – keys, cellphone and wallet. He
stopped for a moment and looked down at me again. All at once he
seemed to make up his mind. In a flash, he pulled his shirt over his
head, slipped his pants down to the floor and peeled off his socks.
He stood there in his white undershirt and red boxer briefs.

I let out a giggle and asked, "Are you comfortable now?"

"No, not yet." Luke tackled me, pulling my blanket around the both of us and adjusted me so I was lying against his chest with his arms wrapped around me. I laid back into him, resting my head on his chest as he lightly brushed my hair away from my face.

"We have to talk about us now," Luke whispered.

As much as I didn't want to have this conversation, I knew he was right.

"Why did you leave me? Did I do something wrong?" Luke asked softly.

I could hear the pain still in this voice. He was always so much better at this than I was. So much better at being vulnerable and expressing how he felt. He was the first one to say I love you, the first one to tell me how he was feeling. It was harder for me. It always had been.

"You did everything right," I finally said between deep breaths. I may have been a journalist who relied on her words, but I wasn't good at this.

"Go on," Luke said, prodding me. He traced his fingers lightly over my arm, snuggling me in closer to him.

"I thought maybe you were too good to be true. You were perfect for me in every way. I was still dealing with how much George had hurt me. Maime was still harassing me. I didn't want to love again or get you mixed up in all of that. I didn't want to leave myself vulnerable to that kind of hurt again. When I felt myself falling in love with you, I wanted to protect you and me so I left. I'm not good at relationships," I confessed. In some ways it felt good to finally say it.

"You were great at our relationship right up to the moment you left," Luke reassured me.

"It doesn't have to be hard, Riley. We had a lot of fun. We were great friends in addition to being great partners. We got it pretty perfect."

"We were," I agreed. "That's part of what scared me. I'd never had a relationship like that before. I'd never met someone with whom I could just be myself and he still loved me so unconditionally. I guess I left before you could leave me. I thought it would hurt less that way."

"Did it?"

"No," I admitted truthfully.

"I would have never left you. Ever," Luke said, stressing the last word. "Where do we go from here? Are you going to stay?"

"I've been thinking about it. My business is slow up in New York. I need a change. I can't promise I can be the woman you need," I responded nervously.

"Let me decide what kind of woman I need. Do you love me, Riley?"

I could almost hear him holding his breath waiting for my response.

I turned my body so I could look into his eyes. He looked deep into mine, and I kissed him. "Yes. I always have. I never stopped. I might have gone away, but I loved you every minute of every day I was away. I love you still."

"You're beautiful. You know that?" Luke said, planting a kiss on the bridge of my nose.

"Do you still love me, even after what I did?" I asked. A part of me knew the answer, but that part of me that had been so hurt still wasn't healed yet. I was waiting for the other shoe to drop. It didn't.

"You never have to question it. I love you and will always love you."

We kissed more passionately this time and when we finally broke apart Luke looked at me and broke into a broad grin, "You know what, I'm not so tired tonight."

He led me up to my bed and left the hall light on so we could still see each other. Luke gently took off each article of my clothing kissing my naked flesh as he went. I stood enjoying every single kiss. I've never been self-conscious with him. I knew he loved every inch of me, every flaw and curve on me.

When we were both naked, he laid me down on the bed, kissed me passionately again and started a trail of kisses down my body. I was impatient though. It had been too long. I wanted to feel him inside me. We'd have time for everything else he was so spectacular at later. I nudged his shoulder and gave him a look he knew all too well. Luke grinned at me, rested his cheek against my belly and laughed at my impatience.

When he finally entered me, he looked deep into my eyes and whispered, "This has always felt like coming home."

I couldn't have said it better or agreed more.

CHAPTER 73

LATER, AFTER WE WERE BOTH SATED, my head resting against Luke's chest, my fingers trailing softly over him, I finally asked what I had been wanting to since the first body was found.

"Are you doing okay with this case? I know it brings up old memories about your sister."

Luke had first told me about his sister's murder two months after we started seeing one another. It was in this very bed one night after making love much like tonight. I could hear in his voice how painful it was for him to talk about and how disappointed he was in himself for not solving her murder yet, even though it wasn't his job.

The Fayetteville detectives still working on the case couldn't solve it. Luke, though, felt he should be better than them and bring his sister's killer to justice. I agreed that justice should be served. But unlike Luke, I didn't think he was solely responsible or a failure for not making it happen.

"I'm okay. It's hard. I can't let another case go unsolved. Other families will suffer the same way mine does," Luke said. "But that's not really my only stress. Norwalk is gunning for my job and out to make me look like an idiot. More women keep dying. I just can't catch a break."

I could hear his frustration.

"We're getting close. I can feel it. I think it's only a matter of time. I think you've made some progress in the last few days. It's just come at you so quickly. I don't think anyone expects you to solve a case like this overnight. Think about how long it took to solve other cases like this. The Atlanta Child Murders. The Green River Killer. Luke, some cases like this go a long time unsolved. You're doing a great job. Don't put more pressure on yourself than what is already there," I explained, trying to reassure him.

"My parents called the other night. You should have heard my mother. I know she loves me, but she always sounds disappointed in me."

Luke's parents lived in Hillcrest about ten minutes from me and about five minutes from him. I knew Luke had Sunday dinner with them every week if work allowed. He was also at their place several times during the week. He had a great relationship with them. I knew what he was saying wasn't true.

I'd met his parents, and they adore him. His parents were more disappointed he hadn't found a nice girl to settle down with and give them grandchildren than they were about him not solving his sister's murder. His parents placed no expectation on him to do that. In fact, they had cautioned him to accept the loss and let it go. The disappointment Luke felt was his own. I told him so.

"Your mother is disappointed that you haven't given her grandchildren yet. I've met your mother, Luke. She loves you," I scolded him, slapping his belly for emphasis.

"You know she loves you, too. She is the one that kept me hoping you'd come to your senses," Luke teased me back. "Maybe we can give her some grandbabies right now."

Luke pulled me up so I was straddling him, looking down into his face.

"Don't say that. I'm not cut out to be a mom, you know that. I can't keep plants alive," I said only half meaning it. Truth is though, I really couldn't keep plants alive. I even broke a ceramic cactus once.

Looking down into his eyes I said seriously, "Come on, really, are you okay? I'm worried about you."

"As long as I have you, I'll always be okay. I won't lie, it was unbearable without you. If you're back, all will be right in my life," Luke said sincerely.

Luke's hands were resting on my hips. He slid them down, grabbing my backside. He squeezed me playfully. I laughed, squirming around under his caress.

Then he got serious again.

"Have you called your mom to tell her I'm back in Little Rock?" I asked.

"I did. She wanted me to bring you by for dinner. I wanted to wait until we had talked and figured out what we we're doing. Are we going to make this official?"

"I guess so, Lucas Morgan, but we have a ton of work to do before we get to really enjoy each other. Someone's got to break it to my mother that I'm moving back to Little Rock."

"That is all you, kid," Luke teased, tickling me. Then he added seriously, "Your mother scares me, and I haven't even met her. I would like to be a fly on the wall when you tell her you are moving back to Little Rock."

CHAPTER 74

LUKE FELT THOROUGHLY EXHAUSTED, but he couldn't be happier. His body hadn't ached this much since Riley had left town. They may have had bumps in their relationship, but the sex they never got wrong. It was more than that though. He hated to sound like a girl, but what he really enjoyed the most was just being close to her. He hated to leave her bed earlier that morning. He had work to do though, and finally, some he was really going to enjoy.

Luke, Captain Meadows and Tyler were finally going to confront Norwalk. Luke couldn't wait to see his smug face crumble. The man deserved everything he got. Cap wasn't taking any chances though. He wanted to hear Norwalk's side before they suspended him.

They had a strict rule about side investigative work, and blackmail was not something he wanted associated with the police force. Cap was willing to let Norwalk either incriminate himself or set the record straight.

"What do you want? Let's get this over with so I can go back to enjoying my Sunday," Norwalk spat as he walked through the conference room door to join the others.

Luke took a seat between Cap and Tyler, directly across from Norwalk. Luke arranged the papers in front of him and asked, "What can you tell me about Dean Beaumont?"

Norwalk didn't even flinch. He looked to the captain and asked, "What is this?"

"Answer the question," Captain Meadows said in a tone that meant all business.

"Nothing. He's connected to Maime LaRue Brewer, right?" Norwalk asked, slumping down in his seat and resting his arm across the seat next to him. It was clear to Luke that even now, Norwalk thought he was untouchable.

Luke pulled out one of Cooper's photos that showed Norwalk heading into Dean's house. He slid it over to Norwalk, tapping the picture and said only one word, "Explain."

Norwalk looked down, but his expression never changed. He pushed the photo back towards Luke. "This is crap. I don't have to answer your questions. I haven't done anything wrong. I'm leaving," Norwalk said angrily and then started to get up.

"Sit," Luke demanded. "Dean Beaumont gave us a statement that said you were hired to do surveillance on Maime regarding her possible drug use. Instead of turning over that evidence, you caught evidence of their affair and blackmailed him."

Before Norwalk could answer, Captain Meadows interrupted and said evenly but sternly, "Before you answer, you should probably know we are only giving you one shot to save yourself. You can either help us with what we need to know or not. Either way, we have enough evidence to suspend you. The outcome is up to you."

"Suspend me then," Norwalk grunted angrily. "I'm not telling you a thing. You think I'm dumb enough to incriminate myself?"

Tyler spoke up. "No, I thought you might be smart enough to save yourself and provide us with valuable evidence that might help this investigation. If what Dean said is true, you could have evidence of who Maime was with when she bought the drugs."

Norwalk sat for several moments. Luke was sure he was probably mulling over whether to tell them what he knew or not. Norwalk finally said, "If I did this, and I'm not saying I did, I never saw her buy drugs."

Then he slid his chair away from the table, scrapping the legs against the tile floor. He stood as if ready to leave.

"Sit back down. We aren't done," Luke commanded.

Norwalk stood still, but he didn't sit.

"Do you know this woman?" Luke said, sliding a picture of Lisa Cramer across the table to Norwalk.

"Yeah the last body you found. So?" Norwalk asked.

"You were one of the last people to see her alive. Care to explain your relationship with her?"

"Wait a minute," Norwalk said, slamming his fists into the table. "That's what this is about? You can't make a case stick on George so you're pointing the finger at me? I don't have to stand around and answer any more of this. Suspend me. I don't care."

Norwalk turned and walked out of the conference room. He slammed the door behind him.

Norwalk had played right into their hands. It was the exact response they had been anticipating. Nobody actually thought Norwalk was going to calmly sit and answer their questions.

Luke picked up the phone and placed a call. When Cooper answered, Luke said, "He's leaving the station. Keep us updated as to where he goes."

Earlier that morning, Luke had been excitedly telling Riley about confronting Norwalk. In their conversation, it occurred to both of them at practically the same time that if Norwalk was dumb enough to blackmail Dean, maybe he was also blackmailing the other guy. If both George and Dean really didn't buy Maime's drugs, and on the slight chance both were telling the truth, that left some mystery guy out there. There was an off chance Norwalk would know who that was. He could be the lead that could break this case wide open.

Riley had suggested that maybe Cooper could find someone else to handle his surveillance case and continue to tail Norwalk since he had already done it so well. Luke agreed. When he asked Cooper to do it, he was all too eager to help.

Now the hard part – all they could do was wait.

CHAPTER 75

SUNDAY NIGHT WAS COLD even for November. I sat on my couch with a fire roaring in the fireplace. I sipped a glass of hot tea. Luke was out running down leads. My hands were tied at this point. I was waiting for my next task. I tried going through the cellphone records some more, but my eyes were tired. I laid my head back and closed my eyes for a few minutes, resting, thinking about a way out of this case, of this mess I'd landed in, sadly of my own doing.

I missed my dog. I even missed my mom and sister. This was my home, but right now I felt really far away from everyone and everything that felt safe. The lock turning in my front door jolted me out of my peaceful solitude. It was Luke.

I stood to greet him with a hug and kiss, but he brushed past me. No hug, no kiss, no warmth. He was so different from the previous night. I tried not to take it personally. I could tell he was stressed. "We need to talk. Cooper will be here in a few minutes."

"Okay, what's going on?" I asked, sitting back down in the chair opposite the couch.

Luke folded the blanket I had thrown over me before he arrived. He sat forward on the couch with his arms resting on his knees, hands folded in front of him.

"We need to get a handle on this case. I didn't make any headway today. All dead ends."

I nodded but stayed silent. I didn't disagree, but wasn't sure what he had in mind. We were doing all I thought we could be doing, given the circumstances.

Luke went on, "There's something we're missing. I'm just not sure what. I need you to put every feeling you've ever had for George aside. I need you clearheaded."

I was about to take offense. I thought we were past this, but just then, Cooper pulled his truck into my driveway and came into the house. He sat next to Luke on the couch. I offered them both something to drink and eat. They declined.

Luke turned to Cooper and started to explain the impromptu meeting. "I was just telling Riley, she needs to get her head in the game. Put all emotion for George aside and look at this thing logically and rationally. There is something we are missing. I think Riley holds the key to solving this."

"I don't know any more than I'm telling you. I thought we had gotten past this," I said disappointed. I wanted to shout and tell him he was a fool, but I didn't think arguing would get us anywhere. I wanted to defend myself that my feelings for George weren't getting in the way. I was worried a little though that maybe Luke was right.

"I don't think I understand either. What do you mean Riley knows how to solve these cases?" Cooper asked Luke.

"Maybe I said it wrong," Luke admitted.

Then he sat silently with a look on his face like he was searching for the right words so we'd understand. After a few moments, Luke explained, "I just think Riley knows George better than anyone. If she can look at this without the emotion, but still use everything she knows, maybe it will spark something. If we can get inside his head, maybe we can find what we're missing."

Cooper nodded in agreement. "That's assuming George is our guy." He looked at me and asked calmly, "Can you do that? Forget how you feel about George and what you think you know about him?"

"I can certainly try. What do you want to know?" I shifted uncomfortably in my seat. I was definitely feeling on the spot.

Luke started, "Think back over your relationship with him. What was he like when you first met? Did anything ever strike you as odd or strange behavior?"

I thought for several moments about when I first met George in Boston and over the course of our relationship. Then I thought about the times here in Little Rock and how he had grabbed me. I didn't want to tell Luke, but other than that, I wasn't really coming up with anything unusual. Nothing too out of the ordinary for a man cheating on his girlfriend and then one that gets caught.

Getting caught. I rolled those thoughts around in my head some more, something was catching. I didn't know if it was important.

"This may mean nothing, but George was always a runner. He ran away from confrontation and discord. He asked me a few times if I wanted to run away with him. I always thought he was kidding, but he might not have been."

Luke looked at me thoughtfully, "Go where?"

"That's just it. I don't know. He never said. He would just get real stressed and ask me to leave everything behind and go with him. I always laughed it off. Once I asked him where and all he said was he had a place. When I pressed him, he never said, just smiled and said it was his secret. He said he'd only tell me if I said yes. I never thought he was serious."

"What else?" Luke asked.

"George was just never confrontational with women. The times we disagreed, he'd just distance himself for a while and then come back like nothing ever happened. I would try to talk about it, but he'd just shut down. Even when he ended it, he dumped me over the phone. Just told me to never call him again, and I didn't. He was the one who initiated contact later but acted like nothing had happened."

"Is that really so unusual given the circumstances?" Cooper asked. He got up and started to move around the room.

"No, I guess not, but to just never speak of it again. It's like cementing a volcano, eventually it will blow."

"Keep going," Luke said, prodding me. "Did you ever hear him fight with Maime?"

"No." I answered quickly. Then I remembered something I hadn't thought about in a long time. "Yes, I did, once. I had sent him an email when he was traveling for work. Just a flirty sweet message like we had always done. But he responded back strangely asking for my phone number. I thought he was kidding so I didn't respond. About an hour later, my phone rings, and it's a woman. A friend of Maime's telling me that George was involved with someone. He was engaged. They called me like twenty times that day. I never spoke to them. I let all the calls go to voicemail. It was all very immature.

"George called me that night and explained that Maime had gotten into his email and read several messages. He asked me to cover for him. He said he was going to call me the next day and tell me off in front of her. Make it look like I was pursuing him and wouldn't stop. But when he called, I didn't answer the phone. He yelled at my voicemail like he was talking to me. I heard Maime crying in the background. He just kept trying to appease her, but she was sobbing and wailing. It was all extremely dramatic. Then I heard a slap and the call ended. I don't know if she slapped him or he slapped her. I guess I didn't want to think about it. He called me later that night after she went home."

"Do you know if there was ever domestic violence between them?" Luke asked, looking between Cooper and me not really focusing on either of us.

"No, to be honest I sort of assumed she slapped him. She was always the more volatile one or at least that's how it appeared. Not one person we interviewed indicated there ever was."

"Based on his actions with Dean, he's got a temper with men, but with women he plays the submissive role or at least he acts like he does?" Cooper inquired, still pacing.

We nodded in agreement. The women had been subdued. They couldn't have fought him.

"I still don't understand the motive," I interrupted. "Even if I could admit he killed Maime, I don't get the motive for the others."

This wasn't about defending George. I just still couldn't find a plausible explanation for how George could kill that many women.

"Maybe he just snapped. Killed Maime and then just lost it," Luke countered. He looked over at Cooper. They exchanged a look I didn't understand.

"What?" I asked tentatively.

Luke patted the couch beside him for me to come over next to him. When I was seated, he said, "Riley, will you please wear a wire and go talk to him? If we have any shot at a confession, you're the one that will get it. Use what you know. Confront him. See what he does. See what you can get out of him. If he really has a secret hideaway, maybe he will tell you. I'll keep you safe. We'll be outside and will come in if anything goes wrong. Please."

Cooper shot me a pleading look and reiterated, "We promise to keep you safe. If you push and he loses it, we are right there for you."

I knew it could be dangerous. I also knew what was at stake. This wasn't just about Maime anymore. There were innocent women who were dead. I felt like a lot was riding on me.

"Yes, I will," I said, finally relenting.

CHAPTER 76

I PULLED MY JEEP TO A STOP in front of George's house. I called him about twenty minutes earlier and told him I was coming by to talk. As I walked to the door, my eyes shifted to the direction of the unmarked police van down the road to the left. I knew Luke, Tyler and Cooper were inside listening, ready to act if things got out of hand. I just couldn't muster up fear of George though. It seemed like such an atypical emotion to have for him, even after everything that had transpired.

"I'm glad you're here. I'm sorry for what happened last time," George said as I walked into the living room. He sounded sincere. I didn't buy it.

I held my hand up, putting a stop to the conversation. I looked at him and shook my head. If he said more, Luke would be in the house before I even asked my first question.

I wanted George calm, loose and comfortable to talk. He had to let his guard down.

"You said you needed to talk?" George asked as we walked over to the couch and sat down. The house was as clean as I had left it. George looked pulled together. He was wearing a blue plaid shirt and jeans.

I sat on the couch, tipped my head back and closed my eyes. I knew George was watching me closely. "I'm just tired. Overwhelmed you know. I thought I was just coming down here to look for Maime, but it's much bigger than that now."

"I know," George said.

He reached over and kneaded my shoulder with his hand. Each time his fingertips brushed up against my collarbone, I had to stop myself from flinching. His hands on me no longer felt comfortable or natural.

"Hey, remember when you used to tease me about running away? I could use that right about now. Skip out of town and pretend all this never happened." I turned my head looking up at him making sure I was making direct eye contact. I let my eyes go soft, gazing up at him with a look I'd perfected through the years of dating when I wanted my own way.

George watched me closely. I pulled his hand from my shoulder and took it in mine.

"It's been so crazy since I got here. We haven't had time to just talk like we used to. It's hard to admit, but I missed that."

"First you're cold, now this? What's changed?" George asked me with a trace of disbelief in his voice.

"Nothing really, but we can't find Maime if we aren't on the same team. I guess you were right. I was listening to Luke and Cooper too much. You hired me. I haven't been very fair. I'm feeling bad about that and thought I'd come over."

"Where's Luke?"

"I don't know. The police station probably. We had a fight. He really believes you're guilty, George. I just can't believe you murdered Maime or any of those other women. That's not the man I remember."

"Well," George said, a smile spreading across his face, "I'm glad to see you are finally coming to your senses. I didn't kill Maime. I didn't kill anyone."

"Yeah, but someone did, George. And it's someone close to you. Think about it. They have the jewelry. Most of the women seem to have some connection to you. Whoever it is set you up good. Got any ideas?" I asked, turning to face him, his hand still in mine.

"No."

"No? That's all you got for me? I'm trying to clear your name here, George. Give me something. Help me out," I pleaded.

"I don't know what you want me to say. I really have no idea."

"Pissed off husband? Bad business deal? Anything? If someone is setting you up there must be someone angry with you. That's all I'm saying."

George still didn't say anything. He stared at me with a dumbfounded look on his face. He wasn't giving anything away. We went round and round like this for several more minutes still not getting anywhere. I wasn't getting any reaction out of him. It was time to push.

"George, if you have absolutely no idea who or why someone is framing you, then you have to have some involvement."

George looked disgusted with me. He pulled his hand away from mine and got up. He walked over to his fireplace, leaned over and poked at the fire with the poker. I walked up behind him and put my hand on his back.

"George, look, things happen," I cooed. "Maybe something was an accident that got out of hand. Maybe you got a call for ransom or something. You just have to trust that I can help you. It's just you and me right now. Nobody else has to know. I need to help you get out of this."

He jabbed at the burning logs more aggressively. He was agitated now.

"We both know that you know more. I trust you. I know that you didn't hurt Maime or any of the other women. I believe you. But I also believe you know more. I need to know what that is."

George turned to me, speaking low and directly into my face. "I don't know any more than I'm telling you. Someone is setting me up. If I knew who it was, I'd have killed him myself, but I don't know. Ask any way you want to. I can't tell you what I don't know."

"Okay, I believe you," I said, holding my hands up in defeat. I turned to leave but wanted one more shot. I tugged on the back of his shirt, leaned into him and asked, "Hey, George, for old times' sake. If I had run away with you, where would we have gone?"

"You're still stumped on that one?" George smiled wide like a Cheshire cat.

"I am, totally curious. I admit it."

George moved to me, wrapped me in a hug, looked down at me and said, "Now, now sugar britches, you remember what happened to that curious cat, don't you?"

CHAPTER 77

THE DAYS CRAWLED BY. We were all a little stunned after my meeting with George. Curiosity killed the cat. I didn't know if George was kidding or if it was an indirect threat. Luke wanted to go and arrest him that moment. It took about an hour back at my house to calm him down. The meeting didn't get us anything other than we were pretty certain nothing was going to break George.

But now, everything seemed to grind to a halt. With so many things that had happened in such quick succession after I arrived in Little Rock, I was anticipating the same dreaded pace. But by mid-day Monday, everything was eerily quiet. The frantic pace was almost easier than the previous days. We were all on edge waiting for the next thing to happen, the next body to be found. But nothing happened.

Even the media was starting to get bored. A few of the national news stations started reporting the story less, weren't hounding the local folks for interviews and comments quite as much. Much to George's delight, his face was getting less air time.

It was a double-edged sword though. The less they played the story, the less pressure George and certainly the cops felt. Luke always felt like he could do his job better when he didn't feel like the eyes of the world were on his every move and every decision. But with diminishing news coverage, the less people were talking about the cases and the victims. When people talk, it triggers things in their memories and potential new leads come in.

From Sunday morning on, Cooper kept a tight watch on David Norwalk. He didn't go anywhere though. He stayed in his small two-bedroom house in West Little Rock. Occasionally, Cooper said, he'd run to the Kroger or Walgreens. Mostly, he just stayed at home. No one stopped by. Norwalk didn't leave much. Cooper said he was starting to lose hope that Norwalk would lead them anywhere. But Luke remained confident, so Cooper kept up the pace. Cooper had called in two other private investigators he knew. They were working in eight hour shifts around the clock.

I would have been offended Cooper hadn't asked me to help, but he knew I lacked patience for stationary surveillance. I was glad he hadn't asked. I was still trying to run down information on the cellphone that was calling in the leads to the media. All we knew was that it was coming from a prepaid cellphone, which for the most part, is next to impossible to trace.

Late on Monday, Luke finally got the reports back from Verizon on Maime and George's cellphones. Maime's had been used once at the location of the rehab. Then it hadn't been used again. The number she called was to a local cab company. At least it explained how she left the rehab. The cab company confirmed her fare from the rehab to her office where we knew she picked up her Land Rover.

From there, it's obvious she met up with someone. We just didn't know who or if she was a willing participant. We were back to having no idea where she had been abducted. I was still going through her cellphone records to see if there was any pattern for unrecognized numbers. There were a few I was trying to track down.

The report on George's phone was less clear. It confirmed he called Laura on Friday night, and then tried Maime's phone several times on Saturday like he said. From the location report Verizon provided, all the calls were made from or at least close to his house. George made very few calls the weeks prior. There was no record of contact with Lisa Cramer or unknown calls we couldn't otherwise identify for the other victim found. George's cellphone pinged at his home location almost all of the time. It was like he didn't leave his house or left his cellphone at the house and potentially had another phone no one knew about.

Leads were just drying up. In addition to the cellphone records, I was still trying to reach out to Maime's friends and others she might have known. I wasn't getting very far. No one wanted to speak with me. Those that did, didn't have much else to add.

George and I had spoken a few times over the course of those few days. He had told me that Edwin had suspended him from the law firm with pay until his daughter was found. He told George he wasn't happy about still having to pay him, but the other partners in the firm insisted that George was innocent until proven guilty. They agreed that it brought too much speculation to have him at the office and to continue to deal with clients. They wouldn't allow him to be fired, which George said is what Edwin wanted.

Things between George and me remained strained. After the other day, I didn't feel like there was much left to say. I couldn't just drop the case, he had paid us. I didn't like leaving work unfinished, but it was hard to speak with him.

Late Monday, I talked to my mother. We had a long and civil talk. I tried breaking the news that I planned to return to New York only long enough to pack up my things, get my dog and move back to Little Rock permanently. She wasn't hearing any of it.

We settled on more neutral topics – my weight, my lack of a husband and the fact that my sister was dating my ex-husband. These were at least neutral topics for my mother. For me, it was same old same old with her.

I wanted to tell her about Luke, but she wasn't hearing that either. It wasn't Luke per se. It was the fact that Luke was in Little Rock. I'm not sure why my mother despised the place so much. I think it was because I liked it, and it was far away from her. I could never gather another reason from her.

During the conversation, my mother was just focused on my sister Liv and her relationship with Jeff. My mother thought they made the perfect couple. She kept cautioning me that I better not make trouble for either of them. I assured her I wouldn't. There was still an edge in her voice cautioning me. I wondered if she was already planning their wedding. We hung up before I got to tell her about Luke.

Each night, Luke came over after he was done with work. Some nights were later than others. I'd leave dinner in the fridge and hear him heating it up and moving around my kitchen. I knew he liked some time to himself after work to just decompress so I gave it to him. When he was done eating, he'd shut the lights off, lock up the house and come upstairs. He'd shower, brush his teeth and climb naked into my bed.

Every night, whether I was asleep or not, he'd pull me into his arms and cuddle against me. If I was awake, we'd make love and fall asleep together. The nights I was asleep, I'd wake briefly as he sweetly kissed my cheek goodnight and would fall back to sleep soundly in his arms.

Tonight, he was supposed to be back somewhat early. When he called at nine to tell me he was still in Hot Springs, I knew it would be another late night. I went to bed on my own again.

At one in the morning, when he finally crawled into bed, I woke up enough to tell him I loved him, but he was asleep before the words even left my mouth.

I laid there watching him sleep. I hoped that I wouldn't disappoint him and that we'd both make it through this case strong on the other end of it.

CHAPTER 78

MY CELLPHONE BUZZED on the nightstand, waking me from my sleep. I reached over, blindly slapping the nightstand trying to find my phone. Before I could get my bearings, the call went to voicemail. They immediately called back.

"What?" I asked, trying to focus my sleepy eyes on the screen to see who was calling. I reached my hand over and hit a cold spot on the bed next to me. Luke must have left already. I'm usually not such a sound sleeper so I was surprised I hadn't woken when he left. It was only seven-fifteen on a Friday morning.

"Can you be ready in fifteen minutes? We need to go somewhere. I'm outside. Let me in," George said, barely taking a breath between sentences.

I hadn't seen him since my interview with him at the start of the week. I didn't really want to see him now, but he was still my client.

"I can let you in, but I don't know that I can be ready that quickly. Where do we need to go?"

George didn't respond. I slid out of bed and pulled on shorts and a tee-shirt. I stepped on the cold hardwood floor and headed down the stairs to let George in the house. I looked out the side window next to the front door but didn't see George or his truck.

"George, where are you?" I asked impatiently.

"I'll be right there. I figured you didn't want Emma to know I was at your place so I parked down the block," George explained. He came into view seconds later. He wore jeans, a heavy sweater, and a ball cap pulled low on his face. I clicked off the call and set my phone on the table next to the front door. I opened the door and stood back, giving him room to enter.

"Hurry. Go shower and get ready. We don't have much time," he demanded as he crossed the threshold.

"What's the rush? What's going on?" I insisted.

George gently turned me around and guided me towards the stairs. "I'll explain in the car. I'll wait here. Hurry. We really don't have much time."

I figured fighting him wasn't going to do much so I jogged back up the stairs, closed and locked the bathroom door and started the shower. I let the hot water rain over me. I showered quicker than I wanted, not because of George's urgency, but because I didn't like being naked with him in my house even with the bathroom door locked.

By the time I was ready to go, my half-dried hair was under my Boston Red Sox hat. I was dressed in jeans, sneakers, and a long sleeve tee.

I bounded back down the stairs and found George sitting on the couch. I grabbed my wallet and keys from my downstairs office and let George walk ahead of me out the door. I grabbed my cell off the table and closed and locked the door behind me.

His truck was down at the end of the block near the side street. As we walked, I demanded that George tell me what was going on. Stopping near his truck, I flat out refused to get in until he gave me an answer.

"I got a call this morning from a man who claimed to know where Maime is," George said, looking over at me, motioning for me to get in the truck.

I didn't budge. "We can't go alone. We need to call the police. I'll call Luke." I reached for my cellphone in my pocket. I couldn't believe he thought we could handle this alone.

"We're fine," George said, putting his hand over mine. "I already called Detective Morgan. He's pulling a team together and heading there. He asked that I pick you up."

I was as sure as I was standing there that Luke had not asked him to pick me up, but my hands were starting to turn numb against the cold. Given Luke was on his way, there was no point stalling. I relented and got in George's truck. Once we made our way out of my neighborhood, I asked where we were headed.

"Down towards Hot Springs," George responded.

After a moment when I didn't say anything, George said, "Just trust me on this."

"Tell me what the guy said when he called about Maime." I knew Luke had been in Hot Springs all night, but we never got the chance to talk before he left this morning so I didn't know whether to believe George or not.

"Just that he had Maime. He is going to release her, but he wants money in exchange. I pulled together all the cash I have and got the rest from Edwin. He's driving down separately. See that bag in the back? It's got the money he wanted. The guy gave me directions. Said no cops, but I called them anyway."

There was a bag I could see right behind the driver's seat on the floor.

"What did Luke say? Why didn't he call me?"

"I said I would call you. He was a little busy pulling everything together. Riley, it's going to be okay. We are going to get her back," George said, trying I'm sure to sound reassuring.

I sat for a good twenty minutes staring out the window. As we exited off city roads and onto the highway, we were definitely headed in the direction of Hot Springs. I didn't like how I was feeling though. Something wasn't adding up. I couldn't quite put the pieces together. By the time we reached I-30, I had a plan.

"George, can we stop please? I know you are in a hurry. I have to go to the bathroom. I was in such a rush I didn't go before we left," I said urgently, squirming in my seat for effect. I was hoping once he pulled over, I could use my phone and get myself out of the situation.

"Not now," George said gruffly and shot me a look. "Let's keep going. We'll be there soon. You'll make it, I'm sure."

I turned my cellphone over in my lap and lifted the screen up to get a better look. I was going to call Cooper to at least let him know where I was and to see if he was on his way. I stared in disbelief when I realized my screen saver was not the scene of huts over the water in Bora Bora. I slid the graphic to unlock my screen and clicked the people tab in the lower left corner. It was blank. My mind flashed back to my cell sitting on the inside table right near my front door. I had left my phone downstairs while I took a shower.

I turned my head, and was about to ask George what he did to my phone, when his hand with a white cloth in it slammed into my face.

He held the cloth against my nose and mouth. I struggled against him, my hands clawing at his arms, but I was confined by the seat belt and the interior of the truck. My eyes darted in panic not wanting to inhale. But in my flailing and panic, I sucked in two short deep breaths. My limbs grew heavy. I struggled to keep my eyes open. I couldn't even turn my head to look at George.

The last thought I had was that I didn't want Luke to find my body like the rest of the women. He couldn't bear it. I couldn't do that to him. Then darkness overcame me.

CHAPTER 79

FOR DAYS LUKE FELT like he was trying to walk through quicksand. The further he got into this case, the more he sunk down into the muck with seemingly no way out. They just didn't seem to be catching any breaks. He thought Norwalk would have led them to the guy that was buying Maime's drugs by now. He hadn't. Luke kept thinking that maybe Norwalk was smarter than he had given him credit for and wouldn't be so easily duped. He kept Cooper on it just in case.

Luke arrived at work at seven that morning. He had rolled out of Riley's bed around six after sleeping for five hours. He had too much on his mind to sleep. He felt guilty each night he went to bed. Luke knew he needed sleep. That he wasn't good to anyone without the proper rest, but each hour asleep meant another hour a ruthless killer was still out there. And there were two missing women's lives still hanging in the balance.

Luke thought he probably should start sleeping in his own bed again. He'd been spending every night at Riley's. He was sure his late nights and early mornings were depriving her of the peaceful rest she needed. She never complained.

Each night, he promised himself he'd go home, but when it came time to leave work, the temptation to sleep next to her won over. Riley looked exhausted the last few days so when he had left that morning, he was extra quiet and just didn't have the heart to wake her. She was sound asleep and looked too peaceful to be disturbed.

He still felt bad for crawling out of her bed without saying a word. Luke looked at his watch and realized it was already close to eight. Riley would be up by now. He reached for the phone. As he did, it started to ring. Luke answered. The person on the other end started speaking before he could even say hello.

"Detective Morgan, we were given your number if any new leads on your case came in. We've had another this morning. Just now in fact," Janelle, the news reporter, said. Her voice was rushed and high-pitched.

"What was the message?" Luke asked, realizing then the dread growing in his stomach.

"It was the same man as before. He said he just threw another woman in the Arkansas River," Janelle said and then paused.

"Anything else?"

"Yes," Janelle said tentatively.

Luke heard her crying.

"Go on, this is important. What else did he say?" he urged.

"He said to deliver a personal message to Detective Morgan. He said to tell him that we took his precious Riley and that she would be dead soon just like the others," Janelle said and then broke into sobs on the phone.

Luke couldn't catch his breath. It was like he'd been punched in the gut. The wind knocked out of him. He wasn't sure what to do first. He waved Tyler over to finish the call and get the rest of the information from Janelle. He needed to call Riley immediately. He needed to get to her. If it was just a joke, she'd answer and be okay.

He sprinted from the office and down the flights of stairs, taking two at a time. He called Riley as he went, but she wasn't picking up. He called Cooper and asked him if he'd heard from Riley. He hadn't. Luke explained. Cooper said he'd meet him at Riley's as fast as he could.

Luke threw on his siren and raced through the city. It was morning rush hour traffic. He weaved in and out as cars pulled over to let him pass. He zoomed through red lights, unconcerned for his safety and the safety of other drivers. All he cared about was getting to Riley. He knew though deep down in a place he didn't even want to think about, that she wouldn't be there. He knew she was gone.

But still he raced. Maybe someone saw something. Maybe he could find her. Just like he knew she was gone, Luke knew he still had a chance to save her.

He squealed his brakes, slamming his car to a stop in front of her house. His siren still blaring brought all of the neighbors into the street. Good, he thought, as he raced to her front door. Let them all know right now that Riley was gone.

Luke unlocked the front door as he had done the previous nights and called her name over and over again, yelling at the top of his lungs. She wasn't there. He was only met with silence. Deafening silence.

Luke raced up the stairs. Room after room he searched. In each closet. In each part of the house. He searched over and over again never ceasing calling her name. He heard voices downstairs and knew that Cooper had arrived.

Luke bounded back down the stairs and said only three words to Cooper and Riley's friend Emma who were now standing in the living room. "He took her."

"Who? How?" Emma asked, leaning on Cooper for support. Cooper put his arm around her shoulders and stared at Luke waiting for a response. The growing concern was evident on their faces.

"He called it in to the news tip line. He said he left another body in the river and that he took Riley." Luke put his hands over his eyes and groaned. "I was just here. I left her asleep a little after six this morning."

They each started looking around Riley's house. Emma noticed immediately that the shower and bathroom towel were wet, like someone had just used it. She asked Luke if he had showered before he left. Luke told them he hadn't. He had showered at home.

Luke's limbs felt heavy as he stood in the living room trying to remember every detail from that morning. Were there any suspicious cars in the neighborhood? Had he seen anyone before he left? Why didn't he just stay a little while longer?

Cooper called from inside the kitchen that he found her cellphone sitting on the kitchen table. Luke willed himself to walk out to his car. He flipped off the siren and pulled out a pair of gloves. Riley never went anywhere without her cellphone. That much he knew.

As Luke walked back to the house, a kid from the crowd that was still gathered in the road in front of Riley's house called out to Luke, "Are you looking for the lady that lives in that house?"

Luke stopped in his tracks and turned to the kid and asked, "Yes do you know where she is?"

"Yep," the boy said proudly. "She went with that guy on the television. The one that killed his wife. He parked way down the block. I saw them leave in his truck."

CHAPTER 80

AFTER HEARING THE KID'S DESCRIPTION, Luke jumped into his SUV and drove directly to George's house. Luke hoped Riley was there. He knew in his gut she wasn't. He needed to rule it out. He needed to see for himself.

There were no vehicles in the driveway, and the house looked dark. Luke tried all the doors. He looked through the windows but nothing. Standing on George's front lawn, Luke cursed himself for not keeping George under twenty-four-hour surveillance. They hadn't received approval for the GPS unit on his truck yet.

Luke kicked the ground in front of him, pissed off at himself for not trying harder, not pushing harder. Screw procedure, he thought. Everyone knew George was guilty.

Speeding back to Riley's house, Luke called Tyler. Luke explained everything he knew so far and asked Tyler about what else they found out from Janelle. Tyler said they already sent guys down to the river to search the spots the other victims were found. Another boat unit was dispatched to search the water. Luke asked Tyler to send another unit to George's house again and break the door down if they had to. It needed to be searched now.

Luke also asked Tyler to try to call George and put an immediate trace on his cellphone.

Luke's next call was to put a BOLO on George's truck. He would have photos of George and Riley on the news immediately. Luke would make it impossible for George to hide.

Just as Luke was hanging up from police dispatch, his cellphone rang. Luke looked at his cellphone screen. It was Ben the reporter.

"Is it true? Is Riley really missing? We just got a tip," Ben asked sharply.

"Yeah, George took her from her house this morning. We need to get this out there now. Can you put this up on the newspaper website?" Luke asked slightly out of breath. "I can have their pictures and an official statement emailed over."

"Sure. Anything to help. I'm at the office right now. I'll watch for it and get it up there as soon as we can."

Luke hung up and walked back into Riley's house. He came face to face with a very concerned and confused Emma and Cooper.

Seeing their concerned looks, Luke explained, "It's George. He's got her."

Emma and Cooper looked at each other and then back to Luke for explanation.

"A neighbor kid just told me he saw Riley leave this morning with the guy he saw on the television accused of killing his wife. We've got to get to her. I don't know what he's doing, but if he harms one hair on her head, I'll kill him myself," Luke said angrily.

Cooper swore under his breath and said, "Luke, listen there's something Riley didn't tell you. It happened the other day. Riley told me not to tell you because she didn't want to add any more stress to your life."

"Just tell me," Luke said impatiently.

Luke knew from experience that whenever Riley kept a secret it was never good. When she was happy, she couldn't wait to share the news. When it was bad, she was a vault.

"The other morning when she told George about Dean, George grabbed her and shook her hard," Cooper said and then hesitated. "He told her he knew you spent the night at her place. He'd been watching her."

"Why wouldn't she say something?" Emma asked, her voice cracking. She looked on the verge of tears.

"Riley just brushed it off like she has been doing. She was upset and shocked but thought it was the stress. Coming by the house, she chalked it up to George being George," Cooper explained but his voice sounded hollow.

Luke knew this wasn't good. He should have arrested George whether they could make a case on him or not. If he'd been doing his job, Riley would be safe now.

CHAPTER 81

AFTER GETTING THE NUMBER FROM EMMA, Luke walked into Riley's home office and sat down at her desk. He wasn't ready to make this call, but he knew it had to be done.

Luke wanted privacy and didn't want to have to talk in front of Cooper and Emma. This was going to be one of the hardest calls he was ever going to have to make. He hesitated, then punched the numbers into his cellphone and took a deep breath.

The phone rang three times before a woman picked up.

"Mrs. Karen Sullivan?" Luke asked for Riley's mom. It was the first time he'd ever spoken to the woman. Emma said she'd make the call, but Luke wanted to do it himself. He wanted to assure Riley's mother he was doing everything he could.

"Yes," she said with hesitation in her voice.

"My name is Detective Luke Morgan. I'm a detective with the Little Rock Police Department. Riley is missing. We believe George Brewer took her this morning. We are doing everything we can to find her."

The woman didn't respond. All Luke heard were shallow rapid breaths.

"Are you there, ma'am?"

Finally, she spoke. "How well do you know my daughter, Detective?"

"Truthfully," Luke paused. He knew this wasn't the time for such a conversation, but he wasn't going to start this call with a lie. "Very well. We were dating for over a year before she moved back to New York. We just picked up where we left off."

"Good, Detective. Find my daughter. If you know Riley, he'll have a fight on his hands."

It was the first time Luke smiled. He knew her mother was right.

Karen continued, her voice strong and even, "If I were a betting woman, I think we all should say a silent prayer for George Brewer. He may very well be the one that ends up dead. You find my daughter, then we can discuss your relationship with her. I'll be on the first flight out."

She hung up before Luke could say anything else.

Luke set his cellphone down. He rested his head in his hands and looked down at Riley's desk. It was clean and neat. Her laptop was open but turned off. There was a pile of papers stacked neatly to the left of her computer. Atop the pile was an orange sticky note with Riley's perfect handwriting. The note read: How is Maime connected to this number 501-555-2734?

Luke immediately recognized the number. It was the number Janelle had just given him. The number the killer was using to call in tips to the media. They had tracked that number to a prepaid cellphone, but then the trail ran cold. He wasn't sure what Riley had meant in her note.

Luke began flipping through the stack of papers until he found Maime's cellphone records. The paper was covered in yellow highlighter. Riley had highlighted line after line of calls coming in and going out to the same number. Luke flipped back through older phone records. More highlights. The calls went back for at least six months from what Luke could tell. Maime was in some way connected to the same guy calling in the tips.

But something wasn't adding up for Luke. George wouldn't call his wife from a prepaid cellphone. There would be no reason. They would use their regular cellphones.

Luke picked up the stack of papers and walked out of Riley's office and down the hall back to the kitchen where Emma and Cooper were waiting. He handed the note and the cellphone records to Cooper.

"What do you make of this? Riley connected the cellphone number calling in the news tips to calls coming and going to Maime's phone."

"Really?" Cooper asked as he flipped quickly through the pages. He looked back at Luke and seemed as confused as Luke felt. It wasn't adding up for any of them.

Luke turned to Emma, put a hand on her shoulder and said, "I know Riley has said that Maime is crazy. She said that all along, but we didn't take it seriously. How crazy is she?"

Emma looked between Luke and Cooper, her eyes darting between them. "It was really bad. It was part of the reason she left Little Rock. Maime got crazy. She called and drove by at all hours. She had her friends do the same. It was serious harassment. Riley never wanted to make a police report. She said it would stop if she just ignored it. It didn't. It continued even after she left. For months, even long after Riley left, I saw Maime drive by the house."

"Is she crazy enough to kill?" Luke asked.

"Honestly," Emma said and hesitated, looking between Cooper and Luke. "Yes. Probably. She would need help. I don't think she'd have the guts to do it on her own. She wouldn't be strong enough."

"What are you thinking, Luke? Maime's not dead, not really missing?" Cooper asked incredulously.

"That's exactly what I'm thinking," Luke said defeated. He pulled out a chair and sat down at the kitchen table with Emma and Cooper. "I think we missed the signs. Maime's been gone long enough that her body should have turned up. Not to mention, we've been so focused on George and the fact that he had motive for each woman. If you think about it, Maime had just enough motive, too."

Cooper said, "It would explain her dropping off her car and leaving voluntarily. It would also explain the jewelry. Unless George is a really good actor, he really didn't know about the jewelry."

Then he asked, "You said Riley left with George?"

"I'll interview the kid again to double check," Luke said and then turned to Cooper and asked, "Can you go relieve your other investigator and keep an eye on Norwalk to see if he leads you to anyone?"

Cooper agreed and headed for his truck.

Luke made one more call before leaving Riley's house. "Send a unit over and bring in Dean Beaumont immediately."

CHAPTER 82

I SLOWLY OPENED MY EYES. They slid closed again. It was a struggle to keep them open. Squinting, all I saw was a dusty hardwood floor. Feeling was starting to come back to my limbs. My arms and legs were burning and itching. I couldn't focus on a thought. It was a little like how I felt once waking up after surgery. My mouth was dry and my head throbbed.

As I struggled to wake up, I realized I couldn't move my arms or legs. My arms were tied behind my back. My legs were tied at my ankles. I tried to right myself into a sitting position, but it was a no go. My right shoulder throbbed from holding my weight on my side. My neck was resting at an odd angle to the floor.

I shivered against the cold air. I had been stripped of my clothes and laid there wearing only my bra and panties. My exposed skin had a rash of goose bumps. Wherever I was, it wasn't heated. The cool air danced across my bare skin.

I stretched my body around and rolled onto my back. Staring up at the ceiling, all I saw was the same kind of wood beams that covered the floor. It was almost like being stuck in a very large wooden box. I laid there looking up at the ceiling trying to recall the last memory I had. I was in the truck with George. I worked over time trying to grasp for details. A voice jolted me back to the present.

"Oh, so you are alive. I thought he might have killed you already," a woman said off to my right. I couldn't see her and couldn't quite make out the voice. It was familiar.

The floor creaked. There was a distinct stomp of a high heel against the floor. Wherever she was, she seemed to be gaining ground coming closer to where I was lying. I felt the cold nudge of a shoe against my bare side. I forced open my eyes and looked up. Maime was looking down at me.

It took me a few seconds to take her in. Maime was dressed in jeans and a long sleeve purple shirt with a white lacy tank under it. Her hair looked freshly washed, her make-up was done. She was even wearing jewelry. I got the impression she was fine and in control. Far from dead or the kidnapped victim we believed she was.

"You're fatter than I remember," she said, looking down at me.

There's a lot she could have said to me, but leave it to Maime to take the easy insult. I wasn't going to give her the satisfaction. I also had to admit a part of me wasn't really surprised to see her alive. She was holding a gun in her left hand. It looked similar to my Glock, which I should have brought with me. I left it in my dresser not thinking I'd need a gun with George.

"What is going on?" I asked, forcing myself up and into a sitting position. It took more strength than I realized I had left. "Where are my clothes?"

"We took them off of you while you were unconscious. Didn't you find all the other women like that? You know you're next," Maime taunted me, waving the gun at me.

Bile rose in my throat. I didn't think there was anyone I hated as much as her — for the things she was doing now and the things she did to me then. I wanted nothing more than to take a swing at her, but tied up, I didn't stand a chance.

I leaned back against the wall for support and took in my surroundings. I was on the floor against the back wall of some kind of cabin. It seemed to be one big room with a kitchen off to my left. The room in front of me had some sparse furniture and a bed off to the far right corner against the opposite wall. The door leading outside was directly across from me in the middle.

As I scanned the room, my eyes rested on George who sat in a chair in the middle of the room. So far he hadn't said a word. He had been so quiet, I hadn't realized Maime and I weren't alone. George looked like someone had beat him within an inch of his life.

"Who did that to you, George? Why did you bring me here?" I asked angrily. I was surprised how hoarse my voice sounded, like I hadn't spoken for hours. Maybe I hadn't. I wasn't sure how much time had passed.

He didn't answer. He looked pretty messed up. There was dried blood caked on his face. His right eye and nose were badly swollen and bruised. More dried blood covered his shirt.

Maime walked over and kissed him on the lips. I couldn't tell if George kissed her back or not. He hardly moved. I realized then that he was bound as well. His arms remained behind his back, and his ankles were also tied. He at least was still dressed.

"Maime, what is going on? What do you think you're doing?" I groaned.

"Kissing my husband. What does it look like I'm doing?" Maime quipped back at me.

I didn't have time for games. I knew there was no way she could kidnap and kill all these women by herself. I was struggling to make sense of it all.

"George, answer me. What is going on? Why did you bring me here?" I asked.

I struggled against the ties on my wrists. I didn't have much room to wiggle them around. I didn't think I was going to be able to get loose. They were tied pretty tight. I worked my hands anyway. I could feel the rope cutting into my wrists, leaving marks and probably making me bleed. I didn't care. I needed to untie myself.

Maime walked over to me. She squatted down and pointed the gun directly at my forehead. I felt the cold metal against my skin.

"You don't tell my husband what to do anymore. Got it? You're a man-stealing loser."

She didn't pull the trigger. Instead, she cuffed me on the side of the head hard with the gun. She drew blood. It trickled down the side of my temple and down my face. My vision blurred, but I remained conscious.

I watched Maime closely. I noticed her eyes. Her pupils were dilated. She looked a little twitchy. It was obvious then she was high on something.

She walked back to George who still hadn't spoken. If I hadn't seen his eyes on me, I might have thought he was dead. He hardly moved as Maime climbed onto his lap and kissed his cheek.

Maime held up George's chin and forced him to look over at me. She whined, "Look at her. She's a mess. She's never been as pretty as me. How could you choose her instead of me, Georgie? Tell me."

"Maybe because I'm not a psycho," I spit out barely above a whisper. She was getting on my last nerve.

She abruptly stood, aimed the gun at my head, and squeezed off a round that passed so close to my ear I could feel the rush of air against my face. The bullet lodged in the wall behind me. Either she intentionally missed or she was a horrible shot. I was only a few feet from her. I didn't think I wanted to try again.

"If I'm such a psycho, why did George trade you for me?" Maime asked with a cold, cruel smirk on her face.

CHAPTER 83

"**WHAT IS SHE** talking about, George? You traded me?" I yelled as loud as my weakened voice would allow.

This was getting ridiculous. I wondered if Luke or Cooper or even Emma realized I was missing. There was only one visible window, but the blinds were drawn. I guessed it was late afternoon as hardly any light came through the blinds, which must have been white at one point. They were now covered in so much dirt, they looked brown.

"Yep, he did," Maime answered for him. "We called him and said that if he brought you here, I'd be released. I don't think it was more than a couple hours, and George brought you right to us."

She turned back to George, a sick smile on her face and asked rhetorically, "Didn't you, Georgie? That's how much he loves me. He was willing to let you die so I could come home."

I stared hard at George. His eyes were averted. He wouldn't look at me. The coward still didn't have anything to say.

"Who are you doing this with, Maime? Did you kill the other women?"

"Of course, I had help. I couldn't do all this myself. I might break a nail," she responded, holding out her hand checking her manicure.

"Who helped you?" I asked again impatiently.

"I'm going to let that be a surprise. He's looking forward to seeing you. He's been saying that this whole time. Seems you are really popular with the boys, Riley. I can't really understand why. It's not like you're pretty."

I ignored her insult. As long as she was insulting me, I was still alive. I wanted to keep her talking and find out as much as I could. I wondered if I could convince her to untie me.

"Maime, you know if you had help, if you didn't do this all alone, you're still a victim. We can get out of here before he comes back," I said. I was still struggling with the bind on my wrists. I didn't think I could get to a standing position like this.

"You can't outsmart me, Riley. He already said you'd try. But since you're going to die anyway, I can tell you what we did," Maime said. She took a seat in the chair next to George and set the gun down on the small wooden end table between them.

"See George can't keep it in his pants," Maime said, patting George's thigh. "No matter what I did at home. No matter what I tried. It wasn't good enough for George. He always needed other women. I got tired of it. I couldn't stop George, but I can stop y'all."

I'm sure she thought she was being rational. She sounded crazier by the minute.

"You can't just kill every woman George is interested in. Why not just divorce him and find someone better?" I asked what I thought was a logical question.

"So you can have him?" Maime scoffed.

"I don't want him, Maime. Trust me. He isn't that great," I said sarcastically.

I wasn't going to rehash what happened or didn't happen between George and me years ago. If anything, he was going to get me killed. I swore right then if I got myself out of this George wasn't going to have any equipment left to entice the ladies. I was going to rip it off his body with my bare hands.

"Where is Laura?" I asked, suddenly realizing she was still missing. My eyes darted around the room. I wondered if I missed her tied up somewhere. I didn't see her.

"She's dead," Maime said matter of fact. "We killed her last night. She was the most fun to kill. She wouldn't shut up until we drugged her. All that begging and pleading, like it was going to change my mind. She deserved to die."

"Where'd you get the drug, Maime?"

"Vet's office, just outside of Hot Springs. Got enough to last for months. My little helper can slip in and out of places undetected all the time. It's a special skill of his. That's how he kidnapped all the women. He got near them and drugged them, carried them out, and no one was the wiser."

It was sick. Maime's voice was full of pride.

I could feel the temperature dropping inside the cabin. My muscles ached from not moving.

"Tell me about them. Tell me about the women you killed. What did Sara do to you? She was just a real estate agent."

"I know, but she was helping George leave me. I couldn't have that. Plus, she looked a little like me. It was only a matter of time before he slept with her, too."

I tried asking more questions. The little energy I had was fading fast. The drug they had knocked me out with was still affecting me. I saw Maime's lips moving, but I couldn't focus enough to hear her answers. My eyes would slide shut, open briefly, and slide shut again. I couldn't force myself to stay awake long enough to get the answers I needed. I couldn't think straight.

I didn't know how much time was passing. It could have been minutes or hours. I was losing all sense of time. Maime kept talking and walking around the cabin. She'd go from yelling at me and pointing the gun at me, jolting me awake and then letting me sleep again. George remained silent the whole time.

In one of my more lucid moments, I yelled at George, "Say something dammit. Don't just sit there and not speak."

His silence was maddening.

George didn't raise his head. He continued to look down. He wouldn't look me in the eyes. Finally, he said, "I love my wife. I've made mistakes. I have to support her now."

They both were insane.

"What about your affair with Dean? You're not so innocent, Maime."

She didn't respond right away. She walked towards the outdated kitchen, opened a cabinet, and pulled out a glass. Maime went to the fridge and poured herself something to drink. She walked back towards me, drinking what looked like iced tea. My mouth was parched. I didn't ask for some. I wouldn't give her the satisfaction of denying me.

"I used him. I knew it would drive a wedge between George and Dean. I did what I had to. But Dean wasn't so fun anymore. He was always getting on me about the drugs. He was worse than George. Ran to my father with every little thing I did."

"You two are sick, you know that? You deserve each other," I said disgusted. I wished I had never laid eyes on George.

Then it hit me. There was one woman we hadn't talked about.

I called out to Maime, "Who is the woman they haven't identified yet?"

CHAPTER 84

"ANY IDEA WHY YOU'RE IN HERE?" Luke asked as he lead Dean into the interrogation room. He sat down opposite Dean at the table.

Luke had been waiting for Dean to arrive, but let the uniformed officers walk him through the building to the interrogation room. Dean wasn't under arrest. Luke just wanted to make sure Dean knew he needed to cooperate.

The officers told Luke they found Dean at the Country Club gym just about to run on the treadmill. This was the most casually dressed Luke had ever seen Dean. He had on running pants and a Razorback tee-shirt.

Taking a seat, Dean answered, "No, I have no idea. What is it? Have you found Maime?"

Luke thought Dean seemed genuinely concerned.

"Possibly, we aren't quite sure. Do you know where Riley is?"

Shaking his head, Dean said, "No. I haven't seen her since we were all at my place on Saturday."

Luke believed him.

"What about George? When did you last speak to him?"

"The same. What's happening, Detective?"

Luke took photos from his file and laid them on the table in front of Dean. There were photos of Shannon, Sara, Lisa and Laura smiling and happy in life. Side-by-side to each, Luke laid close-up shots of Shannon, Sara and Lisa lying on the morgue table. He had another photo of the unidentified woman.

"What are these photos?" Dean asked, looking down and then back up at Luke.

"We'll get to that in a minute," Luke said, waving off the question. "Riley is missing. We have reason to believe George went to Riley's house this morning and left with her. We believe Riley left without a struggle, but we don't know how voluntarily she left with him. Her cellphone, which she'd never leave, was found on her kitchen table."

Dean grew noticeably pale. He spoke after a few seconds. "I really have no idea where they are. I really don't."

"How did Maime feel about Riley?"

Luke believed Dean didn't know where Riley and George were, but he suspected Dean might know more than he even realized.

"She didn't like her. Probably more than any other woman. George had a lot of affairs. They never meant much to him. I think George was truly in love with Riley. That was the biggest threat to Maime. There was a time when I think if Riley had pursued it, George would have left Maime for her."

"Is it fair to say Maime hated Riley?"

"Yes, actually very much. She still talked about how much she hated her after all these years. What are you getting at?"

"We have no reason to suspect Maime is dead or has been kidnapped. Actually, if we look at the evidence, we have reason to believe she is participating in the kidnappings and killings. She has as much motive as George, maybe more," Luke explained.

He paused and waited for strong denials from Dean, but they never came. Luke watched Dean sit back and take it all in.

After a moment, Dean shrugged and said quietly, "It's possible."

Luke pointed down at the photos and said, "I need you to look through these and tell me if you know any of the women or anything about them besides what you heard on the news."

Dean studied the photos and commented on each of them. Luke could tell it was hard for him to look at the photos of the victims in death, but he did. With each one, Dean told Luke what he knew and what he knew from George and from Maime. When Dean got to the last victim, the still unidentified woman, he surprised Luke.

Picking up the last morgue photo and taking a closer look, Dean said, "This is Michelle Banks. We went to college with her."

"You know this woman?" Luke pressed him. "We've been unable to identify her. Are you sure?"

Dean laid the photo back on the table and said confidently, "I'm positive. She was involved with George in college. I would know her anywhere."

"Tell me about her," Luke urged.

"I just remember that she was dating one of our fraternity brothers but came home from a party with George. She spent the night with him. The boyfriend caught them in the morning and there was a big scene. Her boyfriend had a violent temper so it was a big blow out. She wasn't around much after that. I thought they probably broke up. In fact, I don't think I've seen her since we graduated."

"Has George had any contact with her that you know of?"

"No, he wouldn't. As I said, it all ended badly. What I don't understand is how Maime would have known about her. It was way before George and Maime met. I can't imagine George would have told her the story."

"Who did Michelle cheat on? The other fraternity brother?"

"You know him. It's that reporter. Ben Prosser," Dean said calmly.

"Ben Prosser?" Luke asked skeptically, not sure he had heard Dean correctly.

"Yeah, I didn't know he was living in Little Rock, but then I saw him in the crowd at the press conference. I didn't really think much of it. He doesn't look very different than he did back then."

"Tell me about him," Luke said, a sinking feeling growing in his gut.

"He was kind of a weird guy. He'd walk into a room and the whole mood would shift. Nobody really liked him. He was pretty angry, easy to set off. I didn't really know him that well. I tried to spend as little time with him as possible. Until the other day at the press conference, I hadn't seen him since we graduated."

"Did Maime know him?" Luke asked.

"Not that I know of, but it's a small town so you know anything's possible. What are you thinking, Detective?" Dean asked, shifting in his seat.

"I'm thinking I have two people who have pretty good reasons to set up George. You need to keep this conversation between us for now," Luke said seriously.

He quickly gathered his papers and headed for the door. As he walked out, Luke called over his shoulder, "You're free to go but don't go far. I may need you again."

Luke had no time to spare. He rushed to his desk, pulled up the internet and found a recent photo of Ben off the newspaper website. He printed it, grabbed his cellphone and some other files and left the police station.

There was only one person Luke knew that could connect Ben and Maime. Luke was going to get that information one way or another.

CHAPTER 85

LUKE RACED TO THE SOUTHEAST part of the city. He got a call on his cell as he expertly navigated the streets.

"We found a body," Tyler informed him. "I've called Purvis down. He's on his way. Like the last, she wasn't far from George's office. You find him yet?"

"No, but I got another lead. Keep an eye out for Ben Prosser, that reporter from the Times. If you spot him, take him in, and hold him for questioning until I get there. Got it?"

"Yeah, sure. I'll look for him. The news media is all over this. What's Ben got to do with anything?"

"That's what I'm about to find out. I brought Dean in for questioning and learned Ben's connected to George and Dean from college and the unidentified victim. The victim's name is Michelle Banks. Dean identified her from the photo. Seems Michelle cheated on Ben with George in college. I still don't know how it all ties in. Dean said Ben was a fairly odd guy back then, bad temper and so forth. He never came across like that to me, but he also failed to mention ever knowing George. I find that strange."

As Luke sped through town, he caught Tyler up on his speculation about Maime. Luke was finally starting to feel like all the puzzle pieces were sliding into place. He allowed himself a few seconds of hope that he'd find Riley alive. Right now, that was the only thing on his mind.

Luke ended the call with Tyler just as he pulled up in front of a known drug house. There was a group of guys sitting on the front porch. They snapped to attention as Luke walked towards them. Luke knew he only had one shot. He wasn't there to arrest anybody. He didn't care about their crimes today. Just an answer was all he needed.

"I just need Orlando Knight," Luke said, holding up his hands showing them he wasn't reaching for his gun or anything that would put them on guard. "I just have a quick question, and then I'm out of here."

"Maybe I don't wanna answer no questions," Knight called from the middle of the pack.

Luke pleaded, "A woman's life depends on it. You met her. Her name is Riley. She was down here asking questions. She talked to you."

Luke stood down at the edge of the curb and held out a photo in his left hand. "Just look at the picture and tell me if you know him."

"What happen to that girl?" Knight asked as he sauntered down the sidewalk toward Luke. "She was nice. Maybe I'll help."

"Someone took her this morning. You know all those missing women and the ones they found in the river – same guy. I can't find her. I'm trying to save her life. I need your help," Luke said truthfully.

"What's your question?" Knight asked.

Luke thrust the photo towards him and asked, "You know this guy?"

Knight studied the photo for a minute, maybe longer. He looked up to his crew as they carefully regarded him. Luke knew Knight was no snitch, but he was also counting on the fact that Riley had met him to sway if Knight talked or not. Riley could be persuasive and kind. One of her best traits was never acting like she was better than anyone. Everyone was equal in her eyes. It gained her respect. Luke was counting on that respect now.

Finally, Knight spoke, "Yeah I know him. That's the guy she was asking about. Comes down here and buys drugs for that missing white girl."

"Thanks, man," Luke said. He reached out and shook Knight's hand.

Luke turned and headed back for his SUV. Knight trailed after him. He stopped Luke before he got back in the car and said, "We do a lot of stuff down here, but we don't hurt women. If you find him, drop him off and we'll take care of him for you."

"Thanks, but we got this," Luke assured him.

Knight nodded and went back to his crew.

Luke raced back to the heart of the city and called for backup to meet him at Ben Prosser's home.

CHAPTER 86

COOPER HAD GROWN TIRED of being on surveillance, just sitting and waiting for something to happen. He was antsy and wanted to help find Riley. He stayed sitting in his truck though watching David Norwalk's small house. There was little movement the whole time they had been out there. Cooper was starting to doubt there ever would be. Days they had been watching him and nothing.

Whatever Luke thought Norwalk would lead them to, he sure was taking a long time to get to it. Cooper doubted it would ever happen. He was starting to think maybe Luke was grasping, trying another avenue that just wouldn't yield what they needed.

As the hours passed by, Cooper felt more and more powerless. He should be doing something productive rather than sitting there keeping watch over what he was now considering a dead end.

Cooper blamed himself for Riley. He should have kept a better eye on her. He knew George was dangerous, especially after Riley told him what happened. He should have warned her better. Cooper knew no matter what he said, Riley wasn't going to listen. Still there had to have been something he could have done.

Cooper was just about to give up and break off surveillance to go search for Riley when Norwalk walked out of his house. He was wearing a blue hooded sweatshirt and jeans. He had a ball cap pulled low over his eyes. He got in his old Ford truck and pulled out of the drive. Cooper was parked a few houses down and remained unseen.

Cooper put his truck in drive and followed Norwalk the best he could. They navigated through the city streets with Cooper staying two car lengths behind him, purposefully letting a car or two create a barrier in between them.

Following along familiar streets, Cooper thought Norwalk might be heading back to the same motel where he had met Dean. Cooper thought about calling Luke but decided to wait. He didn't want to risk getting distracted and lose him. After all, it was still only a hunch that's where they were headed.

His hunch was confirmed a few minutes later. This time Cooper pulled off the street and parked his truck off a dirt road past the motel. It didn't seem like whoever was meeting Norwalk had arrived yet. In daylight, Cooper couldn't just park his truck on the side of the road as he had the night before.

Where Cooper was parked now was the perfect spot. He had a clear view of Norwalk's truck and the back of Norwalk's head as he waited in front of the motel. Cooper could also see the road coming and going from the motel in both directions. Luckily, the spot Cooper picked was shielded just enough by trees to keep him out of sight.

Sure enough, about ten minutes later a BMW pulled up. Cooper expected to see Dean get out of the car. When Ben Prosser got out, slammed the door shut, and walked over to Norwalk, Cooper wasn't sure what was going on. He watched Ben walk over to Norwalk's truck and stand at the driver's side window. They spoke for a few minutes. All seemed calm.

Cooper didn't see them exchange anything. Then before Cooper even had time to process what was happening, Ben pulled a gun from his waistband and fired one shot into Norwalk's head. Norwalk's head exploded in a mess of blood and brains against the back window of the truck. Cooper didn't hear the gun make a sound. He assumed it had a silencer. It was hard to tell from the angle Cooper was watching. He couldn't believe what he just witnessed. He felt paralyzed, not sure what to do next.

He waited and watched as Ben leaned into the truck and pulled out what looked like a pile of photos. Ben got back in his car and took off out of the lot the same way he came in.

Cooper had to act and instinct took over. He gave Ben a few seconds and then Cooper started his truck and began to follow him.

At the same time, Cooper picked up his cell and was about to call 911. He decided to call Luke. Cooper wasn't sure what had just happened. But he knew he just witnessed the cold-blooded murder of a cop.

Luke answered on the second ring. Cooper explained as fast as he could what he just witnessed and explained that he was in pursuit of Ben.

"Do not lose him. He's our guy. Follow him wherever he goes. But stay back," Luke shouted. "Are you armed?"

"Yeah, just my Glock. It's only got one clip in. Hurry. I'm following close enough, hoping he doesn't notice me. He's headed away from the city not towards it. Where are you?"

"His house. I think he thought we'd never find him. The evidence is everywhere. He has photos of all the victims. He did some surveillance on them prior. We've got rental car receipts for the same make and model cars of both Dean and George. The prepaid cellphone is here and there's a map to a cabin just off Highway 270 down near Lake Catherine. But the map isn't clear, doesn't show exactly where it is. I'm calling the state police. I'm sending some guys that way. I'm leaving right now. Just keep following," Luke demanded.

"We just got on Interstate 30 West. I think we are heading in that direction. He's speeding like a mad man," Cooper explained, trying to block out the image of Norwalk's head exploding. The more he tried not to think about it, the more the image remained implanted on his mind.

"Luke, he killed Norwalk. He shot him in the head in the middle of conversation."

"Just get to Riley. That's all we care about right now. Do not lose him."

The phone abruptly disconnected. Cooper wasn't sure if it was just bad cell service or if Luke hung up. Cooper didn't try to call back. He followed Ben who was picking up speed. He had to be going at least eighty-five. Cooper didn't know if his truck could keep up with Ben's BMW. He was going to find out.

There were a million things racing through Cooper's mind, but he had to remain focused on the task at hand. Minutes ticked by as they cruised down I-30 West. Finally, Cooper saw Ben pull over to the far-right lane and get off the 270 exit, heading in the direction of

Lake Catherine. Cooper didn't know the area well, but he knew it would be pretty desolate this time of year.

Cooper needed to drop back or it would be obvious to Ben he was being followed. If Cooper got into a confrontation with Ben now, they might never find Riley.

Cooper gave Ben some lead time but had his tail lights in his sight. But as Cooper rounded a sharp bend in the road, suddenly Ben's BMW was no longer in sight. It just vanished. Cooper sped up and continued down the road. No Ben.

He made a quick U-turn and went back to the spot he lost him. There were two dirt roads that led into the trees that Cooper missed on the first pass. Cooper couldn't see beyond a few feet.

Ben was gone. That much was clear. Cooper picked up his cell to call Luke, but he had no service. He pulled his truck down one of the dirt roads that seemed to have fresh tire tracks and parked. He'd have to take it on foot. His truck wasn't going to make it through the trees.

Cooper got out of his truck and took off down the dirt road, gun ready at his side. There was little light coming through the dense trees. The more heavily wooded it became, the harder it was to see. Cooper scanned the tree line as he ran. He knew he was a sitting duck if Ben was out there in the woods somewhere. Cooper didn't have much of an option. He had to get to Riley before Ben did.

CHAPTER 87

WE WENT AROUND AND AROUND with the same question. I asked and Maime stalled. I asked the question again, "Who is the unidentified woman, Maime? What did she do to you?"

This time, before she could respond, the front door swung open. The first thing I saw was a guy's hand on the door and then dark dusty cowboy boots peeked around the door frame. When he shut the door and turned to me, I wasn't prepared for the face I saw.

Maime's partner looked over at me. He answered my last question about the unknown victim.

"That one was my own revenge. I had to get a little something out of this deal. I mean the killing was fun, but when you get to kill and have a little payback at the same time, well Riley, there's nothing quite like that."

I never saw it coming. I never suspected Ben.

Ben walked in, hugged Maime and asked her, "Everything okay, beautiful? Got everything under control? I know Riley can be a handful, from what I hear." He looked over at me smirking, his eyes drifting down my body.

"You, you've been doing all this. Why?" I asked. I still didn't quite get it.

"I went to college with Dean and George. Didn't we, George?" Ben cuffed George hard on the back of the head. George didn't respond.

"See, he and Dean thought they were the big shots on campus. We were all in the same fraternity. The whole four years they acted like I didn't exist. If they did talk to me, it was to tease me or give me a hard time. When I finally got a girlfriend, George got her drunk at a party one night and raped her. Go on, tell Riley about it, George," Ben demanded.

When George didn't comply, Ben picked up the gun and pointed it at George. It was clear that it was Ben who beat the life out of George earlier, probably while I was still unconscious.

"For the last time, I didn't rape anyone," George groaned.

George finally met my gaze. Looking me in the eyes, he explained. "I was a senior in college. I was at a party and there was a girl. We were all dancing and drunk. When we got back to the house, we had sex. The next morning, she regretted it when her boyfriend walked in on us in my bed. She cried rape. It was consensual. I swear it."

Ben let out a cruel mocking laugh. "George has always had a problem with the truth. He gets part of the story right, but the rest he makes up to suit his needs. They were dancing and drinking at a party. That part is true. When it was over, George offered to walk Michelle back to our house. He knew she was with me."

Ben aimed the gun at George's head and looked at me as he continued to explain. "I wasn't back yet from the party I went to. George took her up to his room to wait. He took advantage of her. She was too drunk to even consent. He raped her."

"What happened? Did she tell the police? Why is this coming out twenty years later? Where is she now?"

The questions just poured out of me. I didn't even know if I was making sense. I was trying to rapidly add all the pieces together but was still having trouble making sense of it all.

"Oh, she's dead. She's the one you couldn't identify. She was on a work trip in Little Rock. She lived up in Seattle. I called and asked her to meet for coffee to catch up. I hadn't seen her since college. She said yes and well you know the rest," Ben explained calmly like he was talking about a drive on Sunday, not kidnapping and killing a woman.

"But why kill her?" I asked.

"Because she deserved to die for what she did to me," Ben said slowly punctuating each word. "She betrayed me. George may have raped her, but she didn't have to drink with him or dance with him or go up to his room. Choices and consequences, Riley. Life is all about choices and consequences. If you hadn't rushed down here to help George, you might have gotten to live. Since he is still so important to you, now you have to die. It's unfortunate. I like you, but you make really bad decisions."

He started to walk towards me with the gun in his hand, pointing it directly at me.

"Wait!" I yelled. "Tell me first what George drugged me with to get me here."

I just wanted to keep them talking. I knew from Luke there was time between when they kidnapped women and killed them. I didn't think I was going to get that much time. Both George and I were missing. I assumed Luke and Cooper probably still thought it was George who was killing these women.

"Just chloroform. I used it with all the victims. Of course, they trusted me. Most people do. Even the police. I called George, told him to bring you here if he wanted Maime back. I left the chloroform on his back porch last night. I left instructions for him, and he followed them. It was all very easy. You, Riley, are very compliant," Ben said with a beaming smile.

Ben crouched down and spoke directly to me. The gun was at his side. I tried to remain stone-faced. Tears welled up in my eyes.

"But, Riley honey, we aren't going to have a lot of time together. Your boyfriend Luke is already searching for you. In fact, I just talked to him earlier this morning. I called him to ask if it was true that you were missing. Course I knew all along. It was just fun to lie to him. He asked me to post your photo and George's on the newspaper website."

"How did you and Maime meet?" I asked, stalling.

"I've been planning my revenge on George for a long time. I kept up with him. Facebook is wonderful for stalking your prey. It told me everything I needed to know. When I saw how he was neglecting his pretty little wife, I started paying attention. Well, we get along like a house on fire," Ben said.

He stood and reached out for Maime. "Don't we, baby?"

She came over to him and fell into his arms. They kissed. Then he looked down at me and said, "When Maime told me all about what a horrible husband George was I decided he really needed to pay. Maime wanted a little payback on the rotten women who couldn't keep their hands off her man. It was a win-win for everyone."

"Why kill Lisa? Maime, George broke up with her for you," I said. I was trying to understand each kill. I may not get out of this alive, but I wanted to know as much as I could.

"She was in the way. George really liked her. She just kept coming around when we first started going out. She moved away, but then I saw her from time to time in Little Rock. I wanted her gone," Maime said with some satisfaction in her voice.

"You're just going to kill me? It's that easy for you both? What about George?"

"Oh that's the fun part. Are we ready to end our little game?" Ben asked. He pushed Maime an arm's length away from him.

He pointed the gun between us both and said to George, "Okay, George, who dies? Their lives are in your hands, George. Who is it going to be?"

CHAPTER 88

BEN YELLED, "COME ON, GEORGE! We don't have all night. You decide, buddy."

Ben swung the gun between Maime and me, waiting for George to answer. Maime actually looked a little worried, like this wasn't part of the plan, but she didn't say a word.

"Your sweet Maime?" Ben asked, pointing the gun at her.

"Or your feisty Riley?" he asked, aiming the gun back at me.

I couldn't get loose. I was a sitting duck. I squirmed and twisted my wrists, trying desperately to untie myself. I moved my ankles around trying to loosen the bind. Neither was giving an inch. Maime was standing there her hand pressed to her mouth. She looked terrified. I couldn't even save myself. I could barely move. My muscles, weak from the cold and the drug, had stopped cooperating.

I yelled clearly panicked, "Maime, come on. This has gotten out of hand. Nobody else has to die. What do you think Ben is going to do after I'm dead? After George is dead? Maime, you've seen too much. He isn't going to let you live."

She was listening to my plea. I knew she was, but Ben's voice was louder than mine as he swung the gun between the two of us.

"George, stop this. Nobody has to die. Maime, come on. What is wrong with you people? This is insane." I was pleading for my life. Nobody was listening or doing anything as Ben continued to swing the gun, taunting us.

"If you can't pick, George, I will. Or maybe I'll just kill you instead," Ben shouted.

He walked over to George and pressed the barrel of the gun to his temple. Ben nudged it harder against George's head, yelling in his face, "Come on, you coward, who dies? You've got three seconds. One. Two…"

George finally cried out, "Riley, kill Riley. Let Maime live."

Before I knew what was happening, Ben aimed the gun at me and pulled the trigger. I heard the noise almost the same instant I felt the pain rip through my right shoulder not far from my chest. Blood poured down my arm. I couldn't move. I couldn't even reach my hand around to press against the wound. I was in so much pain my breath caught in my throat. Short raspy breaths of air.

Maime looked terrified like maybe she was next. George didn't even look at me. His eyes were closed tight. Ben was laughing, a maniacal laugh. Tears rolled down my face.

"Stop your bellyaching," Ben chastised me. "You'll be dead in a minute. It won't hurt anymore. Good boy, George, you finally picked the right girl. But it's too late, you don't get her. She's mine."

Ben walked over to Maime and wrapped her in his arms. Maime fell into him, but her body was stiff. Not like it had been before. I could tell she was really afraid. Something was wrong other than the obvious. I think Ben was going off script. None of the victims had been shot. They had been drugged and strangled.

With Maime still in his arms, Ben looked over at George and said, "This is how it's going to go. First, I'm going to strangle Riley. Then, when she's dead, I'm going to shoot you. Not a kill shot. No, that's too good for you. A gut shot maybe. Let you bleed out. When you're just about dead, I'm going to call Luke and tell him that I found the cabin and rushed in to save Maime and Riley. I had my gun with me. I accidentally shot Riley in the process and shot you in enough time to save Maime. I'll be the hero. I'll have killed a serial killer and saved a victim."

"Is that why they all had on jewelry, to tie them to George?" I asked. My voice didn't sound like my own. The pain was getting more intense and the blood was pooling on the floor under my right side.

"Of course, I had to make it obvious. You'll have a pretty ring on. You aren't going to be left out, don't worry. George is so vain.

He had to engrave everything with his initials. It was an easy thing to use," Ben explained casually.

I wondered when his first kill was. He was far too casual about this to have just started.

"It will be over soon, Riley. You won't feel any more pain. I promise. Sorry I had to shoot you, but I'm an unlikely hero. I had to set the stage. Make it look convincing."

"You won't get away with this. Luke will figure it out," I said. I knew I was grasping. Luke believed George was the killer. Ben's set up would assure him of that. Luke already trusted Ben. It would just look like Ben was better at his job than they already thought. Ben would get away with it.

"Even if Luke figures it out, Maime and I will be long gone," Ben said definitively.

He walked over to me and looked down at me propped against the wall. He said softly, "Ready to die?"

He shoved me down hard onto my back. I screamed in pain when his hand hit my shoulder. Ben straddled my chest. I felt his weight on me but couldn't do anything about it. He was heavy, and I was trapped under him. He wrapped his hands around my throat and applied pressure.

He was cutting off my air supply with his hands. He was going to choke me to death. I struggled against him the best I could. He was so heavy on top of me. I was losing consciousness quickly. The last thought I had before I blacked out completely was that at least he hadn't drugged me like the others. Even shot and tied up, I could still move.

CHAPTER 89

A SINGLE GUNSHOT rang through the thick dense woods, stopping Cooper cold in his tracks. He stood silent for a moment, trying to figure out which direction it came from. Up ahead to his left. He raced towards it. The sun was setting so it was hard to see much beyond a few feet in front of him.

Just as Cooper was starting to think he might have run in the wrong direction, he saw light up ahead. It was a rustic and very old cabin. One story. Pitched roof with a front porch held up by four wooden beams. There was a door in the middle and two square windows to each side.

Cooper slowed his pace and tried to quiet his footsteps against the leaves and sticks that crackled and popped beneath his weight. The silence made each step boom against its backdrop. Cooper saw the BMW and George's Chevy Tahoe. This was it. The place. He knew Riley would be inside. He said a silent prayer that the gunshot wasn't the end of her life.

Cooper approached the window with his gun drawn. The blinds were closed, and it was hard to see in. He could see what he presumed was the back of George's head. Maime stood off to his left against the wall. They both stared at Riley who was motionless on the ground. Ben straddled her chest, choking the life from her.

Acting quickly, Cooper took a few short strides and kicked the door in, aiming his gun in Ben's direction. He fired off two shots

both hitting Ben, one in the side and the other in the back of his head. Seconds passed too slowly for Cooper. Ben's body jerked as the bullets made impact. He slumped down on top of Riley, covering her. Maime moved quickly grabbing for the gun on the table next to where George remained. Cooper couldn't see his face and wondered if he was dead.

Maime aimed and fired at Cooper barely missing him. Cooper advanced on her and shouted for her to stop. She aimed and got off another shot before Cooper could get to her. A bullet sliced his arm, ripping off skin as it buzzed by. It lodged in the wall behind him.

He tackled Maime to the ground as the glass windows exploded around them, heavy booted reinforcements advanced into the cabin. Cooper landed with a hard thump as he threw Maime to the ground, kicking the gun out of her reach.

Cooper looked up to see Luke running to Riley's side. They pulled Ben's lifeless body off of her. Riley was covered in blood.

Cooper watched as Luke felt for a pulse and wiped the blood away from Riley's mouth. He started CPR. Cooper collapsed his head back against the wood floor. He prayed he wasn't too late.

Officers came in and pulled Maime off the ground and put her in cuffs. She was screaming and shouting the whole time that she was a victim and that her father would have them all fired. Nobody listened.

She wasn't injured in any way, even from Cooper tackling her to the ground. They took her away in a squad car. Cooper could hear the sirens wail as it moved farther and farther from the cabin.

He watched Luke still performing CPR. Finally, another detective working on Riley with Luke nodded that there was a pulse again. The paramedics arrived seconds later and loaded Riley onto a stretcher. Luke stayed by her side. He mouthed a thank you to Cooper as he followed Riley out to the ambulance for transport to the hospital.

Cooper finally saw George's face. Someone had done a pretty good job of giving him exactly what he deserved. He watched the officers untie his hands and then his ankles, which were also tied to the chair. They helped him up and read him his rights as they slapped the cuffs on him.

He may not have killed any women but nobody would consider him innocent. If Riley didn't make it, Cooper was pretty sure both

George and Maime would be held accountable. Either way, Cooper was hoping George was facing some criminal action.

Cooper stood watching George escorted out by two detectives – one on either side of him. When George got to the cabin door, he turned to Cooper and said, "You know I never meant to hurt her. I really didn't. I just loved her too much to let her go."

Cooper wasn't sure if he meant Riley or Maime. It didn't matter now either way.

CHAPTER 90

LUKE PACED THE FLOOR OF THE ICU. Riley was still in surgery. The ambulance had first taken them to Hot Springs Mercy Hospital. The doctors realized quickly the gun shot had nicked part of Riley's right lung and more invasive surgery was needed. They airlifted her to UAMS in Little Rock.

That was three hours ago. The surgeon thought Riley was going to make it, but they tried not to be overly optimistic.

Luke finally stopped pacing and sat down in the waiting room, which the hospital tried to make as comfortable as possible for families. It was empty other than him. The last family had left hours ago. It was nearly one in the morning.

Luke was expecting Riley's mom Karen to come in at any time now. A few hours before, Cooper finally showed up, got a few stitches in his arm, and offered to pick Karen up at the airport.

Emma had been to the hospital twice, but Luke sent her back home. There was nothing anyone could do but wait.

The news story broke about an hour ago. Captain Meadows handled the press conference for Luke. He was surprised Cap had actually credited Cooper with the shot that killed Ben. Luke's cellphone was racking up messages and texts asking about Riley. There were more people than she realized who loved her. He was first on that list.

"You're the young man that breathed life back into my daughter?" Karen asked as she walked into the waiting area.

Luke stood and walked over to her and wrapped his arms around her. He didn't think she was expecting it, but she hugged him back.

Cooper hung back by the doorway.

"How is she?" Karen asked. "I want to speak to the doctor."

"She's still in surgery." Luke pointed to Cooper and said, "He's really the one to thank. Ben would have killed Riley if Cooper hadn't been there in time."

Luke stepped back and appraised Riley's mother. She really didn't look like Riley at all. She was short, small-framed, short blonde hair and clear blue eyes. But the fire, a hot temper burning in her eyes was all Riley. Luke guessed Karen was tougher than she looked.

"The man who tried to kill her is dead?" Karen inquired.

"Yeah, I shot him twice. I didn't have a choice," Cooper explained.

"Please don't be sorry about it. Better you than Riley's father. He would have tortured him first. You gave him an easy death." Karen paused and then added, "Probably easier than he deserved."

Luke never heard Riley talk about her father. Just that he wasn't a great guy, mob connected in Ireland. Luke wasn't necessarily surprised to hear what Karen had to say on the subject, but the direct manner in which she spoke about it was a little shocking.

Just then, Doctor Bill Avery, a trauma specialist, interrupted the conversation. He updated them that Riley was out of surgery and stable. He was able to remove the bullet, reset her shoulder, and close the tear in her lung. It would be a slow recovery, but she would live.

Dr. Avery also said that there didn't seem to be any permanent damage from the strangulation. That the time her oxygen was cut off was so short there would be no long-term damage.

Cooper and Karen looked as relieved as Luke felt.

"Can we see her?" Luke asked.

"Yes, but she's asleep. She won't wake up for hours and won't respond to you now. Let her rest. Don't stay for more than a few minutes," Avery said before leaving.

Luke let Karen go in to see Riley first. She stayed in there for about fifteen minutes. Luke watched as she came out and spoke with the nurse.

Karen walked back to where Luke was standing and said, "She's okay. I imagine you want to spend the night here with her. We both can't, and I think it would mean a lot to her if you were here when she woke up. Cooper tells me my daughter has a house here. I'd like to go there. Cooper said he'd drive me over so you can stay."

Luke nodded and handed her the key to Riley's house. "Are you sure you don't want to stay?"

"I'm sure. Besides, if she woke up and saw her mother here in Little Rock, it might send her into cardiac arrest." Karen broke into the same wide grin as Riley's and then she hugged Luke.

After Karen and Cooper left, Luke walked down the hall and stood in the doorway watching Riley sleep. All he had to do was flash his badge at the approaching nurse. She pulled up a comfortable chair to put by Riley's bed.

Riley was pale and a mess of tubes and monitors, but she looked peaceful in spite of it all. When he arrived at the cabin earlier that night and saw her covered in blood and not breathing, he thought he had lost her.

Luke swore right then if she lived, he'd never leave her side again no matter how much she fought him. He pulled the blanket a little higher around her, moved the hair back from her forehead, and rested his hand over hers. He stayed like that for a few moments. Then he sat back in the comfortable chair planning only to rest his eyes. He fell asleep more soundly than he had in months.

The next morning

"Am I in heaven or hell?" Riley whispered as she woke. It was loud enough to wake Luke. She had her head turned and was smiling at him, waiting for his response.

Luke opened his eyes to see her smiling face. He got up and kissed her lightly on the lips and teased, "That depends. Your mother is in town and staying at your house."

EPILOGUE

Three months later

THE FIRE CRACKED AND POPPED. I was happy to be home in Little Rock. I wrapped myself snugly in a blanket and sank into my couch. My injuries were healing nicely. I still got tired more quickly than I had prior. I wasn't used to having to take it easy.

I hadn't started back to work yet and was living off of savings for now. It was a good break whether I liked it or not. Other than physical injuries, I fared pretty well.

The doctors encouraged me to seek out some therapy to process what happened, but I was doing okay. I still had nightmares of being suffocated. When I woke each night, Luke was right there with me.

Luke and my mother still looked at me like I was going to crack at any moment, but they were easing up. I think they were finally understanding that I was going to be okay.

I would like to say I'd forgiven George, but I'm not sure I ever will. He almost got me killed. Luke and I talked about it. I decided not to press charges against George for kidnapping me. It wasn't really up to me though. It was really up to the prosecutor's office, but after a meeting, the consensus was that it didn't really serve any purpose to make George go to jail.

Ultimately, he was trying to save Maime's life. It was totally misguided and showed me without a doubt how little he valued my own life. Sometimes though, I let myself believe he was probably doing the best he could in his own screwed up way.

If I were to be honest, I'd trade him in a heartbeat for Luke. George's life was pretty much destroyed anyway even without jail time.

Edwin was finally able to fire George outright. He ended up taking a job in a small corporate law firm for less than half his pay. Edwin also kicked him out of the house. George found an apartment in West Little Rock the last I heard. He was still married to Maime at least for now.

Maime was declared incompetent and sent to a psychiatric prison in the northwest part of the state. Her parents were making sure she got clean from the drugs and finally received the mental health services she needed all along. It's unlikely she will ever get out of that facility. If she does, she will be sent directly to Arkansas state prison to serve out the remainder of her life sentence.

I heard from Emma that both Dean and George separately make the trip twice a month to visit her. It's unlikely their friendship will ever be what it was, but it seemed neither could quite get over Maime.

I attended Maime's sentencing. The victim's families all read victim impact statements. They are all still trying to make sense of the violence and loss of their loved ones.

The one remaining victim's family, the one Dean identified, had been notified. Michelle had been on a business trip that was scheduled for three weeks in length. No one knew she had even been missing.

The city of Little Rock placed a nice plaque with the victims' names in Murray Park in honor and remembrance. Luke spoke at the event.

Most of Little Rock was in agreement that Ben Prosser got what he deserved. The evidence in his house was overwhelming. We never really had a clear answer about how exactly he met Maime or how they came up with the plan. Maime wasn't talking.

Cooper is quite the hero around town. His business was booming. He's had more dates than I could count. Cooper tells us he's embarrassed by all the attention. We don't believe him.

Cooper and Luke had some great bonding time when they agreed to drive my stuff across the country back to Little Rock from upstate New York. I was too weak to make the trip myself. I decided to stay after all. I had very little case work in New York. Winters were always slow, and Cooper had more work than he could handle. Plus, Cooper and I both decided that we liked having a business partner. My mother kept my dog. I missed him, but it was my gift to her for leaving.

The biggest surprise of all was that my mother loved my house. She came down for Christmas and had stayed through the New Year.

My sister Liv moved in with my ex-husband Jeff, and by all accounts, they were doing really well. With Jeff's income, my sister didn't have to work, which was good because I didn't think Cooper was going to let her keep the fake job and real paycheck I had been giving her. She'd never say it, but I think my mother was actually enjoying having her house to herself for the first time.

Emma was thrilled to have me back in the neighborhood and kept looking in on me. But the best thing that came out of everything that happened without question was Luke and me. He was currently in the kitchen putting the finishing touches on dinner. Who would get rid of a man that cooks?

"Baby, here you go," Luke said, bringing in warm bowls of chili for the both of us. He set them down on the coffee table, flipped on the television and snuggled under the blanket with me. He handed me mine and watched as I took a big bite.

"Delicious, thank you," I said and leaned over and kissed him.

"That's not the only thing that's delicious," Luke said as he planted sweet kisses on my face. He wore his heart on his sleeve more than I ever could, but it really is a pleasant addition to my life. I'm definitely going to enjoy every minute of it.

READ THE NEXT IN THE
RILEY SULLIVAN MYSTERY SERIES

THE BONE HARVEST

Seventeen years after the disappearance and murder of Lily Morgan, her brother Det. Luke Morgan receives a letter from the killer who calls himself The Professor. The killer claims *"23 pretty little girls harvested dead"* - and he's not done.

It's the clue Luke has been hoping for all these years, but can he really trust a serial killer at his word? When the killer strikes a little too close to home, Luke is hot on his trail – the killer taunting him at every turn. Meanwhile Luke's investigative team – private investigators Riley Sullivan and Cooper Deagnan - work to unravel long-forgotten cold cases across states and uncover decades old witnesses who still have stories to tell.

The cat and mouse game has only just begun. Luke, Riley and Cooper must stop a diabolical serial killer before he goes underground until the next harvest.

Just how far will Luke go to bring his sister's killer to justice?

Access Stacy's Free Mystery Readers' Club Starter Library

Riley Sullivan Mystery Series novella "The 1922 Club Murder"
FBI Agent Kate Walsh Thriller Series novella "The Curators"
Harper & Hattie Mystery Series novella "Harper's Folly"

Sign up for the starter library along with launch-day pricing, special behind-the-scenes access, and extra content not available anywhere else. Hit subscribe at
http://www.stacymjones.com/

Follow author Stacy M. Jones for exclusive information on book signings, events, fan giveaways, and her next novel.

Facebook: StacyMJonesWriter
Twitter: @SMJonesWriter
Goodreads: StacyMJonesWriter

Made in the USA
Monee, IL
21 July 2021

74078253R00187